The right of Shane O'Neill t(
as the author of this work ha:
All rights reserved.
Copyright © 2022 Shane O'Neill.

Cover Licence provided by
selfpubbookcovers.com;
Copyright © Ravenborn 2022.

This is a work of fiction.
Any resemblance to places or people;
living or dead is purely coincidental.

Paperback First Edition 2022

Published By:
Alternative Fiction,
Waterford, Ireland.
Publisher's ISBN: 978-0-9934247

Other books by the author Shane O'Neill:

CAIN

DARK MESSIAH

LEGACY

For Barbara

*"Just because I was present for the birth of human Creation, does not mean I am responsible for the events ... and mistakes which followed. I do not care about the betterment of mankind; neither do I wish for its destruction. I simply work towards my own agenda, for which society admires and despises me in equal measure."*
*Thomas Marsh, Grace's Choice.*

# CHAPTER ONE

Growing up in Red Mountain was a dreary affair, at the best of times. A small town situated on the coast of New England, it was overshadowed by the giant hill which gave the settlement its name, the prospectors who harvested the rare colour-changing alexandrite gemstone long since departed. Isolated by the extinct volcano, the zealous religious community reinforced this sense of aloneness on the weak-willed and especially the young. For its five thousand citizens and the few outsiders who found themselves there, the borough was in essence an open prison.

My nights were dominated by an abusive drunkard father whose only form of expression was to regularly punch my mother with all his strength in the stomach. He'd watch in amusement as she'd double over, then he would kick her raised backside to test if she had ample concentration to put her hands out in time to save her face striking the kitchen tiles. Fortunately she always did manage this, so there was never any facial damage that might allow the town to bear witness to what truly happened behind the closed doors of the home of Charles and Christine Anderson, and their eighteen-year-old daughter Grace. My mother seemed to find solace in the arms of Jesus, which only infuriated my father more, or perhaps this was her sole form of revenge against the man. Her well-known twice-daily visits to the church were enough to send Charles Anderson insane with rage. His fury would probably have been much greater if he knew my mother had been invited to become a member of Fr O'Mahony's private 'Afternoon Club' whose patrons mainly comprised sex-starved middle-aged housewives.

I would like to say I cared about my mother's infidelity but this would be a lie. The whole concept of religion had become alien and poison to me. I steadfastly looked forward to graduating and leaving this town of hypocrites, and never looking back. In the meantime, I would have to suffer the inescapable torture of one more year in the foreboding presence of Sister Greta, a sixty-one-year-old greying nun with a vicious temper and a penchant for a metre-long wooden ruler which she used to devastating efficiency across the unwary heads of my fellow students. A visiting guidance counsellor once made discrete observations of Sister Greta, describing her as a control freak sociopath, in other words meaning she was simply a total bitch.

\* \* \*

"Ladies," Greta said. "I want you on your best behaviour today, if such a thing is possible, as we have a special guest arriving." The normally sleepy heads of eighteen-year-old girls glanced up in interest.

The nun glared across the room in distaste. The class of twenty four young women, ranged from plain to pretty with the majority possessing what the school principal described as average intelligence; destined for casual office work and careers as fast-food cashiers while waiting patiently and dreaming of meeting mister right, but would eventually settle for mister downtrodden; men who would spend most of their spare time either in the bar drinking away their hard-earned wages, or in the porno shop purchasing sexy lingerie or massively oversized dildos they fantasised their spouses would desire, but in reality could not possibly make fit unless they used excessive industrial lubrication normally found on the engines of aircraft carriers.

Greta examined one such student who always seemed to catch her eye, either for the sneer this particular pupil always reserved for the nun or perhaps because of the deep sexual repression the elderly postulant suffered, common to her religious order. Her confessor, Fr O'Mahony, whom she visited once a month, often urged the nun to give in to her desires for the female form, saying such feelings were natural. He even offered to introduce Greta to a few woman parishioners who danced both sides of the sexual fence. She had always refused such requests, much to the priest's disappointment. The nun stared at Grace Anderson for a few moments, the young girl was somewhat pretty, even without makeup; slender with small breasts, about five feet two inches in height with flowing wavy auburn hair reaching just below her shoulder blades and hazel eyes.

"Who is coming to the insane asylum today, Sister?" Grace asked, giving a slight smile of amusement.

"A businessman from New York by the name of Thomas Marsh will be visiting this afternoon," the nun replied. "You girls are lucky. Mister Marsh has a hectic schedule. He has a broad range of business interests, including computers. He has been gracious enough with his precious time to speak with you about technology."

"Ooh, maybe we can ask him about Tinder?" Andrea Schofield laughed, drawing a smirk from her best friend Grace.

The nun glared at the blonde student in disdain. "I know nothing about that," Greta said. "I've always believed the Internet holds fascination only for politicians and paedophiles, and worse."

"What could be worse than a child molester, Sister?" Grace asked as the entire class held their breath, nervously expecting the usual violent outburst from the sadistic teacher.

"The spawn of The Devil," the nun declared. The class stared at her, puzzled. "Homosexuals." Greta stood to attention like a soldier on parade, or Grace suspected, more akin to a Nazi stormtrooper.

"And how do you feel about lesbians, Sister?" Andrea asked and the entire class broke into laugher, all of them aware of their teacher's true sexual orientation.

Greta gave the schoolgirl a cold look that turned everybody silent. "You are quite the smartarse, Ms. Schofield. Ever wonder what it would feel like being thrown down a flight of concrete stairs ten times? You might think the tenth would not hurt as much as the first occasion, but trust me you would be *dead* wrong."

Andrea's mouth dropped open in shock as she realised their volatile teacher was not joking and was fully capable of carrying out such a threat, seizing an opportunity one day when there were no witnesses, not that anybody, even the cowardly principal, would dare object.

Everybody jumped to their feet as the shrill lunch bell tore through the silence.

"Be sure to be back in time, ladies," Greta said. "Mr. Marsh will expect your full attention directly after lunch."

Out in the playground Grace and Andrea sat down on the cold stone alongside other classmates and ate their lunches, watching younger students chasing and kicking a soccer ball on the grass.

Andrea peered into the plastic container in her friend's lap. "An apple, a bruised banana and a packet of crisps," the blonde girl said sarcastically. "What a tasty treat."

Grace smiled. "Amazing what a mother can put into a lunch box with sore ribs, better than anything my father might have done. Of course, if he had put my meal together, it would be swimming in two inches of stale beer."

"At least your mother does not have to suffer the drunken advances of that pig of a man," Andrea said. "I'll bet he slobbers all over the sofa as he is too plastered to get it up."

"I can't tell what the original colour of the couch was, under all the stains of his piss, shit and vomit. Besides, mom prefers the company of the parish priest and those old hags he brings to their Sunday afternoon orgies."

Andrea stuck out her tongue in revulsion. "Jesus, can you imagine that creep and his sweaty palms? I'd rather stick a cactus up my snatch."

Both girls giggled as they watched a large Mercedes drive into the school grounds and come to a halt in the staff carpark. The chauffeur, dressed all in black, got out and opened the passenger door. From out of the back seat came a tall handsome man dressed in an expensive dark suit. Everyone stared as the man gazed across the crowded schoolyard of young women dressed in drab navy skirts, white shirts and once-shiny black shoes, now scuffed by striking soccer balls and riding bicycles. The school principal, William Carson, a small greying man in his early sixties in a cheap horrible brown suit and tie, approached and shook the newcomer's hand and led him towards the building. The man, whom Grace guessed was in his late twenties passed close to her and Andrea, and smiled down at the sitting girls. Grace could not take her eyes off him as he entered the school. He was very attractive, with short dark hair, striking sea-green eyes and a strong distinct jawline peppered with a light stubble. He was tall, at least six feet two inches, with a slender yet robust frame, muscular shoulders and arms.

Andrea grinned at her friend. "Oh my God, he is fit. I thought he was going to be some boring old fart."

Grace smiled.

"Even that bitter dyke Greta will be eating him up with her eyes. Maybe she'll finally get that sexual repression off her chest."

Something caught Grace's attention. "Why is that bitch Lisa Swanson staring at us?"

Andrea followed her gaze to the pretty auburn schoolgirl, leaning against the fence on the far side of the yard, glaring at them. "Maybe it's love, but is it me or you she adores?"

Grace grinned. "Oh, darling, it's definitely you."

"Lisa was always a snob," Andrea said. "Looking down her nose at everyone; especially me, even after her father left her mother for a woman half his age, and disappeared. Now she's just a bitter snob with serious daddy issues."

Both girls laughed as the school bell rang. They followed the crowd into the building and into their individual rooms. Grace and Andrea watched in disgust as Lisa passed by a younger schoolgirl in the corridor, and for no apparent reason other than for her own amusement, stopped and shoved the girl, the young woman striking her face off her locker. Blood began to stream from the victim's nose as Lisa smirked before continuing to her classroom. Andrea handed the injured girl a handkerchief before they too entered their room. The young man in the dark suit already stood in front of the blackboard, beside the principal and Sr Greta.

Once they had settled down, William Carson made the announcement. "Girls, please give a warm welcome to Mr Thomas Marsh, an entrepreneur who is graciously giving an hour of his precious time to tell you of potential career choices in business management and information technology."

"Thank you, Principal Carson, for the kind words," Thomas Marsh said with a smile, revealing perfect pearly white teeth Grace suspected cost many thousands of dollars to maintain. "However, for me, it is not about the money. It's the betterment of society and the advancement of civilisation that drives me."

"He sounds more like a politician than a businessman," Andrea whispered to Grace. "But he *is* gorgeous. I wonder if I could be excused to the bathroom to amuse myself for a few minutes."

Grace gave a light laugh in reply. "Wait until this evening and you can borrow one of your stepfather's many black-on-blonde porn movies."

Thomas Marsh stared in their direction as if he heard their conversation, and Grace looked up into those piercing green eyes, mesmerized for a moment. She felt her face flush with embarrassment.

The entrepreneur smiled briefly before turning to the rest of the class. "My primary focus has been to create mobile phone apps that provide a bespoke one-stop application that covers all the customer's financial and personal requirements; in essence whether the individual desires access to their bank, social media sites or simply to check the weather or maps; whatever the application may be they can just use our program and have instant access to all their information collectively from one place, and no longer require the need to use several apps to view their regularly viewed data and websites."

"Sounds very technical and complicated," Principal Carson said. "I guess I am quite the technophobe; I still rely on handwritten letters. The girls are probably the modern wizards on emails and instantly sending messages and pictures to one another."

"I'm sure they are." Marsh gave the principal a thin smile. "But the Internet is more than simply checking out pictures of your friends getting wasted at a party, or putting half-naked pictures of yourselves on social media as if you were auditioning for an amateur porn film."

The businessman did not see their teacher sneer in disgust or the look of shock on the principal's face. "One of my main reasons for coming here is to seek fresh voices in my company headquarters in New York City. I have three vacancies in my administration department due to staff abruptly leaving. The successful applicants will share a paid apartment and have an expenses account for public travel and groceries. It is a fantastic opportunity for eager minds with significant career advancement possibilities. They will still be able to study online and complete their school education and exams."

Greta turned to him in astonishment. "I am certain there are many and better potential employees in other schools and colleges. The girls in my class have no such ambitions and are destined for low-paid work in the town and surrounds. The only reason some of them can even complete their signature is to sign a lifetime of social welfare cheques."

"I have visited all of the educational centres in the region including universities and successfully filled several positions already; it is not just about qualifications, but the mental suitability of candidates as well." Marsh snapped in reply. "I believe in giving students the chance to prove themselves and not write them off without due cause as you seem to be doing. Many in the class would disagree they are only suited for manual labour, or being baby factories for the local football jock."

Principal Carson and Sr Greta stared at him, open mouthed. Carson recovered first. "I will arrange interviews immediately," he said. "You can use my office. I will assemble the girls in single file and you can have ten-minute conversations with them individually, once I have cleared it with their parents. Will that suffice?"

Marsh nodded in satisfaction as he and Carson left the room, while the class burst into conversation.

"Jesus, imagine being able to work alongside him in New York," Andrea said to her friend. "And a path away from that witch Greta and out of this hick town. I have to get that job."

The girls gathered in the hallway and one by one entered the headmaster's office. The hours passed until Grace's turn came. She was one of the last in the queue, with her friend Andrea in front of her. She watched as Andrea left William Carson's office with a big smile on her face. It was obvious her best friend believed she was in the front running to be offered one of the positions. Grace looked on as Andrea practically danced past the disappointed schoolgirls and out into the yard to await news of her friend's fate at the interview.

Grace entered the familiar office. Thomas Marsh sat behind the large oak table, on which were strewn teachers' monthly reports and Carson's budget deadlines with the local city council. Up close, Grace could see Marsh was indeed very handsome and had a definite air of charisma. Most enticing and attractive were those eyes, which studied her intently.

"Your friend Andrea got the second last appointment, as you might have guessed," Marsh said. "An interesting student that one. Biological father dead from cancer when she was just ten years old and her mother remarried two years later. Above average scores in mathematics and sciences, but it is her singular drive to escape this town which made me offer her the employment. Anyone that desperate to leave this town and their family is sure to push themselves to the limit. Though I'm not sure it was necessary for her to blow me a kiss on the way out."

"Thanks for the opportunity." Grace said meekly.

Thomas smiled. "I read your school and personal report. Your father is by all accounts a violent bully and likely alcoholic, at least that is what the rumours your teacher Sister Greta seemed to imply with much relish in her diligent observations, though I am certain that is beyond her remit as your tutor. Does not appear to like me, which is fine, I do not have a lot of love for religious bible thumpers, especially hypocritical sociopathic nuns with no sense of humour."

Grace smirked. "Any family yourself in this area?"

"I have one sister and five brothers, with one living as an oddball hermit in the woods only a few hours' drive from here. I guess he likes to keep a close eye on me. Another brother is dead, so only six of us remain."

"*Only* six?" Grace echoed. "Still a lot of siblings. Must have been hard on your mother to give birth to all of you."

"Our births were significantly less traumatic than was our rearing. I frequently fought with my brothers and sister because I disagreed often with their strong opinions. One argument finally came to blows, which is why I left. But enough of me, let us talk about you."

"You already seem to know all about me. You have my school reports. There is nothing more I can say. Like Andrea, I'm desperate to leave this hypocritical small town, and I would work hard for you."

Thomas Marsh said nothing at first but stared at her for several moments. "I believe you, like your friend, are fiery forces of nature. Very well, Ms Grace Anderson, you have the job. Welcome to the company."

She gazed at him, perplexed, but then stood up and shook his hand, which was warm and inviting, before strolling out of the office and into the schoolyard to tell her friend the news. The whole interview seemed strange and she got this weird feeling there was another agenda at play, that the businessman had given her the job for other unknown reasons, but for now it was time for celebrations.

Andrea gave her a big hug. "Congratulations, the two of us together heading for New York. Lisa Swanson, that sour bitch, got the other job so unfortunately we'll have to share an apartment with her. Never mind, it's us two against the world."

The two girls left the schoolyard as Grace turned around and saw Thomas Marsh staring at her from the headmaster's office. The room behind him looked jet black, as if a great dark cloud had just descended and surrounded the enigmatic businessman.

## CHAPTER TWO

Despite Grace's jubilation, her parents were less than pleased with her good fortune. Her father treated the matter with the usual nonchalant attitude he attributed to any of his daughter's interests and ambitions. Christine Anderson seemed instead troubled by this sudden interest from the mysterious businessman in her young daughter.

"He is ten years older than you," her mother declared as if she were delivering a sermon in front of a packed church. "Are you planning on fucking him and making a name for yourself in this community, or is it a harem he is planning for the three of you?"

"I know it is hard for you to get that someone might actually value me for anything beyond sex," Grace shouted. "Thomas Marsh and the principal have arranged with the Board of Education that my current test results and completed projects are enough to ensure graduation so I don't need to sit through another year of school. Same goes for Andrea. I thought you'd be pleased that your daughter is intelligent and wants to further herself."

"As long as it is solely ambition that drives you and not the eager advances of an older man you don't even know. What would the neighbours say? I hate to think they'll be looking down on me."

"I'm sure your Sunday afternoon sessions with Fr O'Mahony have already achieved that."

Her mother raised her hand to strike her daughter across the face, but her husband caught it in mid-flight.

"I'm the only one who dishes out the punishments in this house," he said. "Put those energies to good use and make my dinner. God knows how I'm going to get fed once this one leaves."

"You were always such a romantic, father dear. Now much as I love your company; both of you, I have to go pack. I'm going to stay with Andrea tonight so we can catch the early morning train for New York. I am sure you're eager to get rid of me, since I'm such a killjoy. Maybe now you can rekindle your dying sex life."

Charles glared at his daughter as she turned for the stairs to pack her meagre belongings. Grace was nearly finished stuffing everything she owned into a small suitcase when a sudden knock on her bedroom door startled her. Much to her surprise, her mother stood there, the tears flowing down her cheeks.

Christine Anderson stepped into the tiny room and sat down on the bed. Grace passed her a handkerchief before sitting beside her. This was all very strange and unnatural; her mother was usually so distant and apathetic and this display of emotion was surely foreign to her.

"You must think me such a monster," Christine said, wiping her eyes. "And certainly such a terrible mother."

"You've done your best under the circumstances," Grace replied. "Dad has made things difficult. But Mom, keeping company with the parish priest probably hasn't helped."

"Bill O'Mahony has showed me compassion and understanding. He has offered affection when I needed it most."

"You know he's interested in something more sinister than pastoral guidance. His motives are far from altruistic, and having sex with him is only making matters worse."

"You're very cynical for someone of your age, perhaps you truly are ready for the big city. Anyway, I am not going to argue with you about my friendship with our priest. I'm more concerned with our fragile relationship and the choices you're making, which will forever affect not only your life but your family's also."

"There is no future in this narrowminded town. You know I love you, Mom, but I have to go. Please say you're happy for me. And promise you will give serious thoughts to leaving my father. There are places you can go; people you can call for support, like women's shelters."

"I have for some time now been hiding half my wages in a secret bank account. When I have enough I'm going to leave your father. I'll watch his face change from confusion and disbelief when he realises I'm not joking, to sheer panic at the thought of caring for himself. I reckon he thinks the microwave is a small TV permanently stuck on the cooking channel."

The two women burst out laughing, then her mom gave Grace a warm embrace and kissed her forehead. "Go and find your future, my child."

Grace stood up, grabbed her suitcase and headed for the front door, unsure when and if she would see her childhood house again. Her father did not move from the sofa, a can of beer in one hand and the television remote in the other, and gave only a grunt to acknowledge her departure; a microcosm of their entire relationship. Outside, she looked behind briefly to see her mother standing at her bedroom window and smiled.

\* \* \*

After staying at Andrea's house that night, the two girls met Lisa the following morning at the train station. Andrea was dressed in a casual short brown skirt and light orange blouse. In contrast Lisa was wearing formal wear with long dark pants stretching down to expensive-looking black shoes and a white shirt firmly buttoned to the neck. Lisa was reasonably pretty; measuring about five feet three inches with straight auburn hair reaching just below her cheeks and light freckles running under her brown eyes and over her small nose.

Lisa smirked at Grace as she approached. "Dressing down for the occasion, Anderson?" Grace was dressed in blue jeans and a plain navy blouse with black shoes.

"Lovely to see you too, Lisa. Are you hoping to dazzle Thomas Marsh with your fabulous brains in the absence of your beauty?"

"At least you don't look like you're ready for work in the red-light district, like Andrea." Lisa sneered.

Grace saw her friend tensing up, about to strike Lisa. Thankfully, she spotted the train in the distance. "I hate to break up this friendly reunion, but our transport is nearly here."

Andrea had to settle for a dirty glance in Lisa's direction. When the three young women boarded the train, Lisa headed for another compartment away from the two friends, content with her own company.

"What a sour bitch." Andrea said as they sat by the window across from each other.

"You do like to wind her up, though," Grace said and the two girls laughed. "Ignore her if you can. It's bad enough we all have to share not only the same workspace but the same apartment together. She is her own worst enemy. It won't be long before Mr Marsh realises her true personality and sends her packing back to this piece of shit town where she belongs."

Andrea nodded and the two girls stared out at the passing countryside as their seven-hour journey to New York began.

*   *   *

It was late afternoon when the train pulled into Pennsylvania Station and they alighted, leaving behind their former lives. The young women had never seen such a magnificent building such as Penn Station before, the enormous foyer covered with gold-coloured tiles and square pillars at either side adorned with massive screens showing adverts and listing incoming and outgoing trains. A huge American flag hung down from the ceiling. They made their way through the throng of people; a multitude of different nationalities and appearances, from tourists dragging heavy baggage to businesspeople dressed in expensive designer suits. Thomas Marsh had mentioned someone would be waiting for them in Penn Station and amongst the chaos they searched frantically for this hidden guide.

Through the crowd, Andrea spotted a young man, about twenty-five years old, dressed in a plain tieless light blue shirt and navy pants, carrying a placard with their surnames on it. He was holding the two-foot-square sign in his outstretched hands, nearly straining himself, as if he were standing on his toes. A relieved smile graced his face when he saw the three girls approach. He greeted them and escorted them from the massive building, directing them into the back of a black limousine-style Mercedes. An older gentleman dressed in a full white suit placed their baggage in the trunk before taking his place in the driver's seat position.

"My name is Paul," the young man said, turning his head from the front passenger seat to face the women. "Welcome to The Big Apple. Bet you never saw anything like this back in New England."

Andrea let out a schoolgirl giggle and Grace shook her head in amusement. Her best friend was in full flirt mode. Lisa frowned in disgust as her blonde classmate stuck her chest forward. It looked as if she was about to pounce into the front seat and cause a crash. Grace gently pulled her friend back into her seat.

"Yes, there are lots of things that are new to us here," Andrea said softly. "But equally, we're bringing many experiences with us into the big city."

The young man blushed and Grace moved to rescue his embarrassment. "Have you worked for Thomas Marsh for long?"

"I started out as a legal intern about three years ago while I was studying for my Bar Exam." Paul said. "I work in the property acquisition and contract management department, sorting out the small print."

"Sounds fascinating." Lisa sneered.

The young man seemed to not notice her sarcasm. "It can be, but the real perks are working and living in New York. Wait until you see your luxury apartment. We all live in the same block of flats."

"Guess I don't have far to go to ask for some sugar," Andrea smiled. "Or some honey to sweeten my cherry pie."

Grace laughed as Lisa stared out the window, ignoring the smutty conversation.

Soon, the car pulled into an underground carpark and the elderly chauffeur opened the back door for his passengers. The girls waited for their baggage as Paul got out and stood with them. They walked through a set of double glass doors into a small windowless foyer adorned with landscape paintings and small plants. Paul pressed the button for the elevator and he and the three girls got in. He pushed for the fifth floor and a minute later they were walking a long corridor, carpeted in dark purple and lined with several doors. Paul used a white plastic key-card to open the last door on the left and all three girls screamed in excitement at the luxury that awaited them. Even Lisa could not contain her enthusiasm for the new life in front of her. A large living room with adjoining kitchenette filled the main apartment with two three-seater black leather sofas facing an enormous single glass pane. The girls stared out of the huge window at the incredible view of high-rise buildings and the majestic parkland of southern Central Park. A seventy-two-inch flat-screen television was mounted on the right wall and the opposite wall was adorned with a landscape painting of the bay area and Liberty Island. The entire floor was covered in a cream carpet. It was like a dream come true compared to the dreary life they'd left behind.

"Take some time to get yourselves rested and used to the apartment," Paul said. "Mr Marsh will be here at 8pm to take you all out to dinner."

"Does our boss take all his female workers out for meals?" Lisa asked sarcastically and Paul smiled.

"It is routine policy of the company to treat all new employees to a casual dinner to make them feel at ease and to assure them they are part of a family, not anonymous members of a faceless corporation." Paul replied sharply, wiping the grin from Lisa's face. "Now if you have no more questions, I must get back to the office."

The few hours passed quickly as the women unpacked their belongings. Each bedroom contained a large double bed with an adjoining locker, and a fitted wardrobe covered one wall, with enough storage space for the needs of a small family. A six-foot mirror was fixed to each bedroom door, and Grace used the reflection to try out a series of dresses and tops. She settled on a flowery white dress, cut above the knee, and a pink cardigan with matching shoes. Andrea knocked on Grace's door and entered wearing a sleeveless short black dress, showing off her tanned legs and large cleavage.

There was a sudden knock on the apartment door and the girls opened to greet their new employer. He was dressed formally, in a full business suit with brown shoes. Grace and Andrea noticed that Lisa was wearing a long navy dress that almost reached her ankles and a black cardigan, as if to make sure no flesh could be seen that might entice the handsome man before them.

"Settled in alright, ladies?" Thomas spoke in a soft voice that made the girls stare at him in speechless wonderment, the lust quite evident on Andrea's face.

"Yes, thank you." Grace answered for all of them and he smiled.

"Let's be on our way then." Marsh said and held the door for them.

The same black Mercedes limousine from earlier was waiting outside the apartment, and the familiar elderly chauffeur drove them downtown to the restaurant. The girls sat together in the back across from the businessman and said nothing for the entire twenty-minute journey, nervous and unsure of themselves in such company. Grace kept looking to the floor, as every time she glanced up she could feel those piercing green eyes fixed on her. But she could not keep her eyes away from the attractive young man and when she did look he was smiling back at her, seemingly oblivious to the presence of the other two women in the car. Andrea and Lisa seemed not to notice, as they watched the city life outside through the windows.

The Mercedes stopped outside a large building called the St Regis on 55th Street. The girls got out of the limousine and took a minute to gaze at the magnificent structure before them. A lit canopy overshadowed two rotating entrances and four square potted plants lay out in front. The building was several stories high, housing not only the restaurant, but also a theatre. Thomas walked up the red carpet and escorted them through a golden arch and they followed in single file through the rotating door into the main foyer. The girls looked around in awe at the sheer luxury of the interior, unlike anything they had ever seen back home. Grace felt underdressed in such a posh establishment and wished she had worn more suitable attire.

An Italian-looking maître d'hôtel approached them and brought them directly into the dining area. Dark marble tables sat on the grey and white carpet, with brown wooden pillars lining both sides, each holding a large silver goblet filled with green shrubs. Classical-style paintings of men and chariots adorned the ceiling and ran across the top of the walls. Plates and cutlery were already set for the guests as they sat and gazed at the sheer size and majesty of the most expensive restaurant in New York City.

"This place is extraordinary." Lisa remarked.

"Only the best for my girls," Thomas Marsh laughed. "Enjoy this dinner, your allocated employment expenses will have to cover your food after this, which I'm afraid would not afford a four-course meal here."

The waiter brought in the gourmet food and a mixture of red and white wine.

"Should we say grace?" Lisa asked and Thomas burst into laughter.

"You did not strike me as the religious type when I interviewed you back in New England," Thomas said. "Perhaps the chicken and cow before us were grateful for such an accolade when they felt the sting of the butcher's knife, and made the sacrifice of their lives worthwhile."

"Well, they say God moves in mysterious ways." Grace said and Marsh smiled.

"The last time I moved in a mysterious way was in the bathroom after ten beers and a dodgy beef curry." Andrea said and they all laughed except for Lisa who appeared quite affronted that her suggestion had been treated with such crude rejection.

"While I won't go into too much detail regarding my faith," Thomas said firmly. "I will say, during my long and extensive travels I saw enough bloodshed and cruelty to suggest that, if such a deity exists, He or She simply does not care what fate befalls humanity. To give mankind the illusion of free will is simply an enormous evasion of accountability, and an excuse for religious entities like the Christian Churches and others, to deny any divine responsibility while maintaining absolute control, which ultimately is what their insidious organisations are truly about. Meanwhile, your apathetic materialistic selfie-obsessed generation cares only for narcissistic social media where you compete for displays of the most profound pouting, worshipping a boy wizard with a squiggle on his forehead and a conceited mudshark who believes her gigantic arse can shatter the Internet."

The girls stared at him, then lowered their heads to eat their meals in silence. Marsh returned the conversation to small talk to break the ice while they finished their dinner. Afterwards, the limousine waited outside as Lisa and Andrea went to the restroom, leaving Thomas and Grace alone in the foyer. She began to walk towards the main door when he caught hold of her right hand, startling her.

"Please meet me tomorrow," he said softly. "I will show you around the city afterwards."

"What about the others, are you inviting them too?"

"No, just you and me. Tell them you have errands to run that will take all afternoon. They don't need to know, and they might be envious."

Grace appeared hesitant for a moment, but then nodded, just as the two girls returned from the toilet.

"The chauffeur will bring you back to the apartment," Thomas said. "My own car will be dropped off here shortly and I need to go to the office. Get some rest before Monday as you have a busy week ahead."

"Burning the midnight oil, sir?" Andrea asked with a grin. "Or is it something else, or rather, somebody else … that takes up your time tonight?"

Thomas Marsh ignored the question as they got into the Mercedes. "Goodnight, ladies."

Grace glanced through the window and saw Marsh wave at her, though Lisa and Andrea seemed not to notice. When she looked again, he was nowhere to be seen.

## CHAPTER THREE

Grace slept only an hour, her mind buzzing from the previous evening's conversations and anticipation of the day to follow in the company of her charismatic new employer, whose motives remained uncertain. She wondered how she managed to find herself in this predicament and whether such a handsome rich New York businessman could possibly find a young girl from the small town in New England attractive. A whole army of butterflies were fighting to the death in her stomach and she ran to the bathroom, kneeled over the toilet, but nothing was forthcoming. Grace wiped her face and put on her makeup, then put on a long flowery long dress with white flat shoes. She left the apartment, the two other occupants still asleep and unaware of her departure.

Grace was surprised to see Thomas waiting for her at the entrance. He was wearing casual clothes, to make her feel more at ease.

"You look beautiful," Thomas told her and she smiled. "I thought we could walk and take in the sights of the Big Apple." He offered her his left arm and she placed her right hand through the gap. "Did you sleep well? I know it is difficult to sleep in a strange bed."

"Not a wink. But finding peace at home was impossible with my parents constantly fighting so I am used to being tired." She paused. "I'm sorry. I tend to ramble when I'm nervous."

"It is alright, I don't sleep much either, never did. I guess it is a family trait I share with my siblings."

They began to walk slowly through Central Park, admiring the large lake and surrounds, the skyscrapers stretching above them. Joggers ran past them and Grace heard the laughter and high-pitched chatter of teenagers and children.

"Don't apologise for your family, I fully understand how complicated such relationships can be," Thomas said. "That bitter teacher of yours was only too forthcoming with all the background history of her students as if she delighted in the suffering of others. Typical of the Catholic Church."

Grace sighed. "So, you know all about my father's drinking and barfights, and all the gossip about my mother screwing the parish priest?"

"I don't believe the hard copy files the nun gave me were that exact and precise," Thomas replied. "Though she was only too eager to fill in the blanks in a joyful and sadistic manner."

Grace wanted to change the subject. "You said at my interview that you come from a large family. Where are they now?"

"I have lost contact with some of them. I occasionally encounter a few of my brethren as they work here in the city, one in law enforcement and the other a rising politician. But they tend to keep to themselves, the only one I have even spoken to in the last few years lives in woodlands in Pennsylvania. I am more likely to have confrontations with their lackeys, bringing threats from their cowardly masters."

"I don't understand," Grace frowned. "Why would your brothers or sister be threatening you?"

"Like I said, families can be complicated. However, a brief encounter with me sends them fleeing with their forked tails between their legs."

"When did you decide to go into business?" Grace asked, as they sat on a wooden park bench by the lake, basking in the morning sun rising over the skyscrapers.

"I have had numerous employments over the years, too many to mention. For a long time I worked in antiques, accumulating at first pottery for middle-eastern clients before moving into metals and precious stones."

"That is a lot of jobs for someone so young, it almost seems you are much older than you appear." Grace said and then yawned.

She blushed in embarrassment. He grinned at her cheekily. Up close she could see how very handsome he was, the sun to his back, shining over his shoulders and through his dark hair, giving an almost angelic appearance.

"I know the perfect cure for tiredness," he said and she looked at him, puzzled. "Ice-cream; strawberry and vanilla is my favourite."

Thomas took her by the hand and they strolled further into Central Park where a street vendor was selling hot dogs and ice-cream cones. He bought two and they sat on the soft grass, admiring the majesty of the city as children played soccer nearby, their laughter echoing over the grounds.

"It really is quite beautiful here."

"I knew you would like it." Thomas said softly. He took hold of her hand again, his touch warm and inviting. "Are you finished your ice-cream already? Here, have some of mine."

Instead of handing her the ice-cream, he swiftly dabbed the top of it on her nose. Grace frowned and then smiled, before wiping the white blob off with her fingers. She reached over and caught his hand, shoving the ice-cream into his chin, smearing his left cheek. He pretended to shove the entire ice-cream into her face, and she gave him a mock look of disapproval, as he fell forward onto her.

Thomas lay over her, pushing her into the grass as she stared up into those striking sea-green eyes. Grace let out a small giggle and Thomas, taking that as an invitation, gently kissed her on the lips. She could feel his light stubble against her face and the faint taste of ice-cream on his soft lips. He was strong, but also quite gentle and she wanted more, responding to his kiss with an open mouth. Grace felt a strange, unfamiliar sensation run through her body like electricity, as if she was kissing someone from another world.

"Okay," she laughed, pretending to be surprised by his advances. "That was unexpected, and nice."

"I have been wanting to do that for a long time."

Grace frowned in response. "You've only known me for a few days. I'll bet you say that to a lot of young girls."

Thomas sat back onto the grass. "Would it surprise you if I told you I am very picky when it comes to women? My life is complicated enough," he said. Then abruptly he stood up, reaching out his hand. "Come on, you must be hungry, let's get something to eat."

They headed towards the northern exit of Central Park, the Cathedral Church of St John the Divine could be seen not far to their left. However, as they were about to leave the last stretch of woodlands before the busy streets, three men in their early twenties approached them from the trees. Grace could see they were rough looking, dressed in torn jeans and t-shirts, one with a skull and crossbones on his jersey. All three wore cheap jewellery around their necks and wrists. At first, Grace assumed they were simply going to pass them by, but one of them reached out, and grabbing her elbow, quickly put his arm around her neck and the other at her waist, holding her fast. Grace let out a brief scream, before the man placed his hand over her mouth, lest any nearby cops or wannabe heroes heard the commotion.

The other two assailants faced Thomas. One pulled out a small knife and shoved it towards his face. What happened next took the three attackers and Grace by surprise. Thomas grasped the knifeman's hand and twisted his wrist. The thug shouted in pain, dropping the blade, then Thomas bent slightly and punched him in the solar plexus with an open palm, sending the attacker flying several feet across the ground, where he curled up in agony. Thomas whipped around and drove the flat of his right foot against the shin of the second man, breaking his leg, then he used a karate chop on his neck, and the man crumpled to the ground. Thomas advanced on the third attacker, who was still holding Grace, but seeing the fate of his fallen brothers, he swiftly let her go and ran off into the trees.

Grace embraced her saviour and kissed him passionately. He caught her hand and they quickly left the park for the safety of the busy streets, passers-by unaware of their recent predicament.

"My heart is beating so fast. That was incredible. How did you do that?"

"Being a New Yorker requires some special survival skills," Thomas smiled. "Now, let's get some lunch."

"After that, I have a hunger for something else." Grace said and he gave a sly grin in reply.

He flagged down a taxi and opened the door for her. They got in and travelled across the city until they came to a large apartment block. Before her was an enormous seventy-storey glass-clad building deep in the affluent heart of Hell's Kitchen. They crossed a marble courtyard and through double doors where two attractive women in red uniforms greeted them from the reception desk. They clearly recognised Thomas instantly and handed him his key-card, robotic smiles painted to their faces, and Grace was strangely reminded of the insane striped Cheshire cat with the maniacal grin and huge eyes from Alice in Wonderland.

They entered the elevator and it rose all the way to the penthouse suite. Grace gasped at the magnificent view which overlooked the bay at one side and Times Square on the other, giving a vantage point of the entire island of Manhattan. The open-plan apartment was split into two sections; a dining area with a glass table and six chairs to the left side of a central area with a four-seater cream couch and coffee table facing the window; and a huge bedroom to the right which contained a king-sized bed adorned with several cushions. The entire apartment was decorated with various abstract pictures and bronze sculptures of animals and people. Grace was conscious of her shoes on such pristine floors, so she took them off before walking on the soft white carpet. Thomas could see she was nervous and went to the dining area to make coffee.

He passed her the hot cappuccino and she began to sip, feeling a bit more at ease. "I can still drop you home, if you like. I know it feels a bit rushed and intimidating being in my apartment, not to mention the fact I am your employer."

"Thanks for the offer, but I am okay," Grace smiled. "I want to be here. I should mention I am still a virgin, before today the only boy I ever kissed was when I was fourteen. He was equally nervous and gave me a sloppy kiss and even bit my lip. My parents' constant bickering kept the suitors away."

Thomas gave a light laugh and moved towards her. He took the coffee from her hand and set it down on the table. He placed his right hand on her cheek and it felt warm and soft to the touch. He bent down and kissed her on the lips, wrapping his arms around her. Then he ran his lips down her neck, to just below her left ear and she moaned. He reached his hands under her thighs, lifted her up against his chest and carried her into the bedroom. He placed her on the soft duvet and she lay back, her arms outstretched in submission.

Thomas pulled her flowery dress up over her head, and Grace reached up and unbuttoned his shirt, noticing he had little to no chest hair, but broad shoulders and strong arms. He bent down and kissed her again, open-mouthed, their tongues intertwining as he undid her bra and began nibbling at the nipples gently until his mouth completely covered them, and she felt them become hard and firm. He eased off her panties, exposing a small tuft of reddish-brown hair. He kissed her stomach then moved up and sucked on her nipples again and Grace moaned loudly. Thomas pulled off his pants and shoes, standing totally naked above her. His erect penis was large and thick, probably around eight inches with an enormous helmet. His pubic hair, like the rest of his body, was groomed and she guessed he often trimmed it.

He kissed her again passionately and ran his tongue all over her neck, over her breasts and down her stomach, before opening her legs and getting down on his knees as if in prayer. She lay on the bed with her legs dangling over the sides, and he began to lick her labia, before moving up to her clitoris and sucking it gently, flickering his tongue over it and under the hood and Grace gasped, unable to comprehend the sensations she was feeling, experiencing pleasure she had not believed possible. Grace's back arched in ecstasy as Thomas latched onto her clitoris with his lips, holding it in his mouth and sucking hard until she let out a low scream and a flood of warmth ran throughout her body down to her toes as an intense orgasm ripped through her. She began to shudder with the extreme sensation and thought for a brief moment she was going to pass out, such was the intensity and unfamiliarity of the passion.

Grace was still in the midst of orgasm when Thomas pushed her further up the bed into the centre of the mattress and entered her. She let out a high-pitched moan of sudden pain and he kissed her, comforting her. He began to thrust, gently at first before moving in strong strokes and Grace could feel his huge penis fill her insides. Thomas rose on his hands as if doing press-ups and began fucking her hard. Grace moaned very loudly now with every thrust, the sensations in her vagina intense and she came again, her juices flooding her and his penis. She wrapped her legs around his waist and moved in time to his actions. Thomas let out a sudden shout and exploded inside her and Grace felt a warm wet feeling flooding inside her. He smiled and kissed her again, first on the lips and then on the neck, then he gently pulled himself out and she moaned. Grace reached down and felt the wetness and pain.

He fetched her a dressing gown as she went to the adjoining bathroom to clean herself. A few minutes later they sat drinking coffee at the dining table, Thomas naked alongside her.

"I'd better be getting back before Andrea notices my absence."

"What will you tell them?"

"Certainly not that I am screwing the boss," Grace smiled. "I guess it will be our secret ... for the moment at least."

"There is nothing to be ashamed about," Thomas said. "I have strong feelings for you, Grace."

"As I do for you, Thomas. But you know how bitchy young girls can be ... and how jealous."

"I understand. But meet me Monday evening after work, I want to see you on a regular basis."

Grace nodded and got dressed, handing him the dressing gown which he covered himself with.

Thomas called for a car to take her back home and she kissed him at the lift, before exiting the building and returning to her apartment, alone to contemplate her thoughts and the life-changing event she had just been part of.

## CHAPTER FOUR

The following weeks passed quickly, going from work to Thomas's apartment; the humdrum monotony of administrative work forgotten by the nights of passion in Hell's Kitchen. Grace and the two girls settled into working in a busy office environment under the direction of a middle manager. Andrea and Lisa complained often about the long hours and the boring repetitive nature of their assigned duties, moaning at length at every breaktime and in the evening. Grace saw little of her lover during the day and was too consumed by filing business reports to even search him out, though her mind drifted often to him, and she knew she was falling in love with him. It was a strange and unfamiliar feeling; being in love. Books and movies did not do it justice or explained it adequately, all Grace knew with certainty is she longed frequently to see him and felt a flutter and excitement in his presence. Being in his company was the happiest; indeed, the only contentment she had ever experienced and she would do anything to maintain that in her life.

Grace however had not confided in Andrea about her relationship with Thomas, somewhat apprehensive how her best friend might view its secretive nature, and fearing her harsh criticism; perhaps Grace also suspected on some level the only reason she had been given the job and brought to New York was because Thomas wanted to seduce her.

The enormous office block was situated on the bay overlooking Liberty Island and from the windows the employees could see the ferry depart and arrive, transporting tourists to the statue. It was a Friday evening and Thomas had promised to bring her the very next day to visit the island as he seemed to know the derelict immigration buildings intimately, as if he had spent time there in another lifetime. So much of his past appeared secretive and an enigma to Grace, and she vowed to know more. Her mother had led such a secluded life, in effect afraid of her own shadow and never one to ask questions. Of course, given Grace's father's normal state of mind and violent temper this was clearly self-perseverance on her mother's part.

The girls had only just finished their working day and returned to the apartment they shared when Lisa opened the cutlery drawer and threw its entire contents across the kitchen table, scattering an assortment of knives, forks and spoons onto the surface and the adjacent floor. Grace and Andrea who were changing out of their work clothes of straight formal jackets and white shirts and into their pyjamas came running at the sudden crash of metal, expecting or perhaps half hoping their flatmate had passed out onto the floor and injured herself; a few weeks in hospital giving them respite from her incessant moaning and nagging.

Andrea was the first to arrive and frowned at the confusion with Grace following close behind. "What the fuck? Bitch," Andrea growled. "Have you finally lost the plot … do we need to call the men in white coats?"

Lisa glared at them in silence for several moments, before turning to Grace in disgust. "Rumours are swirling about your nightly exploits, slut. Everyone in the office building knows about you and Thomas Marsh."

Andrea stared at her best friend in surprise for a moment, but then started laughing. "So what? Jealous, are we?"

"So, you approve of your friend on the Casting Couch?" Lisa asked. "I have worked hard for my position, not have it given freely for sexual favours."

"What position?" Grace sneered. "You are only a secretary like us, working amongst hundreds of anonymous employees. You're nothing but an arrogant snob."

"What was it like, screwing the boss?" Lisa asked. "Did he tell you how beautiful you are, how gorgeous your naked body is or how your pussy tasted like vanilla ice-cream?"

"No," Grace smirked. "But his kisses tasted like that."

Lisa picked up several items of cutlery and began to throw them in the direction of Andrea and Grace, causing the girls to duck down behind the couch for protection. The girls grabbed cushions off the sofa to use as a makeshift shield and ran towards their assailant, causing Lisa to drop her weapons and flee to the safety of her bedroom. She quickly locked the door with her flatmates in pursuit.

"You have to come out of there sometime, psycho bitch," Andrea shouted, knocking her fist on the door. "And I'll be waiting."

The two women retreated to Grace's bedroom to calm down and assess the situation. They stared out at the Manhattan skyscrapers and allowed their temper and frustration to subside.

"I will talk to Thomas about Lisa, perhaps he can find her other accommodation." Grace said.

"That would be good," Andrea smiled as she sat on the edge of her friend's bed. "Are you seeing him later tonight?"

Grace nodded as she sat alongside her and held Andrea's hand. "I am sorry for not telling you; you are my best friend and I feel awful for not informing you, but we wanted to keep it a secret, at least for the moment."

"It's alright, I would not be critical, just concerned that he might be taking advantage of you. Besides, sleeping with one of the most handsome and richest men in New York has to be complicated, not to mention he is our employer and landlord." Andrea sighed. "Tell me, what is he like? What was your first time having sex like? Tell me all the juicy details."

Grace smiled broadly and said nothing for a few moments. "It was simply magical. He was strong and fierce, yet considerate and gentle. He was both a gentleman and a passionate lover."

Andrea chuckled as her friend got up and began to get dressed. "Does he have any good-looking friends?"

"He did mention having five living brothers. If they are half as attractive as him, they must be beating women off with a stick."

Andrea's eyes lit up as her friend prepared to depart. "You must get me a mobile number for at least one of them."

"Will you be alright here on your own? Lisa can be a handful to control."

"Don't worry about me," Andrea said. "I can handle that bitch."

Grace smiled before leaving the apartment, and taking a taxi to Hell's Kitchen, soon arrived at the luxury apartment where her lover lived. She knocked on the door and after a brief pause, Thomas answered dressed in brown pyjamas with a surprised look on his face.

"I did not expect you until tomorrow for our trip to Liberty Island."

"I am sorry, I hope I did not intrude … things became difficult back in the flat."

He frowned momentarily in puzzlement, and then smiled. "It is a pleasant surprise," he said and gave her a quick hug and kiss, wrapping his strong arms around her. "Let me make you coffee and you can tell me all about it."

Grace sat down at the kitchen counter on a high stool and related the events as they happened earlier that evening. "So, can you find her another apartment? I think she would be happier on her own anyway. I have no genuine bad feelings towards Lisa, despite her attitude. I always felt the animosity was between her and Andrea, and really had nothing to do with me."

"I wish it were that simple. However, Lisa's employment contract is linked to that apartment. It would create a dangerous precedent, every one of my employees who are not entirely content with their accommodation could petition for alternative living standards. I am the Chief Executive Officer and Founder, and it is my name on the businesses and buildings of Marsh Industries, but even I must answer to a Board of Directors who scrutinise everything, not to mention the Internal Revenue Service who carry out annual audits. Much apologies, I know that sounds all business like and formal, but I just wanted you to know there are rules even I have to abide by." Thomas said. "Besides, from what you have informed me, Andrea is more than a match for Ms. Swanson and is only too capable of putting Lisa in her place."

"So, we are stuck with that nightmare bitch forever." Grace moaned, placing her face in her hands in dismay.

"Andrea might be glued to that apartment for the foreseeable future, but you have other options available," Thomas said and she gazed at him in curiosity. "You could move in with me."

"That's a big step. I will have to think about it. You know I love you more than anything, Thomas, but I have to consider Andrea in this decision; she is my best friend after all and I don't want to abandon her."

"I understand completely. It is your compassion and kindness that makes you a good person and one of the many reasons why I love you also," he smiled. "I imagine you are hungry, I will get us a Chinese takeaway."

Half an hour later, they ate at the counter, sitting on high stools and eating chicken curry, Thomas frequently smiling across at her. They then cuddled up on the couch and watched television and chatted into the early hours, before going to bed.

Grace awoke some hours later to find her companion missing from the bed and saw Thomas sitting on the couch, his laptop open on the small table in front of him. She put on a dressing gown and approached him, leaning over the sofa and kissed the top of his head.

He smiled up at her. "I hope I did not wake you. I am just catching up on some work before we leave for Liberty Island."

"I slept like a log, that bed is so comfortable. But I missed your cuddling. Come back to bed for a while."

"Fancy some breakfast?" Thomas asked and got up, making for the kitchen.

She nodded in approval and sat down on the sofa, glancing at the laptop, noticing the foreign language documents on the screen. "Is that Spanish? And the other language ... is that Japanese?"

"Yes, it is Spanish, but the other is Chinese; the Pinghua dialect to be precise. We have important clients coming on Monday from that province."

She stared at him in disbelief. "How many languages do you know?"

"All of them, though my Russian accent is a bit off key."

"That's thousands of languages, never mind local dialects."

"It is a family trait handed down from our mother, my brothers and sister share this ability. Do you like fried eggs and bacon for breakfast?"

"Don't brush that off and treat me like an idiot," Grace snapped, her sharp tone clearly shocking him. "I know it's an old cliché of the secretary screwing the boss, but I am not the blonde bimbo who does nothing all day but file her nails and share stupid Facebook memes. I don't even know the names of your family; never mind their occupations, current locations and feelings towards you, though I sense there is great animosity between you and them."

Thomas put down the frying pan, before kissing her forehead. "I am sorry, I never meant to offend you or keep you in the dark, I am only trying to protect you. They are dangerous and not to be trusted."

"You sound like you are scared of them?" Grace asked, frowning.

"With my sister in particular I have reason to be. I am the eldest and was in essence their leader, but after we went our separate ways she …" he said and paused for a few moments. "Put the fear of God in them." Thomas bowed his head in dismay. "Now all but my brother who lives as a hermit in the woods follow her blindly and without question."

"And your sibling who is dead, did she have something to do with that?"

"That was a combined effort on all our parts; it was 'unfortunate' what happened to him," Thomas said and turned towards the window, gazing out at the skyline and Central Park, and Grace could see he was near to tears on the subject. "But he was very sick."

Grace decided not to pursue the matter, and enveloped her arms around his waist and clung to his back. "Let's have that breakfast."

After cooking and eating, they got dressed and left the apartment block and entered a nearby taxi. A short while later they arrived at the pier, Thomas purchasing tickets for Liberty Island and Ellis Island Immigration Museum. They proceeded onto the ferry and went out on deck, basking in the sunshine and the warm breeze coming across the bay.

"I am so looking forward to seeing the museum," Grace said. "It is such an important part of American history; refugees that built the roads and skyscrapers of New York."

"It is a romantic notion to be certain," Thomas smiled. "However, those same immigrants struggled in appalling conditions on the passage from their country of origin, and many were turned away because of ailments and other factors, sent home to poverty and likely death. The floors and buildings are now pristine and shining, but in those days it was drab, hundreds of desperate people queuing for days; the stink of decay and disease heavy in the air. It was difficult to breathe at times."

"You make it sound like you saw it first-hand, like you were there with them fighting for entrance to the city. I heard the offices were closed in the nineteen-fifties, that would mean you would have to be nearly a century old. I really am dating an older man."

Thomas burst into laughter. "Some of my employees speak of their grandparents' time there, they were quite vivid in their descriptions."

They approached Ellis Island and the ferry docked, letting off their passengers. Grace could see the large red-bricked museum to her right, and beyond the trees to her left smaller buildings which once housed refugee families awaiting processing. Thomas took hold of her hand and they proceeded into the main foyer of the museum, the sounds of crowds in particular children could be heard throughout the structure. American flags hung from the balconies overlooking the bright red-tiled floor and Grace could imagine this huge building once full to the brim with immigrants seeking a new life beyond in the city. Thomas led her deeper into the museum and they observed many posters and displays listing the varied refugees, including Irish settlers fleeing the nineteenth-century great famine and English persecution.

Thomas had wandered off further out of sight as Grace continued to read about the Irish Great Hunger, unaware of the approach of a young man who lent in beside her to gaze at the same literature. Grace stood back, momentarily startled as the individual was barely two inches from her face.

"I apologise for my intrusion, please forgive me." He said in a soft tone and Grace could see he was quite tall, standing over six foot, very handsome having curly blond hair and clean shaven, and wearing blue jeans and a white short-sleeved casual shirt.

"That's quite alright," Grace replied. "Are you Irish?"

"No, but I spent enough time in the beautiful Emerald Isle to become deeply interested in its culture and history, in particular its tragic heritage with England. I am an artist and non-fiction author; writing books for colleges."

"Please excuse me, I need to find my boyfriend." She said, as if to notify this mysterious stranger that her intentions were honest.

The attractive individual smiled in reply and Grace wandered off, soon finding Thomas coming out of the toilet. He took hold of Grace's hand and brought her out into the garden, where he bought ham rolls and soft drinks for their lunch, as they sat on a wooden bench overlooking the bay.

"Having a nice time? After we eat, we will take the ferry to Liberty Island and see the statue."

"Yes, I even got chatted up in your absence."

"A secret admirer?" He smirked. "Still, it is no wonder ... you are after all a very beautiful woman."

"You are some charmer, Tom," Grace said, giving him a nudge on the shoulder. "I am sorry for this morning; for being so sharp. I did not want to intrude, I know your family relations are difficult. I do not need to know about them ... all I need is you."

He smiled and leaning in, gave her a brief kiss on the cheek. They got up and walking back to the pier, got on the ferry to Liberty Island. A short while later they arrived, the enormous statue standing above her.

"This was formerly known as Bedloe's Island, and is surrounded by the waters of New Jersey having a varied history from once being a military fort to being a quarantine zone for smallpox," Thomas said as she continued to stare up at the enormous structure, admiring its magnificent engineering. "Originally the statue was brown, but over the course of three decades it turned green. It contains so much copper it could furnish the American Treasury with thirty million pennies."

"It is incredible, I have never seen anything like it. Can we go to the top of the torch or crown and see the view of the city?"

"Unfortunately, tickets are sold out months in advance. But we can see most of New York City from the pedestal."

Grace snatched hold of his hand and they went into the main building, venturing upstairs until they came to the peak of the pedestal, staring over the bay, the statue so close above her she could nearly touch it. After some time, they came back down and into the garden area. Grace sat down on the grass as Thomas's mobile phone rang.

"Apologies," he said. "It is those Chinese clients, I had better take the call."

Grace smiled in reply as Thomas wandered off towards the opposite side of the garden, engrossed in the foreign conversation. A young man sat down alongside her, and Grace noticed with much surprise it was the same handsome individual she had spoken to in the museum on Ellis Island.

"Christ," she said. "Are you following me?"

"Again, much regrets for the intrusion," the man replied. "It is so good to finally have this chat."

"Do you know I have a boyfriend, and he is only a short distance away." Grace said in a sharp tone and got up to leave, the man also standing, and stared right at her.

"Has my brother asked you to move in yet, Ms. Anderson?"

"Who are you? How do you know my name?"

The mysterious young man strolled off towards the water and Grace ran after him. She grabbed hold of his arm, people nearby moving away as they believed some domestic argument between a couple was about to take place, and wanted nothing to do with it and risk getting involved.

"It is imperative for your own safety you cease your relationship with my brother," he said, taking hold of her hand. "That computer app he is developing is dangerous for anyone in close proximity to him. He is dealing with forces beyond his control. Your boyfriend should remember what happened to our dead sibling, in case the same should occur to him."

"What do you mean by that? Thomas said he was very sick and died."

The man burst into laughter. "Yes, you could say our late brother was unwell. A more accurate assessment would be that he was a violent psychotic. Your lover had no choice when he drove that blade through our brother's chest, killing him."

"Are you saying Thomas murdered his own brother?" Grace asked, her face going white in shock.

"There is so much you do not know, Ms. Anderson. If you are wise, you should get out now.

But if you insist on going down this path, ask your boyfriend two important questions: firstly, about the object that he keeps in his high-security vault in the basement of his office block, and secondly …" he paused for a moment. "Why a handsome rich businessman from the big city would travel all the way to a small town in New England to seduce an unknown schoolgirl when he, and I mean no offence when I say it; could have a harem of models screwing him every night."

Grace appeared forlorn, and on the verge of tears. "He said he loves me."

He grabbed hold of her shoulders and stared intently at her, his piercing green eyes gazing deeply into hers. "Of that I have no doubt, Ms. Anderson. He has loved you for a very, very long time; well before your birth."

Grace glared at him in confusion, unsure what to ask next as Thomas appeared, his business phone call completed. The mysterious individual did not see him approach.

"What the fuck are you doing here?" Thomas snarled, pulling Grace away and shoving the man, causing him to stumble. "You have no right to interfere in my business and relations."

"It is those same affairs that concern me, brother. Before you leave, one last matter; I have been requested by our sister to pass on a message: she wants to meet you at 4pm tomorrow in the Cathedral Church of St. John the Divine. Be sure to come alone."

"I have no interest in meeting her, tell our sister and those cronies of hers that we used to call 'family' to fuck off."

"Remember I am the only one of that 'family' that is still your friend. If it were another brother of ours, this meeting would have been less pleasant. I am neutral."

"Is that not the same as cowardice? Stay out of my business."

"Cancel that computer app you are developing, nothing good will come of it. We are not on this planet to interfere in human affairs, unless specifically directed to do so on the orders of The Source, and the divine origin of those commands died with the lake."

"What I am doing is helping humanity, at least the majority of it."

"The others do not see it that way, they prefer the status quo of good and evil to remain ..." his brother paused. "And they will kill you for that belief, make no mistake."

Thomas grabbed Grace's hand and left for the ferry, leaving his sibling behind. She glanced back, but the mystery man did not follow.

"What is going on, Thomas? Was that really your brother? And those things he said to me, it made no sense. I want an explanation."

"Let's go to the office and I will tell you everything."

They returned to the city and after a short taxi journey arrived at Marsh Tower. He escorted her to his private office and sat her down. Thomas reached into a cabinet and pulled out a bottle of vodka and poured both of them a drink mixed with orange juice he took from a small fridge set into the far wall.

"Here, have this, you will need it," he said and sat alongside her. "The man you met on Liberty Island was my brother Uriel; my sibling who lives as a hermit in the woods," Thomas paused for a few moments, and seemed uncomfortable and even a little sad, his eyes appearing watery. "There is no easy way to say this, and you will not believe me."

"Please just say it. Whatever it is, I can take it."

"My real name is Michael. I am the Archangel Michael," he said and she stared at him with a blank look. "I have been on this Earth for four and a half thousand years, I cannot age or get ill, but to all intents and purposes I am human and can die like any man."

Grace stood up and glared at him, before bursting into laughter. "For a moment, I thought you were going to reveal you are married, or even gay; but this is something else. This is obviously some sort of elaborate joke. And that brother he said you killed?"

"I promise it is no joke," he said. "He was called Samael, but you would know him by the title Lucifer."

"The Devil?" Grace smirked in disbelief. "You mean to say I am dating the man who defeated Satan? You never struck me as delusional, Thomas, but you cannot seriously expect me to believe this incredible story without proof. Just because I was taught by a nun does not mean I believe the Bible is real and its stories. I will need real proof of the divine. I know you showed extraordinary strength and skill in defeating the robbers in the park, and your flair for foreign languages, but even those can be faked. I will need more."

"There is more, much more I can show and tell you. I know you must have many questions and I will answer them all, but first I must tell you some ancient history. I promise I will give you proof and that I am not some madman. I don't have magickal powers, but I will show you something not made by human hands, but fashioned by God itself."

Grace sat back down. "Oh, tell me all, I can't wait to hear this story. I think however you will need another bottle. I am going to be well drunk before the night is out."

Thomas smiled. "For this long tale, we will need to go back to the beginning …"

# CHAPTER FIVE

The waters were warm to the touch and inviting as Michael ran his fingers across the surface of the milky white liquid, before splashing it on his face and his shoulder length straight dark hair. He gazed across the vast lake and could see his siblings scattered over the distance as they talked and gazed into the shallow depths, entranced by whatever was transpiring beneath them. Michael made his way to the centre of the enormous pond, the waters causing waves around his waist and he could see Uriel standing and reading from the Book of Life, its golden-orange binding appearing fluorescent, casting reflections in the liquid below. Nearby a golden flat pedestal lay; the resting place for the supernatural book, standing two feet above the waters. This narrow pillar stood in the very centre of the lake, as if the magickal book was the epicentre of all creation.

    Uriel smiled, closing the large book before placing it on the adjacent pedestal. Michael momentarily glanced at the fabulous codex, wondering as to its inner mysteries, but forbidden to do so; only Uriel as its custodian allowed to examine its contents. The Book of Life contained every minute detail of both the mundane and complicated daily lives of every human on Earth in their present existence and all previous incarnations, as they were reincarnated until the end of time. It did not however state future human manifestations, as the circumstances of when that particular life would cease was unwritten or unforeseen, and the soul moved on into another unborn body.

However, Michael was still mesmerised by its majesty, the book measuring approximately one-foot square and about three inches thick. It was despite this, according to Uriel, quite light and felt warm to the touch, its binding and cover giving off a strange golden-orange colour that seemed to change slightly whatever angle he held it. The custodian had explained how when he laid his hand on the otherwise blank pages contained within, they suddenly filled with words and pictures of the person whom Uriel was concentrating on, the most intimate parts of their life becoming transparent, even their hidden innermost thoughts; all their secrets, fears and hopes laid bare, whom they loved and wished to love, who they despised and hated and even wanted dead, and their dark desires and lusts.

Michael gazed across this vast realm which the humans called Heaven, which for what seemed eternity had been the angels' only home; the enormous circular pond stretching a mile in diameter, its entire waters only about three feet deep, rising to their waists and concealing their nakedness with the exception of Gabriel whose breasts were partially obscured by her long blonde hair. She noticed him staring from a distance and she smiled, the cheeky grin that she always displayed, as if she knew being the only woman among the archangels meant she often became the object of attention, whether because of her extraordinary beauty, or to break from the endless boredom and monotony.

Gabriel's main preoccupation was the dreams of mankind, and like her brethren attempted to influence these sleeping visions to promote outcomes established by The Source; that faceless supreme deity that humans referred to as God which they naively believed had their best intentions at heart, but rather it was in reality rarely so. This creator of the world was more interested in maintaining the status quo; a universal balance of good and evil where one could not exist without the other; a planet where the 'saviour' could not live without the diabolical monster as it were, where good deeds often go unrewarded and bad acts remain unpunished.

Gabriel swept her hand across the surface of the lake, the magickal waters revealing Earth and its denizens as they went about their daily lives, going to work in the fields and tending to their families before retiring to bed at night. It was then like her siblings, that she entered their slumbering minds and whispered; creating for the gullible in their dreams what they would perceive as divine prophecies, and upon waking would act upon these supernatural visions, whether it was to finally marry their childhood sweetheart without hesitation, or murder their neighbour whom they previously only barely disliked.

    Michael turned away and could see the boundaries of the round lake, beyond which lay a brief shore of pure golden sand where at point he could see the naked forms of his brothers Ramiel, Raphael, Sariel and Raguel sitting and chatting, only just departing from the pond to converse and laugh about whatever events they had just seen in the waters. Raguel being the Angel of Justice was the closest to Gabriel and they often consulted and agreed on certain matters regarding vengeance and retribution, and its appropriate response. It was clear to Michael that he was their sister's primary brother and would easily serve as her lieutenant in disputes amongst the others. He was tall and handsome like his brethren and had long blonde wavy hair which flowed down over his shoulders.

    Ramiel had long auburn hair stretching to his broad shoulders and had strong sharp facial features, his large eyes staring across the lake, as if seeing something his brothers could not. His primary duty was reincarnation and he often consulted with Uriel on such matters, including the extinguishing of evil souls when their current life had ceased; their violent past preventing future existences in the timeline of the Universe. The dark deeds performed throughout their life would prevent their soul being reincarnated, they would instead be returned to The Source, and their spiritual essence forever destroyed and removed from Creation.

Raphael in contrast was more concerned with healing and easing the suffering of humanity, though he was bound by strict rules set down by The Source. However, he never objected to such regulations and in fact openly welcomed the unwavering edict as it provided an order to the Universe. Raphael would be the strongest advocate of such rigid rules and believed above all that the status quo of good and evil must be maintained, despite the obvious misery across the planet. This often brought him into direct confrontation with Michael, who stated such pain was frequently unnecessary, and it was Raphael's clear duty to prevent such anguish because it was in his power to do so. Simply observing such heartache and despair and doing nothing to ease it made Raphael in his brother's opinion, as guilty as the evil perpetrators who propagated such agony upon their fellow man for enjoyment's sake.

Raphael brushed back his long dark hair and could see Michael staring at him, and sneered his obvious contempt for his elder brother, before turning to talk to his other siblings. Sariel nodded in acknowledgement to Uriel and Michael, his reddish-brown hair falling across his attractive face. He too brushed it back with a sly smile and laughed, some joke no-one else knew occupying his mind. Sariel was the comedian amongst the family, his crude humour often spoken, whether his brothers and sister wished to hear of it, or not. His primary focus was on the sexual relations between humans and the continuation of the species. He was often amused by the complicated and seedy desires of mankind and had no objection to relationships between same genders; in his opinion if a man wanted to share his bed with another man was not Sariel's concern, there were enough humans on Earth to compensate for this.

If however they desired the bodies of children instead, Sariel frowned on this activity and would endeavour to provide some means to deter them, which included some bizarre and violent outcomes; in particular the child molester suddenly developing a fascination with severing his manhood with a rusty knife or some other blunt implement and feeding the detached appendage to ravenous farm animals, forever removing their lust and impact on innocent juveniles. The man or indeed sometimes woman would afterwards cradle their bloody crotch in a mixture of agony and confusion, as to why they abruptly and inexplicably would cause such devastating injuries to themselves; only aware at the time of the cutting they found the urge to do so irresistible.

This unsanctioned justice brought Sariel into direct conflict with his brother Ramiel, who believed such depravity would have damned the paedophiles anyway and their souls upon death would be obliterated, in Ramiel's opinion it was not necessary to make the molesters carve off their genitals. Sariel was however quick to point out that he was not objecting to their spiritual essence being destroyed, and in fact welcomed it, he was simply preventing further harm upon children throughout the perpetrators' lifetime until their death.

"Look at that little shit," Uriel said to Michael, pointing at Sariel who stretched himself out on the sand. "He thinks I don't see him ignoring his duties and instead gawking at naked farmers' daughters."

"Do you ever wonder if we are doing the right thing, guiding and altering the course of mankind for whatever purpose or reason I cannot determine?" Michael asked, changing the subject.

"Be careful brother, you suggest blasphemy. It is not up to us to question the intentions of The Source, only to do what we are told. Surely such an ancient being that created this lake and indeed the entire Universe knows better than we could ever imagine."

"And the unnecessary suffering such as childhood cancer, birth defects and the like, which are no fault of the victims; is this part of some greater plan that we are too stupid or naïve to understand? One day you will have to stop being a blind observer, Uriel, and become an active participant in ending this barbarity. Otherwise, you are unworthy of being the custodian of the Book of Life and should pass the magickal volume to me instead."

"Being the caretaker of the book is my sacred duty, and while I reside here in this place I will forever respect that responsibility. Perhaps you should instead pay heed to your duties and speak to our brother Samael, I have grave concerns for him; his manner and attitude these past centuries has become more distant and aggressive. He seems to favour you above the rest of his family, and might confide in you the origin of his unsavoury views on humanity."

"We have not finished this conversation, Uriel. You are my closest sibling and I love you, but you are wrong in this matter, don't be a blind sheep and follow Gabriel. I know she has ambitions to be the leader."

"I am my own man and not naïve. Besides, our sister's views are too extreme for me. Raguel and the others might follow her orders without question, but I am content to sit in the side-lines and not get involved in her politics."

Michael began to make his way through the waters until he reached the distant shape of Samael. His brother always stood alone and away from the others, never wishing to converse with any of them, with the rare exception of Michael, whose opinion for some unknown reason he respected. Samael was tall and even more attractive than the rest of his family as if The Source favoured him above the others. He had long straight dark hair that flowed down to his shoulders and possessed strong facial features with piercing blue eyes.

"Welcome brother," Samael said aloud. "What brings you to my domain while the others ignore me?"

Michael embraced him. "I would never do that, and besides, where else would I find such entertaining conversation?"

Samael laughed. "Look at the others, sitting carefree on the beach without a concern. Don't you ever wonder as to the true nature of the Universe and this lake we spend eternity in? How long has it been that we gaze like idiots into the waters and twist mankind's thoughts to our favour?"

"Two hundred thousand years we have spent here, strange to say it like it was a short time. Stranger still is this huge pond is all we have ever known all that time, and the unceasing daylight above us with a clear blue cloudless sky and even no sun to gaze upon. If those brothers of ours on the sand got up and walked out into the desert with their backs to the water, they would travel only a short distance before coming full circle and finding themselves on the opposite side of the great lake from whence they started; as if this constructed magickal home of ours is circular and without end."

"True, but is it our home or our prison?"

"I would not go that far and agree to that," Michael replied. "Yes, we cannot ever leave but it is not that bad."

"And the goat or cow that happily grazes in their small enclosure, do you think they are equally content, unaware that one day their throats will be slit to serve the 'greater' needs of another species? Do you not conceive that is what we are doing here? I know you have a similar viewpoint, but are afraid to express it because of how the others might treat you," Samael said, much to his brother's surprise. "Come, let me show you something."

Samael ran his hand across the surface of the lake and the froth receded to reveal the image of an elderly man seated and reading from a leather-bound book on his lap, the item made from animal skin. As Samael and his brother stared, the grey-haired man closed the book and stared upwards before smiling, and then to Michael's astonishment, he actually waved in acknowledgement that he was being observed from afar.

"That's not possible," Michael said in shock. "They should not be aware of our presence and existence."

Samael burst into laughter. "I taught some of these chattering monkeys to converse with me directly, not just in their dreams but also when they are awake."

"Such actions are forbidden and prohibited. How is such a thing even possible?"

"I am different from the rest of you, I am unique. Would it surprise you that I was trained in this skill and even encouraged to have these 'forbidden' conversations? It was The Source itself that speaks to me daily that showed me how to carry out such accomplishments. It would appear this 'God' the humans so adore is not content to mildly influence mankind through their dreams, but take a more active role in their waking lives. It is proof enough this deity that 'loves' them so much decided to wipe out most of them through a great flood and start humanity over; as if genocide was a well-intentioned cosmic event for their own benefit."

"The Source only speaks to me, and as I understand it from the others, talks to us on occasion, and years and even centuries may pass before it whispers again to me or Gabriel or our brothers, and then only to give short brief instructions before silence reigns again."

"Brother," Samael declared and caught his sibling by the shoulders, holding him fast. "It speaks to me constantly, and often in a roaring voice with the intention I believe to drive me to the brink of insanity."

"That cannot be true. The others should know of this."

"They already suspect I am favourite amongst them, given the highest gifts of beauty, intelligence and status, and are jealous. You are aware that my primary duty is the Angel of Death; it is I that delivers the final moment of departure to the humans; an obligation that I believe segregates and drives me apart from the rest of our family, an isolation in truth that I am most content in. However, it is that role that Gabriel most desires; she tires of her own occupation as simply a 'glorified' messenger of The Source assigned to the declaration of official edicts; she would gladly and without hesitation murder me for my unique position."

"Gabriel would not be capable of such an act, even if such a thing was possible as we archangels are immortal."

"Are you really that naïve, brother? You would quickly change your opinion if you thought she knew about your infatuation with that particular female human whom you guide and protect in contradiction with the supreme rule of non-favoured interference, as we are not allowed to assist one human above all others. I know you frequently consult with Uriel to alter the destiny of that certain girl so as to protect her life down through her successive reincarnations; ensuring she comes to no harm and dies peacefully in her sleep as an old woman. I would wager none of our brethren show such compassion in any specific human. They treat all of mankind equally with cold indifference. Tell me brother, what is it about that particular female that interests you so much?"

"I believe I see in her a potential soulmate, if I could somehow become human and live amongst them. I would surely take her as my wife if such a thing was possible, and find some kind of contentment outside of this sterile brutal realm we reside in."

"I see now the reasons behind your fascination with her, and why you keep her identity secret, especially from Gabriel who would kill the specific human without hesitation, if only to see your misery," Samael said. "And what if I told you such a thing might be conceivable; that we could under the right circumstances dismantle this realm and leave this prison, and descend to Earth and live to all intents and purposes a human?"

"Even if it were possible, what effect would it have on the lake? It could be cataclysmic and destroy this place."

"Would that not be a blessing? Or is it the potential loss of your immortality you fear? More likely we will retain our perennial lifespan because our genetic code is pure and original, not 'watered down' like the humans. However, we will acquire some of their inferior attributes like hunger, thirst, lust and even pain. It might be conceivable that 'a fall from grace' would even leave us open to death, whether that be from a simple knock to the head or something more dramatic. I for one, long to see the many and beautiful various means of fatality up close, instead of killing these chattering monkeys from afar. To see and feel the thrust of a blade entering human flesh and being covered in their blood, entrails and even brain matter would be magnificent; witnessing it from a distance just does not have the same majesty to it."

Michael was shocked by his brother's callousness. "Samael, why do you hate mankind so much?"

"I don't. Killing them is actually a welcome distraction from the monotony and unbearable boredom, not to mention having to entertain the sight and conversation with my 'beloved' siblings. But leaving this penitentiary will hopefully bring an end to the endless roaring voice in my head; it shakes my skull and I frequently want to scream in frustration and agony for it to cease, if only for a moment."

"So, it is The Source you despise? I know not why it speaks to you so often and so loudly, but perhaps I could help you find some peace from the noise."

"I appreciate your offer, brother, but there is nothing you can do to distract from the brutal methods of a supreme being that created the Universe in all its majesty," Samael sneered. "On that note, were you aware those human imbeciles have begun building enormous and lavish temples to this 'God' they so adore and believe has their best intentions at heart? It would appear they rejoice in their misery so much they spend what little money they have in creating towering palaces of gold for their beloved deity, and spend every waking moment on their knees in adoration. Perhaps if I were to visit them in person and show them the true meaning of torment and pain, they would build temples to me instead."

Michael was aghast at his sibling's attitude and turned away, leaving him and returned instead to Uriel.

"Well, what did you discover?" Uriel asked.

"It is even worse than you imagined, he is undoubtedly insane."

"The Book of Life shows clearly and without ambiguity the true animus of every human on Earth, and even fleeting glimpses into the minds of us angels. But when I attempt to see into the reasoning of Samael, the text and pictures are all distorted and my vision is clouded instead with images of extraordinary violence perpetrated not only against mankind, but us immortals as well. It would seem Samael wishes us all dead, or at the very least to suffer indescribable agony."

"He has discovered a way to directly communicate with the humans, and even claims he has found a path out of the lake," Michael said, his voice trembling in apprehension. "Surely such a thing could not be achieved?"

"Some of the more intelligent humans, in particular the mages who have spent a lifetime studying the occult and the dark arts might have envisioned a plan, especially if they were able to pass that information onto Samael in exchange for forbidden knowledge that only an archangel might possess. To what end that plot runs would be difficult to decipher ..."

He halted in mid-sentence as everyone abruptly gazed in the direction of Samael, even the brothers chatting on the beach ceased their idle conversation and stood to their feet, staring into the lake with a mixture of horror and amazement. Samael was screaming as he furiously chewed into his left hand, his teeth gnawing at the flesh, causing a heavy stream of blood to fall from the wounds into the waters below. The dark red liquid began to mix with the lake and seeped throughout the entire pond, even reaching Uriel and Michael. They had never seen the blood of an angel before and always believed such an injury could not be performed against an immortal.

A colossal shudder suddenly ran through the lake and the water began to recede, the liquid reaching below their waists and then to their knees. The sand on the beach was more noticeable now as Sariel, Raphael, Ramiel and Raguel entered what remained of the quickly vanishing pond, running towards their leader Gabriel for answers to this frightening calamity. They could see the water disappearing into a large crack that had opened below the feet of Samael as all approached the injured angel.

Michael noticed the enormous chasm was at least six feet by eight feet across and the liquid was rushing into it at a tremendous rate, being sent to some unknown destination. In a matter of minutes, the entire lake had drained, revealing only wet sand in its wake. Samael was grinning madly, staring at the deep dark hole he had created, the blood from his hand still dripping.

"What have you done?" Michael shouted, grabbing his brother by the shoulders.

Samael pushed him back. "I have set us free, brother." He replied as he jumped into the depths of the gorge, disappearing into the darkness.

A gargantuan quake ripped through the dry lake, sending them flying off their feet and into the moist sand. As they began to stand, they noticed several more cracks had developed, it appeared their home for two hundred thousand years was being destroyed and their angelic lives were now in jeopardy as this 'Heaven' was about to be obliterated.

"We cannot stay here." Uriel said, clutching the Book of Life to his chest.

"We must follow Samael," Gabriel said, turning towards the congregation of her remaining brothers and giving them a fearsome stare. "We must find him … and kill him."

She jumped into the chasm without hesitation and the others followed, leaving behind all they had ever known, and beginning whatever new life awaited them.

# CHAPTER SIX

Grace stared at Thomas, before placing her glass on the table, motioning for him to refill it. "That story you told was extraordinary, and yet still so difficult to believe," she said, sitting back into the office chair. "I have so many questions, not to mention proof of these claims, I still don't believe you are an angel, you must appreciate that."

"Yes, of course I understand. What would you like to know exactly?"

"Everything. What happened afterwards? Did you find and kill Samael?"

Thomas said nothing for a few moments and sighed. "He left me little choice. Even after all he had done and the butchery he committed on Earth by the time we found him, he was still my brother. I was closest to him so it was appropriate I did it. Besides, Gabriel wished to carve him into tiny pieces for destroying the lake."

"How is it even possible to kill an angel? Do you require some type of magical weapon like you see in the movies?"

"It is to all intents and purposes as easy as executing a human. When we 'fell to Earth' we developed the same vulnerabilities as every other man or woman despite our enhanced physical strength, inability to age or suffer illnesses. Suddenly we found ourselves susceptible to hunger, thirst and pain. If you were to pick up that penknife and stab me in the heart, I would surely die as swiftly as if I were to do the same act upon you."

"So, tell me about the death of Samael," Grace said. "And how you managed to stay out of history's way all this time and remain secret."

"I will of course explain in greater detail about the death of my brother later, I need to show you the proof first that I am not making up some fantastic story," Thomas replied, as she frowned in obvious disappointment. "It was not easy remaining incognito, but we quickly adapted to the ways of humans; became involved in simple trade and commerce and even held down jobs of every kind, from carpentry, masonry, etc. But we stayed away from politics and the military; anything that would draw attention to us and suspicions about our immortality, in essence remaining in the shadows … until now."

"I would not refer to you or your siblings as the same as us mere humans. I for one would not mind living forever."

"Do not wish that upon yourself so readily. Watching everyone around you dying while having an unnaturally long life in comparison to normal mankind was at times not easy, for I had become fond of some particular humans down throughout history. Those terrible moments of grief were mixed with long periods of loneliness as I wandered this planet, much of it alone."

"So that scar you have on your side is proof you are vulnerable and can feel pain?"

"Yes," Thomas sighed. "We angels can sustain injuries like an ordinary person and even die. Many centuries ago I was stabbed there and took weeks to recover."

"What about the speech of this supposed deity? What exactly did the voice of God sound like?"

"That is difficult to describe, certainly from a human perspective. Imagine the strange tone of the wind through the trees, not human and yet having an air of magick to it; a supernatural whisper unlike anything on Earth and yet you found an irresistible compulsion to obey its instructions."

"You never refer to the place as Heaven. Why is that?"

"Because that biblical description does not fit accurately. It was never Paradise as priests or clergy would see it; no humans ever entered and we were never joyful or content to be there. It was simply our duty for eternity to monitor and guide mankind. We would interfere only at the strict instructions of The Source, never at our own behest or benefit; to do so was absolutely prohibited."

"So, God through you and the rest of the archangels would decide the fate of every human; every facet of their lives from the mundane daily chores to their rare big life choices?" Grace asked. "And why drive Samael insane by shouting in his head; no wonder he believed to all intents and purposes he was schizophrenic, that he never had peace of mind to hear his own thoughts?"

Thomas stared out at the New York skyline for several moments in silence, before turning back to her. "I have debated the craziness of that logic with myself for millennia, and found no easy answer," he said and sat down alongside her so they were face to face. "Imagine a deity with limitless power that created a vast and complex entity like the Universe, with its perfect balance of chemicals necessary to propagate life on billions of planets across the cosmos; it would be therefore simply illogical and impossible to conceive this God would not be able to foretell what consequences could arise from such interference in both humanity and the deliberate persecution of Samael, unless of course The Source intended it to be so."

"So, evil beings such as murderers, rapists and paedophiles are all part of the *Grand Design*?" Grace sneered.

"Yes, that and much more; all the diabolical acts committed by mankind down through the ages can ultimately be attributed to God, despite what modern theologians and psychologists tell you; that evil acts are solely from man alone. It is true humans are capable and indeed perpetrate terrible things upon each other, but the most wicked crimes are committed because from birth their souls are jet black with corruption; in essence they are born evil and no matter their normal upbringing, parentage and education they will perform heinous acts. One only has to examine certain serial killers like the cannibal Jeffrey Dahmer who was doted on by loving parents, but despite this raped and ate every man he could find. It is easy and convenient to label such individuals as deranged, however it is worth noting that Dahmer himself was declared legally sane by the Court. These people come from all walks of life with varying parentage and education, however they share one thing in common; their eyes betray their true nature, being cold and devoid of any emotion as if they were soulless. I firmly believe however there is a simpler and more sinister logic to it all; that this is all part of a grand experiment; that humanity is placed in the very centre of a 'laboratory maze' like mice searching for the exit, and humans are put through a labyrinth of hurdles and pitfalls designed to see how they react to given circumstances often outside of their control like cancer, famine, miscarriages and many other miseries that dominate this life for God's own amusement, for surely there ultimately can be no other reason. I can understand why some people become atheists because the alternative is despairing, and to think most of mankind praise this existence of torment, which I find mystifying."

"It's understandable you essentially lost your faith, for anyone who witnessed what you have and even been part of that grand deception would have turned their back on all forms of religion. So, do you care about what happens to us humans?"

Thomas sighed. "Just because I was present for the birth of human Creation, does not mean I am responsible for the events … and mistakes which followed. I do not care about the betterment of mankind; neither do I wish for its destruction. I simply work towards my own agenda, for which society admires and despises me in equal measure. The few occasions humans have known about our true existence has not always been positive, either for them or us. Our awful experience at the hands of the Spanish Inquisition was proof of that."

"So, like us, you and your brethren are just passing down through the ages with no purpose other than to make the best of it?"

"Partially," Thomas replied. "But I have a plan to at least make the world a better place, if only to put an end to the unnecessary suffering and the crazy balance of good and evil."

He rose to his feet and putting out his hand, took hers and they left the office for the direction of the lifts. Entering the elevator, he removed a key from his pocket and placed it into the slot below the floor numbers and entered several digits into a console. The elevator began to descend as they watched the floor numbers decrease.

"One thing I don't fully understand is how a God who created humans in Its image could treat them so cruelly and with such apathy as to their misery and hardship?" Grace asked. "Surely such a parental figure would look kinder upon Its children?"

"Well said, and a very educated response," Thomas smiled. "What the Bible teaches about the creation of mankind is false, and only a person with absolute blind faith would take it at face value and not examine its obvious contradictions. Consider for a moment why an all-powerful deity would forge a Universe billions of years old which only recently gave birth to humans; surely if this cosmos was solely for their use, then mankind should always have existed. Do you think us archangels also existed for all time and were the guardians of first amoeba, then insects and lower animals and finally dinosaurs before mankind arrived? The simple and obvious truth is that we angels were created first, and from our genetic code mixed with apes, humans were established through careful manipulation of evolution; that is the scientific missing link separating apes from mankind. The biblical God you believe in never lived in any fashion as a man; for any creature that could exist everywhere simultaneously could not do so under the limitations of a human. The Source could be more accurately described as a gas or matter more akin to Dark Energy which comprises the majority of the Universe."

"So, God never appeared as a human to prophets as mentioned in the Old Testament?"

"I don't know anything about that. However, such an omnipotent deity could conceivably appear as any individual or animal. Gabriel once told me The Source did materialise to her in the form of a beautiful young woman with flowing silver hair and piercing red eyes, but I was dismissive and believed my sister was simply mistaken, confusing the dreams of mankind with her own aspirations to finally witness such a vision and give meaning to the archangels' existence."

"Imagine if you could actually talk to God, the questions I would love to ask."

"Indeed," Thomas replied. "But conversations were impossible, such requests always went unanswered as if on deaf ears. The commands from The Source were one direction only and the gaps between each orders could be years, or even centuries. Only Samael seemed to be the perpetual receiver of such divine speech. Of course, one could question whether in fact such communications were real, or simply part of his deranged mind."

"Tell me, how did you manage to avoid the Catholic Church all this time? Surely they would have become aware of your existence through rumours and stories down through the centuries?"

Thomas burst into laughter and she glanced at him in puzzlement. "The Roman Church hierarchy is more concerned with acquiring wealth and the subjugation of women. They are intrinsically corrupt; more akin to American politics. The Cardinals tell you they have a 'hotline' to God and only through them can you achieve salvation, but in reality they don't believe their own sales pitch, and the few that are not actually atheists themselves know with certainty none of them are going to be saved; their sins far too plentiful and extreme to guarantee anything other than damnation."

"If Sister Greta and Fr O'Mahony are indicative of what the Church has to offer mankind, then surely it is with a sense of karma that they deserve their fate in the afterlife," she said and decided to change the subject. "What was it like after leaving the lake?"

"Uriel and I remained together for many years while Gabriel with the others went their separate ways after the death of Samael. Initially we used what meagre skills we had in the sense of understanding all languages and survived by acting as translators between traders and foreign merchants, eventually we became business owners ourselves offering everything from goods to carpentry and metallurgy after we learned the value of international commerce."

"So, when you said you sold pottery in the Middle-East you were not being sarcastic. Obviously you didn't remain selling common items forever, there are after all other ways to become rich, even in ancient times?"

"Indeed, we managed to establish trade routes for our merchandise to Africa and the Egyptian empire. However, constant wars in the regions meant we were always on the move. I worked in dozens of various employments from stonemason to gravedigger to even being a scribe for the Romans under Julius Caesar. With the onset of the Industrial Revolution I discovered by investing in cotton and coal it was easy to become wealthy. But I still had to frequently relocate and change my identity as people became suspicious as to why I did not age or get sick, especially when one considered the living and working conditions of Victorian London."

"I would love to hear more about these stories; your personal first-hand insight into historical events."

"I want you to know it all."

"And what about your siblings?" Grace asked. "What became of them?"

"Uriel and I parted ways after several millennia together, we had a difference of opinion about what our roles should be and as angels he was adamant we should not marry or have sexual relations with the humans. I explained to him to all intents and purposes we were almost the same as mankind and it should not matter. The lake and The Source were long gone and that life would never return. Only a few times did we encounter Gabriel and our brothers and those brief meetings were formal and cold. It was evident she did not want anything to do with us and our brothers were now only too willing to adhere to her orders without question. Uriel did not object to her ranting but wished instead to be a silent observer and remain neutral. It has been over a century since I met her and our brethren that follow her like lapdogs."

"No wonder you are nervous about meeting her tomorrow," Grace said softly and grabbed hold of his hand. "I will go with you and offer what support I can."

"Thank you," he smiled. "But it is not necessary. I will be alright, and besides, Gabriel can be harsh and has very little time and understanding for mortals. I don't want you to be placed in any danger."

Grace held his hand tighter and turned to face him. "We are in this together."

The elevator door opened at that point and they exited into a short corridor where a single plain white door lay at the opposite end. There were no windows on the featureless walls and a brown concrete floor was beneath their feet.

Grace glanced at him in curiosity as they approached the door and another numerical keypad was on the adjacent wall. Thomas pressed more codes and they entered beyond into a large circular room. Five heavily armed men greeted them and she was suddenly frightened, but he took her hand and motioned not to be concerned. All of the men wore bulletproof vests and were armed with a side pistol and sub-machineguns. They saluted Thomas in acknowledgement as Grace observed these new surroundings. Another plain white door marked lavatory and canteen lay opposite, meaning the black dressed guards only had to leave their posts for a few minutes and were at all times only a short distance from this main area of the bare concrete reinforced basement. Like the corridor leading to this large circular chamber, there was no furniture or decorations on the walls of any kind. It was however the main item in the room that instantly caught her attention; an enormous round metal vault she recognised from movies usually belonging to large banks where they would store gold, money and the deposit boxes of preferential clients lay to their right. Grace was reminded of what Uriel had said on Liberty Island about the vault and its mysterious contents.

Thomas approached the huge door and Grace noticed another keypad and a small screen on the safe above the wheel-handle. He placed his hand on the console and a series of lights began to highlight under his fingertips before he entered another series of codes, again completely different from the elevator and the keypad on the door in the corridor.

"Is all this security necessary?" Grace asked.

"Something more valuable and precious than all the gold in Fort Knox lies inside," he replied. "And like that fortress, many men would die and kill for its contents."

She stared at him, both surprised and intrigued by his comment as he turned the wheel and the enormous metal door slowly swung open. Thomas escorted her in as he closed the safe behind them. What she saw next caused her eyes to open wide in amazement. The room beyond was approximately twenty feet length and width, and filled with fantastic ornaments and weapons of varying descriptions hanging from hooks on opposite walls. She could see medieval swords, knives and axes above various antique gold and silver chalices and pottery on the floor alongside jewellery and rolled up tapestries. The entire chamber was adorned with such treasures including open caskets of what appeared to be Roman gold coins and even older currency which she could not decipher as she got on her knees and examined such splendour.

"This is extraordinary," Grace said in astonishment. "This stuff must be priceless. You have gathered an archaeologist's dream here."

"The remnants of a long lifetime spent as a trader and merchant. However, the real treasure lies behind the next entrance." Thomas smiled and pointed to a single metal door opposite the enormous gateway from which they had entered this chamber.

Grace noticed the single metal door had no handle, but yet another small computer console on the adjacent wall. The only other items of interest were a one-foot square window just above the centre of the door at head height allowing both the persons inside and outside of the room to see the other, and a metal grille to the left of the aperture for ventilation and transition of speech for same, which Thomas explained.

"The metal in this door is composed of one-foot thick chromium and the window is several inches thick and bulletproof. Both could withstand the effects of a grenade or even rocket launcher."

Thomas said. He suddenly took her hands in his and stared at her fixedly. "Grace, I know this has all been a great shock to you and has been difficult to absorb, and I am certain a part of you still believes this is all a great fantasy of mine, and that I am delusional because quite simply from your perspective how could these things be possible; talking about angels and God, and the fact your boyfriend is ancient and virtually immortal."

"I could not have put it better myself," Grace smiled. "But I am ready to see whatever is beyond that door."

"I am very pleased you said that, because what comes next is the most extraordinary thing yet. Before we enter, I have something incredible to tell you. It must have occurred to you that during my long lifetime I would have had many, even hundreds of different lovers, but what if I told you there was only one; that I shared my bed to all intents and purposes with the same and only woman down through history from the moment I left the lake to this very moment."

Grace stared at him in confusion. "I am flattered. But you cannot make me seriously believe I was your only sexual conquest, that you have existed on this planet for several thousand years and saved yourself until you met me recently. Besides," she laughed. "You are simply too good in bed to have been a virgin like me."

"You misunderstand, I watched your former lives for aeons from 'Heaven' and guided them safely through their life until your successive reincarnations, forever protecting and loving you / them from afar in the lake, until I met your incarnate soul in person and became your Earthly husband until your / her death, and when you were reborn and reached of sufficient legal age, I then married you again and again down through the millennia until this current moment. I have loved you, and only you since the dawn of mankind."

Grace stood motionless in shock for several moments. "That's impossible," she stuttered. "Even if such a thing were possible, surely I would be different each life, I would not be the same woman you met first time around."

"True, your appearance was different each incarnation; you were from many different races across the millennia, but your fiery personality was surprisingly similar each existence, and in each and every lifetime you loved me as passionately as if it were the first time."

"If what you say is true then I suppose it is romantic. Of course, others might consider it incredibly creepy as if you were a perpetual stalker and manic obsessive," she laughed, which he found disconcerting. "I am joking with you," she smiled. "That explains what Uriel meant back on Liberty Island when he told me you specifically picked me out at the school to come work for you in New York. However, while I understand how you managed to keep tabs on me in Heaven by gazing into the lake, I am somewhat perplexed on how you tracked my incarnations throughout history as you would be unable to ascertain where and when I would have been reborn."

"This is where the secret room comes into play." Thomas said and keyed in the numbers on the console adjacent to the door.

He opened the door outwards, revealing a strange sight. Grace gazed into the small eight-foot length and width concrete chamber which was the complete antithesis of the area behind them. While that contained an enormous array of ancient antiques and weapons, this room was the absolute opposite; filled with modern technology. A computer tower, keyboard, mouse and monitor were placed on a metal high table on the far wall, an assortment of thick cables running from the computer tower into the ceiling, and further wires from it attached to a single two-foot length and width square metal box seated on a separate wooden table in the centre. The cables from the computer appeared to be directly connected to the mysterious crate through various holes in its outer surface. Grace carefully stepped over the cords and could see moving data on the monitor of what appeared to be people's personal information including current employment, spouses and children if any, accompanying their face which was similar to a police mugshot. She stepped back as Thomas lifted the lid on the box, revealing a large one-foot square book, the colours on the cover changing and seeming to alter as she stared upon it.

"Behold the Book of Life," Thomas declared. "From the moment of creation of mankind to its final demise, here within lies all the intimate and hidden secrets of humans from their birth to death and their subsequent reincarnation. Every moment of their lives from the mundane to the important is written here; no small or large detail is omitted, no matter how they wished certain embarrassing or criminal events were ever recorded and instead were forgotten."

"How can such a small book contain all the details of every human to have ever lived? Surely you would need a computer database the size of a house?"

"Just like the Internet where the information is vast, it is also controlled and directed to the precise knowledge you seek, like a search engine. It will reveal only the details of the particular person you are enquiring about. Let me show you."

He lifted the cover of the book, careful not to disturb the wires attached with circular pads similar to what doctors used to monitor heartbeats. Thomas encouraged her to touch it and as she felt the mysterious book, she noticed it was warm, and the paper felt very strange; almost alive as if you were stroking a sleeping animal. Grace lifted the pages and saw the manuscript was blank throughout, each leaf revealing no information. She glanced at him in puzzlement and he smiled as he took her hand and placing it flat on the surface of a bare page, put his own hand on top of hers. What happened next filled her with amazement as the vacant leaf suddenly came alive with words and pictures. Grace began to read, astonished as the book revealed what she was doing at that precise moment, deep in the basement of Marsh Tower as if she was reading her own life story as it was unfolding. It described how she and Thomas were standing at that very moment reading from the Book of Life, even mentioning her curiosity at the contents and how they entered that room and the preceding chambers; her very actions and thoughts outlined in minute detail as if the supernatural book was reading her mind.

"This is extraordinary, not to mention a bit Big Brotherish," Grace said. "Why was it at first blank and its contents obscured from me?"

"Only an angel can reveal the inner workings of the Book of Life. After all, it was created for us to facilitate our job of overseeing mankind, that is why only through my touch in combination with yours were the details lay bare. As regards privacy issues, I can understand your concern, but The Source never considered 'political correctness' when forging the sacred manuscript. Through my intercession I can reveal to you not only your current life from birth, but also the forgotten details of your former incarnations if you so wish. You can read how you were a maid in Victorian England, assisted me as a scribe in the Roman Empire and even as a nurse in the Second World War, and many other lives down throughout history, and in all you were by my side until your mortal death. It was through the book I was able to ascertain your next incarnation, and be there to safeguard that destiny until you came of age so we could be together."

"How on Earth am I supposed to take all this in? Only yesterday I was in love with a handsome rich businessman, to today discovering that same boyfriend is an archangel who is in possession of the mythical Book of Life, is being hunted by his heavenly siblings, to stories of God from a first-hand perspective, and I have been reincarnated many times and lived with you as your 'soul-mate' for all eternity. How is it I have no memories of past lives? Surely some flashbacks would carry over, given that I always had the same life partner?"

"It is the same for everyone, and rightly so. Imagine being born remembering dead spouses and continuing grieving for them, or children from your last incarnation still alive; you would search them out and all this would impact both your current life and theirs also as they would not recognise their dead parent with a different face, in addition a much younger version of same. I know it is a lot for anyone to absorb," Thomas said softly and embraced her, holding her close. "We will return to the apartment and you can rest and let all this sink in. However, before we leave I need to show you one more important item. You noticed the computer system and the knowledge displayed on the screen. That device is directly connected to both the Book of Life and the enormous mainframe several stories above, feeding personal information related to every man, woman and child on the planet from the supernatural book to the computer storage archives."

Grace stared at him in puzzlement. "Why would you need that knowledge collected from the Book of Life? Surely the American National Security Agency already has such data, why not just ask them for that? And governments of other nations?"

"Because it is the sole reason why the Book of Life is so unique that makes it so valuable and can harvest data no government agency could ever collect, though certainly in their wildest dreams they wished they could," Thomas replied. "Imagine being able to not only know the time and circumstances of the birth of every person on Earth, but also know whether that individual would do good in the world or commit foul acts from early childhood until their death."

"I thought you said the book could not foretell the future? How could you know for certain if a person will commit evil deeds or not?"

"I don't. But the Book of Life does. It alone knows for absolute surety who is destined to be a murderer, or rapist, or paedophile…or even worse. It alone knows who will grow into a dictator or serial killer; their innermost thoughts laid bare to the book like an open palm. Consider knowing and having that knowledge who is born evil and will do terrible acts upon the world. Then envisage being able to kill those people before they commit these deeds; when it is barely a dark dream in their twisted minds. No longer only to read afterwards in the Book of Life or much later in newspapers and the Internet whom these monsters were, and wish if only you could have stopped them murdering that innocent child, you could have saved the family that dreadful heartache that will follow them throughout their lives."

"So, is that what you are doing? Collecting the personal details of evil souls?"

"I am more proactive than that," Thomas smirked. "That computer app I have been developing when it goes online will integrate itself into every modern device from laptops, to mobile phones, tablets and even the electrical brains of all vehicles from trucks; to caravans and all makes of cars, and especially all the thousands of satellites in space. Shortly you will have to be living in the Amazon Rainforest to be immediately outside of its influence, and when it goes onstream, it will seek out those same evil people and stop their hearts forever no matter their age or personal circumstances. From babies to the elderly, if you have a predestination towards depravity, you will die instantly and the Book of Life will extinguish those souls and prevent any future reincarnations. In essence, I can rid the world of evil in an instant and make the planet a better place, leaving only good humans behind to propagate the Earth."

"You are talking about mass murder," Grace said in shock. "I am not sure whether you are a genius or a lunatic. You are considering probably killing millions of people."

"Fourteen million, three hundred thousand and twenty-seven individuals to be exact, which includes three thousand, two hundred and fifty-five politicians ... and two former American Presidents; one Democrat who had a fondness for blowjobs in the Oval Office, and a so called Republican who is an outright bigot narcissist."

"That's not funny. I now know why Uriel was so concerned as to your activities. The other angels do not approve of what you are doing with this computer app."

"Gabriel and the others after we left the lake simply wanted to ignore the plight of mankind. Uriel and I used the Book of Life to travel and exact retribution on those humans who had committed terrible acts. Sometimes it would take us months, even years to traverse such large distances and find the preparators. Contrary to the teachings of the Bible, we did not have wings on our backs, but legs and limitations like any other human. I had to wait millennia until technology such as this was finally invented, especially the microprocessor and the birth of the Internet, before I could develop my computer app and put into practice what I had always wanted; a way to once and for all destroy evil people."

"Why stop with the diabolical individuals?" Grace asked, shrugging her shoulders. "Why not just go further and kill all humans and rid the world of the stain of mankind completely?"

"The app was never intended for that. Neither do I wish that."

"Seriously, I am not joking. When you see what mankind as a species has done to the planet from animal extinctions to the plastic destruction of the oceans, would this world not have been a better place without humans. If it was up to me to choose, I might very well consider the complete annihilation of all humans; not just the evil ones, for at times I have a difficulty seeing the difference between good and bad … even if it meant my own death as well."

"I guess we will agree to disagree on that one. However, based on that opinion, does that mean you believe in what I am doing and I have your blessing?"

"You don't really need my absolution," Grace sighed. "Though I do *believe* it's of paramount importance to you and your conscience as your soul twin that I grant it. I told you we are in this together, whatever the outcome; whether this computer app succeeds, or brings about our own destruction."

## CHAPTER SEVEN

Grace and Thomas returned to the apartment in Hell's Kitchen and she sat down on the sofa facing the magnificent skyline as he made coffee for both of them. He handed her the mug and she began to sip, letting out a huge sigh.

"Are you alright?" Thomas asked with a nervous grin. "I'll bet a part of you would like to run for the door and go back to Andrea, and even the misery of that small town in New England somehow seems appealing, because it is far less complicated and everything there appears normal, even if it is utterly depressing."

"That is an interesting way to put the fantastic story you just told me," She smiled. "I think I believe you, but it will just take a long time to absorb it. Can I ask you something?"

"Of course. You can ask me anything."

"In all those lifetimes we shared together throughout history, how many children did we have? Surely it must number in the hundreds; those grandchildren and their descendants must be in the tens of thousands over the millennia."

Thomas said nothing for several moments before getting up and gazed out at Central Park, the sprawling lights of New York stretching into the horizon; its many streetlights flashing in the darkness and the snakelike lines of cars making their way through the night towards their destination. When he turned back to her, Grace noticed tears were streaming down his face and she rose from the couch and hugged him fiercely, wrapping her arms around his strong frame, and yet despite his supernatural strength, could distinctly feel his fragility, and in that moment, he seemed to her more human than anyone she had ever met.

"I'm sorry," he sobbed as she held his face in her hands. "We angels can never have children. While we have the appearance of mankind with all its attributes, that 'spark' was missing. It is a brutal irony that our genetic code was sucked from us and used to create that evolutionary jump from apes to humans and forge the society you see around you today; whilst simultaneously denying us the ability to have direct offspring of our own. It is both the gift we gave to the world and the punishment bestowed upon us for leaving the lake."

Grace sighed. "It is not your fault. Besides, I am only eighteen years old, it is not something I have really thought about; having children and raising a family. Perhaps we can adopt or other methods of conception … in time."

"You must think me terribly selfish; a cruel monster who would deny you this right because I always wanted you for myself." Thomas said, wiping his face.

"I don't blame you, sincerely. The true fault lies with a divine architect who would deliberately design you this way, as if God wished you also to be part of his grand experiment. I must admit I am not an atheist, but neither am I a strong believer. I am a sceptic, but I keep an open mind; I have never seen a ghost but that does not mean there is for definite no life after death, neither have I set eyes on an extra-terrestrial, however one would be naïve to be resolute and say for certainty no aliens exist considering the sheer size of the cosmos. Many scientists admit privately there must be an intelligent engineer behind the creation of the Universe considering its complexity and the exact balance of chemicals necessary for life. One belief is if the expansion of the galaxies after the Big Bang had been a millisecond faster or slower, then this world and many others would never have existed; in essence if you were to count sheer chance as the deciding vote on life being created, you would need to roll seventy consecutive sixes on a single dice to match the same figure that scientists have established is the odds on the requirement for the expansion of the Universe; a number calculated as one in many trillions."

"It may sound insulting and offensive to nonbelievers, but in my extensive experience I have found most atheists are begging for someone to finally prove them wrong. Despite the terrible acts carried out over the millennia and even today in the name of religion, I have discovered people are generally desperate for proof of the divine; for something greater than themselves to ultimately give their lives meaning outside of the mundane, and what little pleasures they can garnish from their short existences on this planet."

"I have been meaning to ask you on that topic, is this the only world that life exists? Somewhere out there in the cosmos are there other guardian angels watching over other planets and interfering in their lives?"

"Yes, life of a sort exists on many other worlds. But humans are unique in the entire Universe; nowhere else does a species exist that matches the intelligence and capacity for love, the arts and literature. Neither are there any angels watching over the simple animal and sea creatures that roam those planets. We too are unique and our fates are intertwined with mankind, for after all we are their true parents being both their protectors and from our genetic code their very existence was established."

"Should I still call you Thomas Marsh? For that is not your true name, is it?"

"I have not used the title of Michael for centuries. It has been necessary as society has become more obsessed and focused on legal paperwork to create false personas for business reasons and to simply interact on a daily basis. The taxman for one is consumed with bureaucracy and despises oddities in audits; I had to create fake identities that were perfect and able to stand up to scrutiny. I have had dozens of names over the millennia. But the title of Thomas Marsh like the others is completely legal, and to all intents and purposes is my name. It is right and proper to call me by that persona, and to be perfectly frank, it is one I prefer over my archangel title."

"Let's leave this heavy talk until another time. It will be dawn soon and we have that meeting with your sister ahead of us. I want it to be just you and me again for a while like it was this morning before all the madness of angels and demons; of gods and supernatural books, and when all I knew was this simple life, and not many other forgotten existences."

"You should get some rest. I may not need sleep, but you have a long day ahead."

"How does that work exactly?" Grace asked, sitting on the couch. "You never get tired?"

"I suffer fatigue like any human. However, it is a trait I share with my siblings; never being able to fall asleep, but meditation usually brings me back to full strength."

"I wish I had that ability. Not to mention what I could achieve with gaining those extra eight hours lost through sleeping."

"Perhaps, but I always wondered what dreams I would have experienced, given the chance."

"Mine are usually nightmares of the convent school or my horrendous family life."

"I know you said you wanted no more heavy talk," Thomas said. "But on that subject, you never asked me if anyone you personally know will die as a result of the activation of my computer app?"

"You mean will Sister Greta, or perhaps even my own father perish?"

"Would it surprise you if I told you they are not among the fated evil souls? The terrible acts committed during their lives are a consequence of bitterness and injustices they perceive were perpetrated against them long before; abuse in childhood and similar times. They are simply acting out those grievances upon others weaker than themselves and under their control. The absolute darkness that has doomed others was never present on their souls."

"I guessed as much," Grace sneered. "Despite my father being a drunken wife-beating bastard, even I would not wish him dead. He would lose the opportunity to mend his ways, even though that is probably unlikely to occur."

"I could show you indications of how he became the man he is today by reading from the Book of Life."

"No, that is not necessary, I already know the answers to that pitiful tale," she said and sat up on the couch. "Thomas, if I am to be part of this world-altering event and could potentially put myself and others I care about in harm's way, I need to know more about the book and that computer app you are developing."

"I am sorry, I assumed because of how passionately you believed in this cause in your previous incarnations to rid the planet of evil, you would naturally desire the same in this lifespan."

"I am not those *people*," Grace replied sharply. "I am my own person with my own mind, and will make my singular viewpoints based on this life alone."

"I understand completely. What is it you wish to know exactly?"

"How can you be so sure that this app will even work? What makes you believe with such certainty that a person is truly evil from birth with no possibility of redemption, especially as this will kill children, even babies?"

Thomas said nothing for several moments before responding. "Not to be patronising, but I have experienced all aspects of humanity over four and a half thousand years, not to mention what I witnessed from afar in the lake. I have encountered people forced to commit vile acts and suffer lifetime scars as a result; child soldiers compelled to murder their parents and siblings, fathers execute their families rather than face certain torture by their enemies, and none of these were because of an ingrained evil nature. A warrior who kills another combatant does so because of orders and duty. But it is the person who delights in the suffering of others, and murders for fun does so because his soul is black from the moment of creation, and no amount of love and understanding will want him or her to think otherwise. I have met many like this throughout history; from Hitler and Stalin to modern despots like Assad and Kim Jong-Un. Their sole happiness and joy is the pain and torture of others and only their own death will make them stop these heinous acts. I was a member of the select audience at the trial of the serial killer Ted Bundy, having bribed the press corps into allowing me entrance. He blamed society, in particular an addiction to pornography as an excuse for raping and murdering all those women. But never once expressed remorse for his crimes. It was certitude enough that when he escaped, instead of fleeing to Canada or Mexico and the surety of the electric chair, he was compelled to sate his hunger by killing three women in one night. Even his own attorney described him as the definition of heartless evil after not only raping and murdering over thirty women, but keeping the severed heads of a dozen of his victims as souvenirs. I stared into his eyes; those cold emotionless pupils and saw only empty blackness there; the identical abyss I witnessed in Jeffrey Dahmer, Adolf Hitler and many others throughout the ages. That is why they say the eyes are a reflection of the soul."

"I understand you have that unique perspective, both being immortal and an angel, but how certain can you be that the Book of Life will seek out those same evil humans and wipe them out? How sure can you be that only the guilty will be punished?"

"I have spent millennia studying the book, I know what it is capable of. I am confident technology has become so advanced it is now possible to achieve my aims, and I have employed the greatest scientific minds to the task. I even carried out a test run on the app in its early stages and managed to kill a Syrian soldier from thousands of miles away; his life snuffed out in an instant, proving it is a success. When the complete app goes online, I will be able to kill millions."

"So, your staff are aware of what they are creating?" Grace asked, shocked. "You could conceivably have a traitor or anarchist within those ranks and undermine the whole endeavour?"

Thomas smiled. "All they know is they are involved in the creation of a revolutionary application that will combine all social media, emails, programs and even the computers behind modern televisions, vehicles, tablets, laptops and mobile phones into one cohesive structure that will help unify the planet like never before. They are unaware of the connection to the Book of Life, and if they did know, many would describe such a religious 'myth' as pure fantasy; any employee even mentioning such a thing would be treated with utter ridicule and contempt."

"So, you can count computer coding amongst your languages?"

"I have watched the advancement of technology with great interest. I was a consultant with British Intelligence during the Second World War when they invented the Enigma machine, responsible for decoding German submarine activity, and was instrumental in pushing that forward with politicians and technicians, making them aware of the importance of such a computer and its future potential."

"I thought you and your siblings tried to avoid getting involved with mankind, and events that might shape history?"

"We did, but certain monumental occurrences like World War Two inspired me to participate. The Nazis were the greatest manifestation of evil I had ever seen, not even the Romans could have matched them in ferocity and efficiency in the way they organised the Holocaust. I can be killed like any human, so becoming an active combatant like infantry was unwise, but I could still use my enormous intellect in other ways; like the Enigma machine, and feel like I was in some capacity being part of the fight to destroy Hitler. Though in recent times, Islamic State have surpassed the Nazis in cruelty and warped nature."

"That brings me to an interesting point ... I thought the Old Testament Bible said the Jews were blessed in the eyes of God? How could The Source allow the persecution and genocide of that people, as in The Holocaust?"

Thomas laughed, much to her surprise. "Like I mentioned before, our 'all-powerful' deity cares as little for the Jews as it does for the rest of mankind; God has no favourites and does not discriminate between races or nations, treating every human with equal contempt."

"And you instead care so much?" Grace asked which shocked him. "You told me before you also ultimately are not concerned whether society fails or succeeds."

"I have been witness to the rise and fall of the Roman Empire, the age of the Egyptian Pharaohs and the birth of American influence and capitalism," Thomas replied. "All these societies once burned brightly, and then suddenly their light went out. People are being born and dying every day, but it is the unnecessary suffering I despise."

"So, *unlike* Samael, you are not doing this just to get back at God?"

"My brother was insane and worshipped violence in all its 'glorious forms' as he saw it. He had his own twisted agenda and hated mankind and The Source for what happened to him. Contrary to Samael, I do not kill for pleasure, and this planet and indeed the entire Universe is forged in such a way that to uncreate it is impossible. I am simply trying to make the world a better place, sincerely."

"Okay, my love," she said softly and held his face in her hands. "I am sorry, I did not mean to upset you. I just needed to clear some things up before we proceed in this life-changing adventure."

"I know I said that I won't allow you to come to harm, as I have done in all your previous incarnations, but I still don't think it is a good idea for you to come to the meeting with my siblings at the church," Thomas said. "Gabriel will see you as a weak link and a way to get to me, threatening you to influence my decision with the app."

"I understand," Grace replied flatly. "But I am not afraid of them. I have lived with the threat of violence my entire life with my father and won't be so easily intimated. Neither will I put you in a compromising position, I will stay be your side, now and always."

Grace brought him to the bed and cuddled herself into his strong robust frame and they laid together in that same position for hours before it passed into early afternoon, Grace drifting in and out of deep sleep. They rose and quickly dressed as Thomas made them sandwiches. After eating, they left the apartment and walked through the city; not taking a taxi, their minds occupied on the meeting with Gabriel.

\* \* \*

They finally arrived at the Cathedral Church of St. John the Divine with a few minutes to spare before the appointed time. Thomas stopped dead in his tracks as they approached the entrance, and Grace glanced at him in puzzlement, before seeing three figures standing as if on guard duty at the doors to the church. Grace took his hand and they continued towards the gothic building, determined not to show weakness.

"Long time no see, brother," one of the three men said as Grace could see they were all like Thomas very handsome and tall, and all appeared a similar age. They all had short hair and were dressed in expensive black suits as if ushers at a funeral. "You were told to come alone."

"I am my own person. I do not answer to you or our sister," he replied sharply and turned towards Grace. "May I present my brothers Ramiel, Raphael and Raguel."

"So, you have confided in mortals our identities," Raguel declared. "Your treachery has no boundaries. You should be on your knees girl, for you are in the presence of three archangels."

"I am sorry for not bowing," Grace replied in a sarcastic tone. "I was waiting for the Heavens to open and announce your existence with a thunderclap, or perhaps even trumpets from the skies. But if it helps, I can whistle *Danny Boy* quite nicely."

"And like you Michael, she is also insolent." Ramiel said.

"Where is our sibling Sariel?" Thomas asked. "You are missing the full set for me to be fully intimidated and quaking in my boots."

"Our brother the comedian has been absent without leave these past two years and his location is unknown," Raphael said. "You wouldn't happen to know anything about that, would you, brother?"

"Despite our legendary rivalry and the spectacular falling out millennia ago," Thomas paused for a moment. "I would not harm any of you."

"That is why you will always be weak; you lack the strength to do what is required," Raguel said. "We would not hesitate in killing you, if so ordered."

"Spoken like a true politician, you fill the requirements of United States Senator perfectly," Thomas said as Raguel glared at him in rage. "Being a bully and tyrant makes you an ideal successor to our former American President. Now if you don't mind," Thomas sneered as he brushed past them with Grace. "We have an appointment with your leader."

"We will meet again soon brother, and in less hospitable circumstances." Ramiel said.

They entered the magnificent Cathedral Church of St. John the Divine and saw before them hundreds of small chairs laid out to the left and right of the central isle. Above their heads was a huge dome supported by massive stone pillars, and in front in the distance was the altar behind two opposing rows of high seat stands where priests and bishops would sit for mass for the Archbishop for special occasions that demanded their presence. Grace was amazed at the size and majesty of the gothic building, and could see a single figure seated near the front of the small chairs on the left side. She glanced at Thomas in nervousness as they made their way down to the sole individual.

The seated person did not turn around and Grace could barely identify the shape of a woman wearing a long black coat and hood which obscured her features. Thomas sat next to the mysterious woman as Grace moved into the row directly behind, but a few seats away, so as not to intrude but would be able to still hear the conversation quite clearly.

The individual removed her hood and Grace gasped at the extraordinary beauty before her; gazing upon the most attractive woman she had ever seen. Gabriel had long flowing blonde hair stretching down to her shoulders and perfect features with pale white skin and eyes as blue as the ocean. She was tall, nearly six-foot Grace guessed in her seated position, with very large pear-shaped breasts atop a slender frame, and dressed beneath the long coat in a striking green dress and white high-heeled shoes.

"This conversation is not for mortals, Michael," Gabriel declared in a tone that was almost musical. "Even if your girlfriend is the reincarnation of your lifelong love. Yes, we are aware of Grace Anderson's true soul heritage. We have been keeping tabs on you all this time."

"You seem to have lost Sariel in your travels," Thomas sneered. "Your *intelligence agents* appear lacking in that department ... very sloppy."

"Sariel has a fondness for the flesh of young women ... not unlike yourself," she smirked and glanced coldly at Grace with eyes that almost seemed to enter Grace's very soul, sending a chill down her back. "He will inevitably find his way back, he always does when trouble comes to his door, which invariably he cannot handle."

"This cathedral is one of the most popular tourist destinations in New York," Thomas said. "You must have made quite the impression with City Council to guarantee such exclusivity."

"Ramiel is Assistant Director of the New York State Police Department, it was a small matter for him to ensure this privacy."

"I don't appreciate you using Uriel as a messenger, especially through Grace. Any future notes meant for me can be communicated directly."

"You are not an easy man to obtain, Michael. Your tight security at Marsh Tower does not seem to like us."

"They have been given your likenesses and various identities, ensuring prying eyes stay away."

"And you really believe because of that the Book of Life you have in the basement will be secure?" Gabriel laughed. "Do you naïvely think I will allow that computer program to go online?"

"It does not concern you, sister. It is none of your business."

"None of my business?" Gabriel shouted and stood to her feet. "It is my solemn duty given to me by The Source to maintain the status quo; we are here to observe and not interfere."

"And what was it we were doing in the lake, if not intruding on every aspect of mankind?" Thomas replied fiercely, also rising to his feet. "When are you going to open your eyes, sister? We were manipulated from the beginning; we were slaves to God's will, but no more will I be a blind servant serving an evil master."

Gabriel turned and with a brush of her hand, sent twenty or more metal chairs scattering across the church. "Be very careful, brother, lest you end up like Samael; dead and forgotten, and buried in the desert in an unmarked grave for all time." With that, she quickly exited the cathedral.

Thomas let her go and did not follow. Grace approached him and gave her boyfriend a strong embrace.

"You were not joking," Grace said. "I have never met anyone so intimidating and frightening in my entire life, and I have seen my father in his most violent and meanest drunken moods."

"Let's get out of here." Thomas said and they left the church.

They returned to his apartment in Hell's Kitchen and sat on the sofa in silence for several minutes, absorbing the content of the meeting they had just attended.

"So, what was the point of that confrontation?" Grace asked.

"It was a final warning, not to implement the app. Gabriel is a self-righteous hypocrite, she wants to use the program herself to wipe out half of mankind. Despite that however, one should not underestimate her." Thomas replied. "I will drop you home, Andrea will be missing you and you need to rest before work tomorrow."

"Before I go, I need you to tell me what happened to Samael. I want to know what Gabriel meant about those threats."

Thomas buried his face in his hands, before turning to her. "You won't like parts of this tale."

Grace took hold of his hand. "I need to know everything. The bad with the good."

"Very well, let me tell you of life after the lake …"

# CHAPTER EIGHT

The sand felt hot and coarse beneath his naked skin and the blazing heat of the sun fierce against his unprotected back and legs. Michael opened his eyes and found it hurt to see; a strange sensation, feeling pain for the first time and knew all at once in that moment he was now to all intents and purposes human; and no longer an angel, the lake gone forever.

Michael slowly rose to his hands and knees and with much trepidation, finally to his feet to take in these new surroundings; so very different and completely alien to the life just gone. An endless desert filled his aching vision in every direction. He could see no sign of his siblings and began to stumble through the sand which burnt his feet with every step. Michael began to walk for what seemed hours until in the distance he could see through sweat-drenched eyes what appeared to be a small village containing about ten single-storey huts constructed from clay and straw and at least two dozen camels. He was nearly on his knees when he entered the village square, surprising the locals, never before seeing someone so totally white of skin from head to feet, never mind naked and without water or transport.

Michael fell flat on his face as two figures ran towards him. He barely managed to open his eyes, and with delight recognised Ramiel and Sariel gazing down at him. He noticed they were clothed in light brown robes and sandals, appearing to have been made from some type of desert animal. They picked him up and after waving off curious children and their anxious parents, brought him into the shade of a palm tree. Sariel rushed and gave Michael a jug of water from the village well and he began to drink it down furiously, coughing.

"Take it easy," Ramiel said. "Your body has never experienced liquids before. You will make yourself sick."

"Where are we?" Michael asked as Sariel wrapped a similar rough brown robe around his naked sibling. "Where are the others?"

"This is Egypt, about ten miles from the capital Memphis," Ramiel replied. "This is the era of Pharaoh Khafra, son of Khufu who built the great pyramids at Dahshar and Giza. When did you fall to Earth?"

"I don't understand your question," Michael said in puzzlement. "I arrived this morning. Didn't you two also leave the lake this very day?"

Ramiel and Sariel looked first at each other and then stared down at their eldest sibling. "Michael, we arrived at this planet two weeks ago," Sariel declared. "Fortunately, I saw Ramiel fall nearby and at the same time as me, so he was easy to locate. There has been no sign of the others. A passing merchant found us and brought us to this village, and we carried out repairs to these huts and the well in exchange for clothing, accommodation, food and water."

"For someone new to this planet, you certainly managed to land on your feet as it were."

"In this harsh environment, you learn fast or die quickly." Sariel replied.

For the next few days the brothers laboured and waited, scanning the desert in hope of seeing another of their siblings, but there was no sign. The days were long and hot, the nights cold and dark, but full of amazement like young children as they stared up at the moon and stars, trying to count their number and distance from Earth.

"It is simply astounding," Michael said to his brothers. "I could never have imagined such beauty; it is all so different witnessing these sights from the other side of the lake."

"Hey, try this," Sariel said, handing his eldest sibling a flask of sheep skin. "The locals call it wine."

Michael took a swig and promptly spluttered, and the other two brothers burst into laughter.

"It is an acquired taste," Sariel smirked. "But it grows on you."

"Certainly after several flasks it does." Ramiel added and patted Michael on the back, causing him to cough more.

More similar nights followed and Michael began to feel a new understanding and kinship with his brothers he had never, or rather not being allowed to experience back in the lake; a closeness forged in a new world and lives that were not set and open to mystery.

When it seemed they would have to wait years or even forever for a sign, two riders arrived and the three brothers rushed to the camels, eager for any news. To their delight, a hooded figure descended from the humped animal, and throwing back his hood, revealed the bearded face of Raphael. All three siblings embraced and laughed in joy, as they led their new arrival into the village and poured him some water.

Raphael drank quickly from the flask. "I am so pleased to see you, my brothers," he said aloud. "I was afraid you had perished in the desert."

"As we had feared the same for you," Sariel said and the others nodded. "What news have you of Gabriel, Uriel and Raguel?"

"Gabriel and our brother Raguel are safe and well and reside in the capital city Memphis. With the exception of Uriel, we three arrived about two months ago and swiftly found each other. The city could be seen in the distance, so it made sense to make for there and safe refuge. You cannot imagine the surprise of farmers seeing three naked white strangers. Especially with Gabriel, as laying eyes upon an unclothed female is taboo and forbidden."

Sariel smiled in response. "And Uriel and Samael? You did not mention being in the company of them."

Raphael said nothing for several moments and the three other brothers stared at him in anxiety, fearing the worst. "Uriel we believe arrived approximately three months ago," he said. "Because he landed much earlier than even Gabriel, I and Raguel, he was left to fend alone and probably felt at times he was the only surviving archangel, stumbling through the desert, starving and thirsty … and afraid."

Michael grabbed hold of Raphael by the shoulders. "Are you saying Uriel is dead?"

"No," Raphael replied and they sighed in relief. "He was picked up by royal guards on the outskirts of Memphis, and because they believed he might be a spy from Assyria they put him in the dungeon, and there he still resides."

The three brothers were stunned.

"And you simply left him there to rot?" Ramiel asked sharply. "We must barter for his life."

"It's not that easy," Raphael replied. "He is detained at the pleasure of the Pharaoh Khafra, the Heretic and the Cruel."

"I don't give a fuck if he is the Stupid and the Cowardly," Michael sneered. "We must do everything to free him. Besides, Pharaoh or not, he is a mere human and they are easy to manipulate, or kill."

"Not this one," Raphael replied. "We believe the real Khafra is dead, and has been replaced."

"I don't understand," Michael said. "You say this man is a usurper, surely the people of Egypt would not allow that."

Raphael paused for a moment. "The new Pharaoh Khafra is our brother Samael," he said and they stared at him in shock. "He arrived around six months ago. After sneaking into the city and realising the importance of the position of Pharaoh in Egyptian hierarchy and culture where such an individual is essentially regarded as a god, Samael entered the palace under cover of a sandstorm and after fighting his way through several royal guards using his superior angelic strength, killed Khafra in his sleep. He dragged the body into the desert and fed it to jackals."

"And the people did not know the difference?" Sariel asked in puzzlement.

"Khafra had no wife or children to question his identity," Raphael replied. "The Pharaohs wear heavy jewellery and a headdress, further hiding his appearance and he even shaved his head to finish off the swap. It would be an act of treason to contradict your 'god' and would surely result in your death. The true Khafra was of a similar age, making the transformation easier. Launching battles against the nation's enemies with increasing ferocity and brilliance has only reinforced his claim, especially as Samael himself leads the army and shows a savagery that terrifies Egypt's foes. He has a particular fondness for torturing and beheading captured prisoners by his own hand which seems to unsettle even his hardened generals."

"That makes perfect sense," Michael said. "Back in the lake, he had shown a great interest for inflicting violence on a personal level. This must be a dream come true for him."

"The Assyrians have a nickname for him," Raphael said. "They call him The Devil which only seems to delight him further."

Michael shook his head in distaste. "Why does he not simply kill Uriel? Why keep an archangel alive which could upset his plans?"

"He appears to know the rest of us are alive and aware of his enterprise for Egypt and the rest of the world," Raphael said. "If he keeps Uriel alive, he knows we will attempt to rescue him and Samael can then capture us all in one fell swoop. He even parades Uriel publicly every few days with mouth gag so he cannot question the Pharaoh's real identity. Furthermore, Uriel is shown to be beaten and whipped regularly so increasing our intensity to set him free."

"The bastard," Michael growled. "I cannot wait to get my hands on Samael, and to think I once called him brother and friend."

"As did we all," Ramiel said. "But he is no longer either of those, and must be treated like a rabid animal and killed."

"There's more," Raphael said. "Uriel had the Book of Life in his possession. It is clear Samael has it now and is using the insights the book offers to destroy Egypt's enemies, knowing their troop movements and strategies by effectively reading the minds of their commanders."

"So, what is the plan?" Michael asked. "I presume there is one being formulated by our sister, given her massive intellect and the time passed since her arrival to this planet."

"Gabriel thinks a full-frontal assault would be suicide given the large bodyguard detachment the Pharaoh has, and the fact the people think of him as a god and would surely protest if we attacked his identity in public," Raphael said. "She has instead made contact with the High Priest of the Temple who suspects the Pharaoh is not the true Khafra, and is hungry for power as he would likely succeed to the throne if this usurper was killed. Gabriel has only given the priest enough information for the plan to come to fruition, lest Samael is also reading his lifespan from the Book of Life and arrest him. This so called holy man will order most of the guards away from the palace, and allow us entry through a secret passage that Khufu used to ferry prostitutes in the night to his private quarters which Samael now uses as his own bed chambers. We will capture him, bring our brother to the desert and exact retribution."

"Agreed." Michael said and they all nodded.

The brothers rested for the night in one of the clay huts and the following morning bartered camels for the journey to Memphis. They arrived at the capital two days later and were greeted on the outskirts by Gabriel and Raguel. After a brief embrace, their sister led them to a house in the poor district overshadowed by the outer wall and rich buildings of Memphis.

"Take these," Gabriel said, handing out short-swords to her brothers. "Do not be afraid to kill. Despite our enhanced physical strength, we are vulnerable on this planet and can die from a mortal injury like any human. Do not think for a moment the guards will hesitate in using their weapons. Our lives are infinitely more important than theirs, and reincarnation is not something gifted to our kind … unlike them."

"Nevertheless their lives are no less significant, and we should consider that when we butcher them." Michael replied.

Gabriel stared at him in rage. "Michael, I need to know you are fully committed in this venture. This requires no hesitation from any of us."

"I want Samael punished as much as anyone," Michael said sharply. "I am after all the eldest sibling and should be in charge of this undertaking."

"You may be the oldest," she replied. "But I doubt your conviction in doing what needs to be done. You were the closest to Samael in the lake."

"Are you accusing me of being a traitor, or even complicit in the lake's destruction?"

"No," she said after a few moments of awkward silence. "But we are no longer in the lake and now not guided by The Source; the same rules held there do no longer apply. Perhaps it is time to elect another leader."

Michael turned to his brothers. "Are you all in agreement?" He asked, looking at their faces one after another. "Let us then put it to a vote and majority wins."

"Agreed," Gabriel echoed. "Let us vote for strength and force like The Source taught us, and not for weakness and indecisiveness which your brother believes is the right course of action."

"That's a bit unfair, not to mention completely inaccurate," Michael said. "I simply believe there is more than one alternative to how we proceed."

"There is only one path. In the absence of The Source, I am now its messenger on Earth," Gabriel declared. "Now, let us vote. Who is with me?"

Michael watched as one by one his brothers raised their hands in solidarity with their sister. He sighed in dismay and realised at that moment that things would never be the same between them; that immortal bond forever damaged, perhaps irretrievably.

"Now to work," Gabriel said. "Samael obviously knows at least some of us are here, considering his daily parade of Uriel; displaying his humiliation and encouraging us to show ourselves. I have asked the High Priest to distract our brother with domestic boring matters lest he read from the Book of Life and know our plans. It is imperative we clear our minds of this scheme after this discussion. We have only a narrow window of opportunity before Samael realises he is being deceived and captures us. Michael, I want you to make for the dungeons and free Uriel. Ramiel's task will be to secure the book while the rest of us will take our errant sibling into custody."

They all rose and departed from the small house and made their way through the labyrinth of buildings and gardens of Memphis. As they travelled through the large city, they marvelled at the majesty and beauty of the dwellings and statues situated throughout the massive region, as it appeared so different gazing down from the lake. Thirty foot effigies built to worship the gods Horus and Osiris, and other minor deities adorned the entrance to the main gate to which they managed to sneak through, passing off as merchants selling wine and grain. Flat roofed two-storey buildings filled the capital, accommodation for wealthier residents and beyond off to the centre of Memphis the barracks for the hundreds of guards who patrolled the city, dressed in brown light chainmail, sandals and a leather cap covering their entire scalp. The soldiers brandishing short-swords and long spears passed them by as the group of angels hid in adjacent alleys and empty houses as they slowly approached the enormous palace situated in the very centre of the province.

The dwelling of the Pharaoh was simply colossal, its decorated white walls and inner square structures stretching hundreds of feet into the air and dominated the entire city given its massive size. The palace's only apparent entrance was a huge ramp and stone stairs for soldiers, chariots and appointed dignitaries. They now knew with absolute certainty why Samael immediately sought ownership of this empire, and from it could launch a military campaign on the entire world. Egypt was undoubtedly rich in gold and resources and as the Pharaoh was considered a living god, his orders would be accepted without question; it was the perfect platform for global domination.

"A small army could not penetrate this structure," Michael said, staring up at the pure white wall towering above him, its smooth surface decorated with a chariot and rider going into battle, the soldier's spear raised high. "I hope that information the High Priest gave you was true."

"His deviousness is superseded only by his ambition," Gabriel replied. "The fact our desires coincide ensures his compliance; he is simply fulfilling his own thirst for ultimate power and is willing to take risks by trusting we will complete our end of the arrangement."

With that, she led them around the eastern side of the enormous wall for some distance before stopping near a group of palm trees. Her brothers stared at her in puzzlement, before their sister pressed in on a lightly coloured brown brick and to their amazement, Gabriel began to push a two foot by five foot section of the barricade inwards, revealing a long tunnel obscured by darkness. She pushed the wall sufficiently to allow them all access before closing it shut behind them. From beneath her robe she took a small torch and gave it to Raphael, before using two pieces of flint to light it. He gave the blazing stick back to their sister and she began to lead them down the narrow passage which was only six foot high to the stone ceiling and three feet across, meaning they had to follow in single file.

They made their way through the tunnel for several minutes until they approached another seemingly blank wall. Gabriel pushed on the barricade and it opened outwards, revealing a small plain room containing empty wine flasks and boxes of straw which were filled with scraps of fruit and nuts, the remains of meals meant for visitors to the palace. An arch lay at the opposite side, opening into a grand corridor. Gabriel discreetly peered and could see statutes of the gods filling the marbled large passage, but could see no guards or any other sign of life. The High Priest was also not to be seen and she hoped his absence was because he was keeping their brother busy.

Gabriel turned to her siblings as they exited the tunnel and crowded into the tiny room. "Michael, head down the corridor to the right and go down the steps leading to the dungeon," she said as she revealed a small parchment on which a crude diagram of the inner layout of the palace was scribbled. "The guards are due to patrol every twenty minutes so it is vital we make haste so to avoid any unnecessary conflict; surprise is key to the success of this venture and remaining alive. Ramiel, this chamber …" she whispered, pointing to a section of the map, "is likely where the Book of Life is stored as it is located close to the Pharaoh's bedroom and is hidden from visitors and soldiers alike. The rest of us will apprehend Samael in the adjoining area and all meet back here shortly. You have your orders, let's get this done."

Michael nodded and exited the room, making his way down the corridor as quickly as possible, all the time keeping to the wall to avoid being seen. A few minutes later, he could see stone steps leading down into darkness and carefully creeping, soon found himself in a large region of reinforced wooden doors which filled the circular dungeon. A small latch was positioned near the top of the many entryways. He approached one of the doors, gently knocking on the wood and listened for a response. There was none and he moved to the next. He could hear faint moaning coming from the cell and opening the latch, peered in and could see the form of a man huddled in the far corner dressed in a rough brown robe and sandals. Michael called out in a low tone and the figure responded, getting to his feet and approached the exit. He gasped in shock when the familiar face of his brother Uriel came into view, his face so bruised and bloodied that he was almost unrecognisable.

Uriel limped, almost falling as he drew near, but still managed to smile. "You are a welcome sight, brother," he stuttered. "Unless of course you are here to join me in my misery."

Michael stuck his hand through the narrow hole and placed his palm against his sibling's damaged cheek. "No, we are here to free you."

"We? Are all the others with you? And Samael, where is that bastard brother of mine?"

"Yes, we are all safe and well. And Samael is soon to meet punishment for his crimes."

Uriel smiled in reply as his rescuer briefly departed and grabbed the ring of keys off the opposite wall from a hook. Michael unlocked the cell and helped his injured brother from the filthy dungeon. They could hear faint cries of pain coming from other doors, mixed with the scratching of what was likely rats feasting on the corpses of prisoners who starved or were beaten to death. But they had neither the time to free other unfortunate residents of the prison, nor could not risk their escape without alerting the guards.

They made their way slowly back up the stairs and down the corridor towards the room and the tunnel to freedom.

"I will leave you here and find the others," Michael said. "You will be safe and hidden until we return."

Uriel snatched hard onto his older brother's arm, holding it fast. "No, I want to come with you and witness my persecutor's fate."

Michael could see he was adamant on the matter and it was pointless to argue. He helped his younger sibling down the opposite side of the corridor towards the personal chamber of the Pharaoh. Michael could still see no sign of any patrol and was beginning to question where the guards may be when they heard a great commotion coming from the large room ahead. They approached the ruler of Egypt's quarters and were shocked to see Gabriel, Raphael, Sariel and Raguel on their knees, the blades of soldiers standing above them at their exposed throats. Four more guards advanced on them and disarmed Michael, before ushering he and Uriel into the alcove and also to their knees. Uriel groaned in dismay when he saw Samael in the centre of the crowd, smiling his enormous pleasure at having the siblings who had so much power in Heaven, now helpless before his feet.

"Now we have almost the full party," Samael laughed as his captives stared up at him in rage, but could do nothing in the presence of twenty armed soldiers. "My men are searching the palace and will find Ramiel shortly. You are all so predictable, I did not need the Book of Life to read your stupid minds, and you never wondered why the palace and dungeon had no guards, so you would walk right into my trap."

"You are a disgrace to the title of angel," Gabriel sneered. "To think you were once the wisest and most beautiful of us all, but look at you now; an evil shadow of your former self."

"At least I am no longer a slave to the wishes of a ranting tyrant. Here on Earth there are no screaming voices in my head and I am my own master," he said as he placed his multi-coloured headdress on the floor. "Did you really think you could deceive me and leave your ill-conceived plan in the hands of a mere human whose intelligence is puny compared to my own? See for yourself your *greatness* undone." Samael declared as he briefly left, only to return with the dismembered corpse of the High Priest, a heavy trail of blood in its wake. He unceremoniously dropped the mangled body on the floor in front of them. "This 'chattering monkey' naïvely thought he could bare-face lie to me, but you would be amazed how eager and swiftly the real truth came from his lips when I began to cut off his right arm. The other limbs I removed slowly just for fun."

"You are a monster." Raphael said.

"I have discovered with these humans one man's demon is another man's god," Samael smiled. "And they are quick to change their mind as to which when it suits them. They are far bigger hypocrites than we could ever aspire to be. I believe many of the Egyptians suspected I was not the true Pharaoh, but they promptly forgot that when they saw the military victories and the conquered wealth flowing into their greedy hands."

"You have found your perfect path," Michael said. "You could never have been happy in the lake, but here on Earth you have discovered your true destiny of bloodshed and are finally content."

"I could not have said it better myself," Samael grinned. "And now nothing will stand in my way of using this great empire to vanquish the whole world."

The captives watched in surprise as Ramiel appeared behind the fake Pharaoh and swiped Samael across the back with the Book of Life. Their captor let out a cry of pain and the guards responded, advancing on this attacker to their ruler. However, Ramiel reached his fallen brother first, dropping the supernatural book on the floor and placing his short-sword to the neck of the usurper.

"You were so preoccupied in your 'victory,' and having your audience of soldiers and captives to hear your ranting, you did not see me steal the book and creep up behind you," Ramiel smiled. "Tell the soldiers to disarm and free Gabriel and our brothers."

"I won't do that," Samael replied. "You don't have the nerve to kill me, especially as you and the rest of the angels will surely perish."

"To see you dead will be enough and worthy of our sacrifice." Ramiel replied and the others nodded in silent agreement.

Samael sneered and said nothing for several moments, before motioning for the guards to drop their weapons, which they did so, allowing their spears and swords to hit the ground with a tremendous clatter. The captives collected their short-swords and Raphael picked up the Book of Life as they exited the alcove and into the main corridor. Ramiel slowly followed, the blade still at his brother's throat, his back to his siblings and keeping a close eye on the assembled Egyptian soldiers, who stared at him fixedly. As Ramiel and his prisoner began to make their way down the hall, the guards bent down and retrieved their weapons before following their captive ruler, keeping a few steps away but ensuring no escape would be possible, and any chance of fleeing out the main entrance of the palace would be suicide for the intruders.

Ramiel motioned for his siblings to open the entrance to the tunnel and all should enter the narrow passageway, their safety paramount as only his life and that of his prisoner would continue to be in jeopardy. Gabriel called out to him in fear and Ramiel quickened his pace, dragging Samael into the hole in the wall, the soldiers following close behind. When she was sure they were all in the tunnel, Gabriel reached past Ramiel and his captive, pulled the barricade back and sealed the entrance to the tunnel, before shoving her sword under a gap in the floor, jamming the section of the wall meaning the guards would find it impossible to access the secret passage from their side. Nevertheless, they began pushing on the brown brick that opened the tunnel and hammering on the wall with their weapons. The angels could hear the soldiers screaming in rage and frustration as they struggled to gain access to the intruders and their pretend Pharaoh.

The angels exited the tunnel, as Raphael used the blunt handle of his short-sword and struck Samael across the back of the skull, knocking him unconscious. They rapidly made their way through the city, careful to avoid any patrols as they heard shouting coming from the palace, the soldiers searching for them, carrying their captive along with them.

Once they were in the desert and sufficient distance from Memphis, they deposited their brother on the sand and waited for him to awake, wanting him to be fully conscious to receive his rightful punishment. Some hours passed before Samael awoke and stared up at his siblings, before rising to his feet. He realised with much amusement they had stripped him, removing any reference to being Pharaoh, even though he had usurped that title.

"Well played," Samael said, rubbing the back of his head and feeling a large bump. "Even though there was more blind luck involved, than skill and intelligence in the strategy."

"It was enough to get you here," Gabriel replied. "The place of punishment and ultimate justice."

Samael stared at her in amusement. "What exactly do you have in mind, sister? Are you going to kill me and leave my corpse to be devoured by the desert rodents? Of course, you know leaving me alive would be a colossal mistake; one I would make sure you regretted later."

"No more than you deserve for destroying the lake," Michael said. "But you are our brother, and angels do not kill their own kind."

"Why not?" Samael smirked. "I would surely torture each and every one of you to death and have no hesitation about the act."

"Exile is not what we agreed," Gabriel snarled. "And you all voted me leader."

Uriel glanced at her. "I was not present for that vote. I am with Michael on this matter. Despite the beatings, starvation and imprisonment with only rats for company, I believe we cannot be judge, jury and executioner for our fallen sibling. That divine decision rests alone with The Source."

"We are no longer in Heaven," Gabriel said. "And in the absence of that spiritual guidance, here on Earth … I am God."

"Be careful my brothers," Samael said. "Our sister shows all the signs of being far more dangerous, and all the qualities of a megalomaniac … more than even I."

"Shut your mouth," Gabriel growled. "And now I will close that evil cavity forever. Hold him down, I am going to remove his limbs one by one, like he did for the High Priest."

Michael and Uriel stood in front of their naked sibling, preventing their sister access. "You go too far," Michael said. "We are not the monsters that Samael aspires to be, you all should be ashamed of yourselves to so readily agree to this torture."

Gabriel stared at them in fury. "When this is done, you two are banned from the group, I never want to see your faces again."

"That is fine by me," Uriel said. "Give me back the Book of Life."

Ramiel did not move for several moments, but finally Gabriel nodded in his direction and he relinquished the supernatural book to its true custodian. "It is only because you, Uriel, have been its appointed guardian that I will allow you to have it back, otherwise I would keep it for myself."

What happened next surprised them all, even Uriel. The book began to glow in Uriel's hands and to their amazement, his wounds began to heal and disappear, as if he had never been beaten; the scars on his face, back and chest vanishing.

"Well, that is interesting," Samael said. "Even I never knew the Book of Life had the attribute of healing."

"There will be no resurrection for you," Gabriel declared. "I am going to chop off your head and bury you here in the sand. I have paid off the locals, they will build a giant statue resembling a sphinx having the body of a lion and the head of a Pharaoh complete with headdress over your corpse, and this place will be forever cursed; stories of visitors being devoured by monsters will become legendary; a fitting gravestone for the ultimate evil."

"That's so sweet," Samael grinned. "I never knew you cared so much. Did you know the Egyptian people call me the Morning Star, and the Assyrians named me The Devil. I would really appreciate that plaque being my memorial, in gold would be appropriate."

"You mistake me, brother," Gabriel replied. "No one in history will know you are here, not strangers and not the foolish people of Egypt who were deceived into believing you were their true ruler. You will be forgotten, and mankind will not know you even existed. Now stand aside, let me exact justice."

"I won't allow you to torture him to death, he is still our brother," Michael said. "I will kill him and make it quick."

Michael turned towards his naked sibling and began to raise his sword, but hesitated.

"You are such a coward, brother," Samael said. "I read from the Book of Life, I have seen that human woman you adore so much, she lives in the city of Babylon. A farmer's daughter; quite beautiful and so young and innocent. I could visit and introduce her to the pleasures of the flesh. I however may be somewhat less gentle than you," he laughed. "Perhaps I will rape her and then flay her alive, remove her skin like an onion. Or better, I will flay her first and then rape her, how exciting would that be; which screams would be louder? The agony of skinning, or me ravishing her?"

Michael stared at him motionless for a moment, before driving the short-sword through Samael's chest, the tip of the blade protruding from his back. The act seemed to take the pretend Pharaoh by surprise, as if he believed his brother could never actually do the act and kill him. Samael said nothing, but simply smiled much to Michael's shock as he fell back onto the sand, the weapon exiting his body. The life had nearly left him when Gabriel sidestepped past her two brothers and leaning down, swiped her sword and removed Samael's head from his neck, the skull rolling across the desert, leaving a bloody jet in its wake. Michael could not bear to see the head of his former friend and sibling, the lifeless eyes turned upwards, and the grotesque stump on his mutilated body; that great intelligence and angelic heritage lost forever.

"Now we bury him," she said. "I will drive my sword into the sand as a marker for the locals to know where to begin construction of the sphinx."

"That is your business, I never wanted any of this," Michael stated. "Uriel and I will take our leave."

"Remember what I said," Gabriel replied. "Our lifespans may be long, but I never want to see either of you two again."

Michael nodded as he and his brother left their former brethren, and carrying the Book of Life, disappeared into the desert.

## CHAPTER NINE

"I can see how Samael gave you no choice," Grace said. "It was the only way his evil was going to cease."

"Gabriel was wrong however; she believed our brother would be forgotten, but a cult soon formed not long after in Mesopotamia, and over the millennia spread across the globe; Satanism. It became clear Samael had revealed his true angelic heritage to at least some of Egypt and he is now worshipped by many deluded groups throughout history, even performing animal and human sacrifices in the hope of his return. It is an irony that is now Samael's legacy, and I believe he would not be entirely disappointed."

"You miss him, don't you? Despite what he did."

"I enjoyed the intelligent conversations. Samael had an incredible intellect and a sarcasm that was at times amusing."

"It is still difficult for me to grasp that The Devil actually existed and you knew him, and even killed him. However, it is also quite interesting how legends are born and become part of history."

"Now you see why I was so reluctant to tell you what happened."

"And that young woman he threatened to harm? Was that me; my first incarnation, as you call it?"

"Yes, that was you; in a manner of speaking, or at least the first incarnation of you that I met here on Earth. I could not allow you to come to harm, for he would certainly have carried out the threats, if we had let him live." Thomas sighed. "I will call a taxi to bring you back to your apartment, I would say you have experienced enough excitement for the weekend and need rest."

"Yes, and work tomorrow will seem even more boring and mundane than usual, imagine the breaktime conversations about what everyone did over the weekend; getting drunk or laid will seem ridiculous and even more funny by comparison."

"Indeed," he laughed. "And work must continue on the computer app. Gabriel's appearance after all these years, not to mention her threats give an even greater impetus towards its urgent completion."

"On that very subject, how soon before the program becomes active?"

"At current beta testing, I expect it to become operational in two weeks. To think in merely a fortnight, we will change the world forever."

"And you are certain no one I personally know will be affected? I don't relish the sight of work colleagues suddenly dropping dead in front of me."

Thomas burst into laughter, which she found alarming. "I was very thorough with my interview selection process, I can assure you no employees of mine are on that list. The *victims* are total strangers, you might have encountered them in the shopping centre or on the train, but they were simply passing by. On a separate point, if you don't mind me asking a personal family question; I am curious as to why your parents never had another child."

"Does the Book of Life not mention the reasons?"

"I am sorry, I do not wish you harm," Thomas said and put his arm around her, placing her head on his chest. "I of course can infer the logic from the book, but I wanted to hear it from you in your own words, not second-hand from the book as it were."

"My mother told me my father was not always a drunk; he was once tender and kind to both me and my mother, and they had talked about not making me an only child and the pressures associated with same, caring for elderly parents and sharing the burden with siblings. However, after he hurt his back falling off a ladder working on a construction site, he swiftly became mean and bitter, spending what compensation he had received in the bar and sharing his former 'glory stories' with other alcoholics who only cared as long as my father kept buying rounds. My mother's pity only seemed to enrage him further and she was an easy punching bag for his frustrations. I found comfort in a few friends, especially Andrea. Her stepfather may not be a vicious drunk, but he also has little time for parenting so I found in her a fellow compatriot as it were. It was easy to confide in her my secrets and fears, and she likewise in me."

"I appreciate you filling in the 'blanks' that the book was vague on, I know that can't have been easy to disclose."

"It's okay, I want to be able to tell you everything, and you also reveal anything of concern to me."

"I will always be honest with you, no matter how difficult the subject. I want to say one final thing before you go. Our destinies are forever intertwined; you may have experienced many separate lifetimes in contrast to my one long lifespan, but our souls are eternally connected throughout the ages, and nothing or nobody can change that." He smiled before putting on her coat and escorting Grace to the elevator. Thomas watched her leave before returning to the apartment.

A short journey in a yellow cab brought her back to the flat she shared with Andrea and Lisa. Upon entering, Grace dropped her overnight bag adjacent her bedroom and proceeded to make herself coffee.

Andrea heard her friend arrive and came from her room to greet her. "Welcome back, well, how did it go?"

Grace glanced around the apartment. "Are we alone? Where is Lisa?"

"Not here," Andrea replied. "I think little miss snob might have got herself a man, or at least whatever passes for a boyfriend in that bitch's world; maybe a sugar daddy too blind and horny to care what a gold digging nasty cow he has shacked up to. Wonders never cease that she might have found someone to listen to her incessant moaning, and certainly not groans of pleasure; he must obviously be a masochist."

"I know trying to be friends with Lisa is hard work, Andrea," Grace sighed. "But perhaps we should give her more leeway, we don't know her history and problems. She could have had a hard upbringing, maybe you cut her some slack."

Andrea stared at her friend in anger, which surprised Grace because they almost never had fights about anything, and could always speak openly about any subject. "You don't know her like I know her. We were once friends, not as close as me and you; but good friends nevertheless. I knew a boy from the town for many years, his mother and mine were work colleagues. Anyway, I liked him; he was cute and funny, and I *really* liked him. I told Lisa about him, made the mistake of introducing them, and she stole him from me. Broke off the relationship only a few weeks later, because she really did not have any interest in him. But because she and I were friends, the boy wanted nothing to do with either of us. And she did this only because she could, and because she found my tears so amusing. She is an evil bitch, make no mistake, Grace, and she will chew and spit you out like a chicken bone."

"I am sorry, Andrea," Grace said softly. "I never knew, you should have told me, despite how painful that story was."

Their conversation was interrupted by loud knocking on the front door. The girls glanced at each other in puzzlement, thinking it was either a late night delivery of pizza meant for someone else in the apartment block, or perhaps their flatmate had lost her key. The hammering appeared to cease and they relaxed when they heard what seemed like a key in the lock. Both girls turned, expecting to see their obnoxious work colleague enter the apartment, but to their shock, three masked men dressed all in black rushed into the main area of the flat and quickly approached them. Andrea ran for her bedroom and the men did not pursue her, their interest seemingly focused entirely on Grace.

Andrea began searching for her mobile phone in panic to ring the police as she could hear her best friend screaming in terror. Grace meanwhile ran for the kitchenette, attempting to evade her captors, putting distance between the assailants and herself by way of the countertop, but two of the men simply went at opposite ends and grabbed her. The third man took cable-ties from his pocket and proceeded to bind Grace's hands behind her back. Grace was shouting at the top of her voice in fright and struggled furiously.

One of the men bent down and held her head, as if preventing Grace from hurting herself off the tiles or counter. "Please calm yourself, Ms.

Anderson," he said in a rough voice that Grace thought sounded east European, perhaps Russian. "We have orders to take you alive and well, we are not here to hurt you."

Grace glanced over the man's shoulder and with relief saw Thomas suddenly appear. Her lover wrapped his arm around the assailant's neck and pulled him upwards and hurled him against the far wall, before striking him on the top of his head with his clenched right fist so hard it fractured the attacker's skull and broke his neck. Thomas let the lifeless man fall to the floor as his two friends stood up and stared at their fallen comrade.

One of the assailants moved to attack Thomas, but his colleague snatched hold of his arm. "We have our commands. We are not here for him, only the girl, and we don't get paid if we are dead."

"Fuck you, he just killed my brother," he said as he revealed from a pouch a ten inch bowie knife. "I have a score to settle."

His friend nodded and began to pick up Grace from the tiles, believing his colleague would keep Thomas occupied enough to secure his escape with his prize. However, Thomas sidestepped the swipe of the knife and grabbing the man by the forearm, turned the blade upwards and with one swift motion, drove the weapon up through the base of his jaw, through the mouth and into the brain. The attacker fell to his knees, the tip of the bowie knife protruding from the top of his skull, and Thomas smiled as the final assailant dropped his captive in panic, realising he had a somewhat better chance of escape without his burden, his fright evident as he was shaking in fear. The masked man reached for the Glock 90 pistol strapped to his waist, but Thomas quickly stepped in and held his wrist with such force, it shattered five of his eight carpal bones. The assailant cried out in pain, before Thomas struck him with his right fist squarely in the face with such strength that his spine was severed from his skull, killing him instantly.

Thomas let the man fall to the floor before removing Grace's bindings with a kitchen knife. "It is alright," he said softly as she burst into tears and wrapped her arms around him. "You are safe now."

Thomas lifted her up and placed Grace on the couch as Andrea came out of her bedroom, believing the commotion had ceased and the attackers had left.

Andrea ran to her friend and embraced her fiercely. "I am so sorry for running and leaving you alone," Andrea said and started to cry. "I was so scared and didn't know what to do. I knew I had left my mobile phone in the bedroom and went to ring the cops."

"It is okay, I would have done the same thing. It is fortunate for us both that Thomas had dropped me home and heard all the noise." Grace replied, attempting to explain Thomas's sudden and inexplicable appearance.

"Strange, I thought you got a taxi home on your own," Andrea said in puzzlement.

"Nevertheless, I am glad you were still nearby. I owe you a month's wages for saving our lives."

At that moment two uniformed policemen with handguns drawn entered the open apartment and Thomas and the two young women put up their hands in submission. Their employer swiftly explained the situation, leaving out some potentially 'inconvenient' details as regards the deaths of the three masked men.

"We will need to file a report with the Federal Bureau of Investigation," one of the cops said. "This was a potential kidnapping and so falls under their jurisdiction. I know you said it was self-defence, and so no charges are likely against any of you if that is proven to be the case, but we must adhere to proper procedure. Can I ask a question? How the hell did you kill three assailants and not suffer a scratch? Are you related to Bruce Lee?"

"Just lucky, I guess," Thomas smiled. "Those karate lessons came in handy."

"Well, you certainly got your money's worth in those exercises," the second cop laughed. "This is now a crime scene. You will all have to reside somewhere else for the next few days. Are you two women the only occupants of the apartment?"

"No, there is a third woman," Thomas said. "We will wait for her outside of the flat, and I will take all three women to stay in a hotel. It is probably not safe here anyway."

"That is best," the policeman replied. "You seemed to be the obvious target for these men, Ms.

Anderson. Given Mr. Marsh is one of the richest people in the city, it probably makes sense they wanted ransom for your eventual release."

"I suppose that is probably the reason," Grace said. "And I am certain I am not attractive enough to be sold into the sex trade."

"Very amusing," the cop replied. "But from my experience they find a place for everyone in that line of business. These men were professionals judging from their attire and the door shows no sign of forced entry as if they had a key for the apartment. Did they mention any names in the course of the attack that might indicate who their leader was?"

Grace glanced at Thomas in nervousness and it was he who spoke for her. "They mentioned nobody, officer," Thomas said. "Whatever secrets they had, they took it to the grave."

"Understood," the policeman replied. "You may go, but do not leave the country and be easily contactable, further questions are certain from higher authorities."

Thomas nodded and they left the flat as the two cops sealed up the apartment, placing yellow tape across the door and baring entry. They allowed the young women to acquire basic clothing for the next few days and whatever belongings into a bag for their absent flatmate also. Thomas got Lisa's mobile number from Grace, and she promptly appeared on the scene.

"What the hell happened here?" Lisa shouted. "I go away for one night and you wreck the place, inviting drunken bastards back to make a whorehouse of the apartment."

"That's enough," Thomas said sharply. "You can all stay in my luxury flat in Hell's Kitchen tonight until we decide what to do next. I have a house in New Haven, just outside of New York City, perhaps we can stay there for a few days."

"And are we all sharing the love bed?" Lisa sneered. "A 'ménage à quatre,' how very sweet. Just to let you know, even if I was into lesbian relationships, these two skanks would be the very last on a very long list."

"Dream on, bitch," Andrea laughed. "I would file all my teeth first to shark razors before eating your dirty pussy."

Lisa reached out in rage and grabbed hold of Andrea's hair, attempting to pull it out by the roots and Andrea responded by trying to kick her work colleague in the shins. After some moments, Thomas and Grace managed to separate them.

"I said that's enough! We already have three dead bodies only a few away, let's not add more to the mix. Grace and Andrea can have my bed, Lisa you sleep on the couch. I will watch over all of you to prevent World War Three from occurring," he said and Lisa nodded in agreement. "Grace and I need to go briefly back to my office. Since you two can't contain yourselves, you will have to tag along and stay in separate work stations in Marsh Tower until we are finished and go to my apartment."

"One last quickie, is it?" Lisa laughed. "Christ, you two are like rabbits."

"That is none of your business, and remember I am still your employer, I am sure an ideal waitressing or garage service job awaits you back in New England. You can always remain here in the corridor alone for the next week if you like until I organise your transport home."

He could see Lisa was holding her mouth shut in silent resentment, and when Thomas was satisfied that peace of a sort was finally restored, he escorted them downstairs and into a taxi before they arrived at Marsh Tower. Thomas left Andrea and Lisa in different offices at opposite ends of the corridor, before he and Grace entered his personal office.

"Christ Almighty," Thomas said as he shut the door. "You were not kidding when you said living with Lisa was a nightmare, and the venom between her and Andrea, not to mention their appalling language. I don't understand, I thought the three of you were best friends?"

"What on Earth gave you that idea?" Grace replied, perplexed, her back to the glass window adjacent the entrance. "I am guessing you invited Andrea along to New York to be certain I would come, knowing our close companionship, but did the Book of Life not mention anything about the hatred between Andrea and Lisa?"

"Where else did you think I ascertained this knowledge? Like I mentioned before, your educational documentation did not mention such interpersonal relationships between classmates. I had to rely solely on the book for this information, and it was most clear you were all friends."

"How is that possible? Did you read it wrong? Did the book deliberately lie to you, and if so, for what reasons?"

"I have carried and read from the Book of Life for thousands of years, and never has it led me astray. It always showed me with pinpoint accuracy events and people throughout history, explaining in minute detail the location and exact acts occurring at that particular time. Without such meticulousness, I would have never known about your reincarnations; you could have passed me in the street and I would have never known you existed, I would have been none the wiser."

"Let's get to the real business at hand; who were those men back in the apartment and why did they want me? I have never been so scared in all my life."

Thomas embraced her. "I am not sure, my guess is they were mercenaries of some kind, presumably paid to kidnap you."

"Could Gabriel or this missing angel Sariel be behind this attack? I thought he had vanished about two years ago."

"I don't really believe he has 'disappeared,' as my other siblings mentioned. I have no reason to trust them, and they certainly would not be so forthcoming with such knowledge considering the ancient animosity between us. It is more likely he is carrying out Gabriel's dirty work so she can remain 'innocent' and free from any collateral damage arising from his actions. The Book of Life should reveal their plans; I tried before to see what they were up to, but the pages were vague and difficult to read, as if they were attempting to block my vision, like we did when rescuing Uriel in Egypt. Stay here and have a drink, I will go to the basement and find out the nature of their schemes, I will see through their attempts at blocking my vision. Make no mistake, blood and angelic heritage aside, if I discover they had intended to harm you directly or indirectly, then they will pay for it dearly, I promise you."

Thomas left while Grace took a glass tumbler from the shelf and poured herself some vodka and coke from the small fridge next to her boyfriend's desk. Nearly half an hour passed before her lover returned, and she stared at him in concern noticing his apparent confusion and state of mind as he entered the office.

Grace rose from her seat and moved him to the chair instead to sit in her place. "What is the matter? What did the book say?"

"That's just it; the book said nothing at all, it is like a great black cloud covers the pages and obscures my visions completely of my siblings. I cannot see them at all now, where before it was vague if I so wished to see them, it is now hidden entirely as if the book is deliberately keeping this knowledge from my eyes."

"How can that be? Thomas, I am now really frightened."

"It will be alright. Don't be scared. I think we should go straight to my house in New Haven in case the Hell's Kitchen apartment has been compromised, I bought the property under a false name and have been very careful in hiding its location. There is plenty of space and Andrea and Lisa can have their own separate bedrooms. I have a caretaker who maintains the property, I will ring him and make sure everything is ready for our arrival."

"And what about the book? Is it safe here? Has this 'fog' obscuring your reading of the book ever happen before?"

"I made a phone call," Thomas said as if in response to her question. "He will be here in the next few minutes. Meanwhile, I really need a drink."

Grace could see the apprehension on his face and knew her soul mate was hiding something, probably for what he believed was her safety. "Thomas, you promised no more secrets," she said, watching him pace nervously around the office. "Tell me what is going on."

"The Book of Life is perfectly safe here in the basement of Marsh Tower, no one can gain entry except me. My brother can hopefully fill in the blanks."

Grace stared at him in puzzlement and wished to question further, when they heard a soft knock on the door and in walked Uriel.

The angel glanced briefly at her, before turning to his eldest sibling in temper. "I should not be here, and you especially should not have called me. I warned you not to start down this road; you brought all this chaos upon your own head, and now have involved these innocent humans who will get caught in the crossfire."

"It has happened again," Thomas said. "That black cloud filling the pages of the book and denying me access to our siblings and their activities."

"Frankly I am not entirely surprised they have managed to find a way to block their thoughts. It is now clear they are preparing to make a move against you, and those mercenaries who tried to kidnap your girlfriend only adds weight to the assumption that those plans are already being undertaken. I also don't believe Sariel has vanished from the face of the Earth; he is obviously integral to those strategies, he is not the same jovial brother we knew back in the lake, full of laughter and fun; Sariel is now very dangerous and is as committed to the cause as his other sibling-followers under the absolute leadership of our sister Gabriel."

"And what cause is that, may I ask?" Grace asked.

Uriel turned and stared at her fixedly. "The complete control and domination of mankind under a single ideal; that humans are unwilling or fundamentally incapable of forging their own destiny. Gabriel has come to believe that technology has brought the planet to the brink of catastrophe, and democracy is an illusion created by the super-elite to make low-paid slaves of the masses. The manipulation of society and individuals we practiced without hesitation or thought for consequence back in the lake has become the foundation of Gabriel's cause; that as angels we have the unique authority, even moral obligation to continue this oversight and a select 'culling' of the humans is necessary to curb overpopulation that is destroying the world."

Grace stared at him in shock and disbelief. "So, Gabriel is a hypocrite. She despises Thomas for wanting to change the world and rid it of evil, and yet she wants the book to do virtually the same thing, but on a much larger scale; to kill billions instead of millions, and damn the innocent with the guilty."

"Yes, she does not want a piece of the pie," Uriel replied. "But the entire pie itself for her own means. That is why the book is so dangerous and valuable, and why I was sole guardian of it back in the lake; it is the greatest weapon of mass destruction ever created, and governments and criminal organisations would most dearly love to have possession of it, if they knew such a manuscript existed."

"You say you were the sole custodian of the book, and yet you gave it up to Thomas, why would you do that?"

"I believed at the time that it would be safer in the hands of Michael. After we parted ways with Gabriel and our brothers, we wandered for many millennia trying to right wrongs wherever we travelled; protecting the innocent and punishing the guilty, but it eventually brought us to the attention of the likes of the Roman Empire and later the Nazis who were obsessed with the occult and ancient mystical cultures; Hitler had sent spies all over Europe searching for legendary items like the Grail and the Ark of the Covenant, and he had somehow discovered the Book of Life's existence. I gave the book to my brother after it was briefly seized by Julius Caesar, knowing Michael would hide it and keep it out of the Roman Empire and later in history the Fuhrer's grubby hands."

"I understand. And this 'dark cloud' that is preventing the reading of the book?"

"Of that I am not entirely certain as to its true origin or meaning," Uriel said. "This has happened a few times before throughout the ages, the most notable when we attempted to use the powers of the book to discover the exact location of key members of the Nazi party during the Second World War for the Allies to use strategic aerial bombing, especially to eliminate Hitler, Goering and Himmler, but we always appeared to be thwarted in our endeavours."

"Could Gabriel have been behind that also?" Grace asked. "Maybe the prevention of mass-murder hindered her plans for culling the population. If World War Two came to an abrupt end, that would have saved the lives of millions."

"Perhaps. However, I have discovered the book has almost a 'mind' of its own, as if it were sentient and have its own consciousness, as if it were aware of our plans and hid these visions from us, for what reasons we cannot determine."

"Have we ever considered the most bizarre explanation," Thomas said. "That The Source itself might be behind this; that this is some type of divine strategy to maintain control from afar?"

"I suppose that could be one explanation," Uriel replied. "But if our actions were so objectionable, then The Source would have taken our lives immediately; it is certainly within its powers to do so, or called us back to the lake, whatever the consequences of returning us to that dead wasteland might be. No, this is something else entirely. It is worth mentioning that the Book of Life was forged with extraordinary magick simultaneously at our creation, and I believe it is at least partly organic; in essence having a life of its own, no angel or human ultimately knows or will understand its full powers, secrets and even limitations, and even if it is capable of having same. But enough debate, let's get to the core of why you invited me here; you wish to identify the location of Gabriel and our siblings and know their intentions. However, the fact is I know neither and if I knew, I would be hesitant to disclose such facts as I am and always have been neutral in these matters."

"Christ, when are you going to take a stand? Nobody is nonpartisan in these matters; neutrality is another name for cowardice. I know you disagree with Gabriel and her plans."

"Disagreement is one thing, being an active participant in family civil war is quite another. I have a compromise, why don't you hand the book back to me? I will hide it and keep it safe from everyone, bury it somewhere where no one will ever find it."

"The book is quite safe with me," Thomas replied. "Goodbye, brother."

"Very well, Michael," Uriel said as he made for the door to leave. "If it were up to me, I would fill that basement with a mountain of cement and forget about the book forever, but you have made your choice and must accept the consequences for same. Perhaps we will meet again … and then maybe not."

Grace watched Uriel leave before turning to her boyfriend. "I guess we are on our own. It isn't even possible to destroy the book; is it?"

"Uriel in a fit of rage once tried to stab it and even burn it, nothing worked. There was not a single mark afterwards. You should have seen his face; the frustration."

Grace smiled. "You miss them, don't you? It's understandable, you were altogether for so long and united back in the lake."

Thomas put his head down in momentary dismay, but then seemed to shake himself out of it. "Well, the past is the past, and that time is gone forever."

"Uriel said he left you possession of the book," Grace said, changing the subject and not wishing to see him in such emotional pain. "Why would the ancient guardian of such a valuable and important supernatural manuscript simply give it up?"

"It was in danger of being stolen by the Roman empire, and the concept of those megalomaniacs having such a document would have been a catastrophe for humanity. The second and most obvious reason is I needed the book to keep track of your reincarnations, and Uriel realised I was never going to let you go."

"So you ultimately did it for selfish reasons," Grace frowned. "One final thing I must ask, how did you know I was being attacked back in the apartment?"

"My computer here in the office is directly connected to the mainframe which receives signals from the Book of Life in the basement; anything which is of concern immediately flashes on the screen and likewise is transmitted to my laptop at home and mobile phone; an alarm sounds off so I am instantly notified. The minds of the mercenaries became open to me as they were outside the building; planning their assault, giving me time to arrive, fortunately for you and Andrea. I told you before, nothing and nobody is more important to me, and your safety is paramount."

"That was certainly convenient; that they spent so much time planning instead of just coming in, it's like they were waiting for you to arrive," Grace frowned. "Let's just get out of here and go to New Haven."

Thomas nodded and they collected Andrea and Lisa from their separate offices and departed from Marsh Tower. He ushered them into the back of the Mercedes and instructed the driver to take them out of New York, and begin the near two hour journey to their new home.

"My country home is located overlooking New Haven East Rock Park in Connecticut; the area is quite beautiful and peaceful, and especially secluded, ensuring our safety and privacy." Thomas said as they left New York behind, Andrea and Grace sitting across from him with Lisa adjacent her employer, staring out at the passing landscape and ignoring her fellow passengers.

Lisa turned towards her boss. "Are we still going to get paid our wages while on this involuntary excursion? And when the fuck are you going to explain why my flat was raided by cops and is now home to the bloodied remains of three robbers?"

"That is all being taken care of," Thomas replied. "New York can be a dangerous place, but I want to ensure your safety and wellbeing is of primary importance."

"That does not really answer my questions." Lisa growled.

"Just be thankful you still possess that worthless life of yours." Andrea said.

"Isn't New Haven supposed to have a high crime rate?" Lisa asked. "New England might have been boring, but at least it was relatively murder free."

"Everywhere has its problems," Thomas replied. "Where we will be located near the large parklands is quiet. There will be no trouble on our doorstep."

"Only the conflict inside the doorstep," Andrea said. "I don't understand why we have to tag along little miss snob with us."

"All three of you were tenants in that apartment, therefore you are all victims in that attempted robbery," Thomas said. "My primary concern is the safety of all."

All the passengers remained silent the remainder of the journey and arrived sometime later in New Haven. The three young women were exhausted and Thomas escorted Andrea and Lisa to separate bedrooms, before he and Grace retired to the master bedroom. He let them sleep in the following morning and went for a walk in the park for some hours before returning and finding Grace and Andrea sitting in the kitchen, drinking coffee.

Thomas smiled at them both before starting to prepare breakfast, throwing sausages from the fridge into the frying pan. "I hope you like these well done," Thomas said, but heard no response and turned around to see the sheepish look on Grace's face, and the furious stare on Andrea's. "Okay, what is going on? Are you vegetarian?"

Andrea reached over and suddenly struck her employer across the face, much to his shock and bewilderment. "You lying son of a bitch, tricking me into coming to New York and putting our lives in danger for your ancient feud with your fucked up family!"

Grace saw Thomas glance in her direction in a mixture of confusion and anger. "I am sorry, my love," she said softly. "I did not mean to betray your confidence, it just became so overwhelming with the attack and attempted kidnapping back in the apartment. I have never been so scared and Andrea and I have never kept secrets from each other. I told her everything while you were gone. Please say you forgive me."

Thomas said nothing for a few moments, taking the frying pan off the hot plate. "It is alright, I forgive you," he said and kissed her forehead. "I should have guessed it might be all too much for you, it is me that needs to apologise."

"I have some questions, angel boy," Andrea said. "You owe me that much. Don't worry, there is no one else here. The chauffer has returned to New York and Lisa has gone into town. Grace has never lied to me, but even I find it all incredible and somewhat unbelievable. Can you do any magic tricks to prove your identity?"

"Contrary to what the church may have told you, I don't have wings and carry a flaming sword, but I cannot age unlike a human and am immune to any diseases or infections from the common cold to cancer. I can also be injured like any common man."

"That is certainly handy. You must have lived an extremely 'charmed' life to have lived so long and yet be so free of any obvious injuries or scars, unless of course as you mentioned you spent most of that extensive lifespan in the comfort and safety of Grace's former incarnations' bedsheets."

"Be careful what you say, girl," Thomas replied. "I am still your employer and deserving of proper respect."

"We are far from Marsh Tower and our daily boring jobs," Andrea said. "And considering your arrogance has put our lives at great risk, I believe that entitles me to speak my mind freely and without constraint. It must have been in a way a 'blessed' life, or rather perverse existence that you always lived a monogamous habitation with Grace's incarnations; never having to find other totally separate partners unlike the rest of humankind when their spouses died; always in a fashion having Grace in your bed, but at the same time loving different women throughout history, having the smug comfort that you were never cheating on Grace because you were always her exclusive soul companion. In essence, you had the best of both worlds. One would question whether she as an individual was ever really given a choice of someone else; you might call it 'romantic' fate or destiny that Grace's former incarnations were always your life partner, but others may label it obsessive controlling of the worst kind."

"Christ, you see things so black and white. It is worth pointing out that I too was totally loyal to Grace and her former lives, never wanting another woman, no matter the large gaps between those incarnations; in essence for the majority of history I was alone."

"So you say, and we will just have to take your word for it as proof to the contrary is impossible. Tell me about these so called evil souls that you will purge from the world, why do you possess this exclusive right to determine who might be wicked and fated for damnation? I don't understand why you don't simply use that knowledge gained from the Book of Life to place these people in prison, after all this is the proper environment for such vile individuals, and it is fitting they spend all of their life in captivity. The public would be safe from their evil desires and they would know they would die old men or women in jail."

"From a naïve viewpoint that appears so straightforward and easy. However, many of these people commit their deeds without punishment, whether that be because their identities remain unknown to the proper authorities, or they are protected through influence and wealth. Some will never act on their compulsions because of lack of opportunity, but nevertheless their nightly dreams will be filled with diabolical thoughts, and they will be reincarnated into another life, as The Source only extinguishes the souls of individuals whose lives were filled with evil acts; henceforth more favourable circumstances may arise in future incarnations and they can commit these deeds without hesitation. Besides, in my experience, such perpetrators never or are even capable of reform; re-education is a waste of time, all these people think about when incarcerated is fantasies of reoffending when released. In fact, they simply cannot or will not allow themselves to believe they had ever done anything wrong."

"And how do you discriminate what is truly evil, for that is so subjective and open to interpretation?" Andrea asked. "Religious leaders have long used that as an excuse for genocide and persecution, like the Crusades."

"I do not hold views representative of hypocritical religious leaders like the Catholic Church, and the 'holier than thou' extremists they pander to. What I find most interesting as regards evil souls is the predestination of aspiring corrupt priests and in particular nuns to gravitate towards the Christian faith, as if it were a prefect platform for their compulsive violence and sexual depravity, knowing it would at the very least be overlooked, and at best hidden and even encouraged. One only has to examine religious events in history like the Crusades and especially the Spanish Inquisition to understand sadists and psychopaths had in the Catholic Church an ideal home for their diabolical desires. Unlike blind justice in so many countries, I will not persecute the innocent. I am not naïve; I am fully aware given the proper circumstances anyone is capable of violence and even murder if provoked enough, but they feel awful guilt and remorse afterwards, and that will follow them throughout their life. The truly evil; the sociopaths and psychopaths in this world feel no such emotions and often relish in such cruelty; it is them and them alone that are on the Book of Life as requiring oblivion. All I am doing is providing a shortcut; not waiting for these monsters to die of old age long after the crimes have been committed, but to simply wipe them out now, and save those families the unnecessary agony of burying loved ones killed for the wanton pleasure of such brutes."

"And what about the suffering inflicted on the families of those you plan to kill? Surely they will not have the foresight or understanding to comprehend the moral necessity that their child, or even baby dies so young to prevent some predestined future where that loved one commits a terrible deed."

"I am doing this for the greater good. Terrible choices have to be made; it is similar and no worse a decision when President Truman ordered the deployment of the two atomic bombs, murdering hundreds of thousands to prevent the killing of millions."

"I understand. On a different note, if there is no true salvation for 'sinners' as regards regular mass attendees, do you consider them blind idiots simply wasting their time?"

"I think anything that gives a person some comfort is never entirely a waste of time," Thomas replied. "But in reality they are only going to regular mass because they are either scared of the unknown; out of habit, or because of what the neighbours might say of them for not attending. Praying to a deaf God is like an adult sending a Christmas Wishlist to Santa, hoping for a favourable answer from their imaginary friend. The ultimate truism is they are simply hedging their bets; playing Pascal's Wager."

"I am curious, in any of Grace's reincarnations, was she ever born a boy, for I imagine that provided somewhat of a dilemma for you; unless of course for that lifetime you jumped the fence?"

"That is enough, Andrea. Thomas has answered enough of your questions, we are going to take a walk and get some fresh air." She said and her friend nodded in agreement and let them depart, somewhat satisfied her interrogation had provided enough information, at least for the moment. Grace took her boyfriend by the hand and they began to walk into the park, admiring the striking red leaves on the trees and the beauty around them. "I am sorry again for that, I should never have broken your confidence."

"It is truly alright," he smiled as they sat on the grass and admired the landscape. "She has spirit and fire inside her, and wants to protect you. I understand and respect that."

Grace laughed. "Yes, she certainly has that. Thomas, tell me a story of us in another life; take my mind off our current situation and transport me to another time …"

## CHAPTER TEN

"Uriel, what exactly are we doing here?" Michael said, standing to his feet in the tent and staring out at the endless forest before them, a fine mist obscuring the distant weeds. "Surrounded by barbarians on one side and the Roman army on the other, not to mention it is so fucking cold and wet out here."

"As scribes and advisers to Gaius Julius Caesar, did we really have any choice in the matter?" Uriel replied. "We are here to record his campaign in Gaul, and disobedience is not looked kindly upon. I am only too aware the real reasons for this war is to further his political ambitions and pay off his huge debts through stolen gold and slaves. He seeks our advice because we have a unique insight into the minds of his enemies, and our lives would be in serious jeopardy if he ever discovered the true source of that special knowledge."

"He is unable to read the Book of Life," Michael said. "Which is fortunate for you as he might be aware of your scrying in favour of the Gallic Chief Vercingetorix; playing both sides and ferrying information via that barbarian small boy that visits the tent with food every day."

"I know all too well you think such endeavours are both insanely foolish and dangerous, but I cannot sit idly by while these Roman monsters butcher everyone in sight," Uriel responded sharply. "Is it really necessary for an invading army to kill all men, women and children in every village they pass through; it is no wonder the whole world fears and despises them."

"And is this really our concern? How much longer must we babysit humanity and protect these mortals? Ten thousand years from now they will still be murdering each other and never learn from their mistakes."

"You are a hypocrite, brother. You say you care so little for these humans, and yet you obsess over that young slave girl you dragged away from the relative safety of Rome and into the jaws of the savages, not to mention the Imperial Roman Army whose brutality and contempt for all of mankind outside of their narrow viewpoint is infamous."

"I understand your fake concerns, brother," Michael said. "I know all too well as you have expressed it so frequently, that you consider me foolish or deluded to care for Adina and her former incarnations, not to mention 'dragging' as you see it us across the world to protect those departed lives of hers. Please try to comprehend my true feelings for her throughout history, and it is not irrational desire that I have; if you had ever felt something like it for any human you might understand."

"Just because I have no interest in lust or love does not make me an emotional eunuch. I am simply more focused on the divine mission I was given by The Source. Even though I no longer hear

The Voice, I am still committed to its success, and hope my sincere endeavours can help guide mankind on the right path."

"At times you sound like Gabriel and those cronies we once called siblings that hang onto her every word. I sometimes wonder why you did not go with her also?"

"Our sister's agenda is far more extreme in nature, as you well know. She is more concerned with controlling humanity and would actively encourage someone like Caesar, believing he keeps overpopulation in check, despite his savagery; in essence the ends justify the means."

His elder brother was about to respond when the man in question suddenly entered the tent, flanked by half a dozen soldiers and two Decurios. Gaius Julius Caesar was an imposing figure of a man, despite his obvious physical shortcomings; standing at five foot seven inches with brown greyish hair. He was prematurely nearly bald given he was only forty six years old which he was very conscious of, and frequently combed what little top hair there was over the ever increasing vacant scalp. However, what captivated people's attention was the piercing dark eyes coupled with his extraordinary military intellect; and whose brilliant strategies had secured for Rome numerous victories over the years, particularly in the long campaign against the many tribes of Gaul.

"I require your advice, Uriel," Caesar said and the angel nodded simply in response, knowing all too well such a request was an order not to be disobeyed. "We are soon to engage the tribes of the Belgae, in particular the very powerful Nervii, whose ferocity and cunning is well known throughout northern Celtae."

"Do you require refreshments, my lord?" Michael asked. "I will have Adina bring some wine and bread."

Caesar smiled briefly in acknowledgment, as his close friend Mark Anthony entered the tent. The angels watched his arrival with some apprehension, knowing his mood swings and his distrust of anyone not clearly recognised of being Roman. Mark Anthony was very handsome with a large head of curly hair and like his comrade Julius, wore a golden breastplate and matching shorts, brown sandals and a large helmet with a ten inch high red plume rising above it.

Mark Anthony placed his shortsword and headgear on the plain wooden table in the centre of the tent before turning to the two advisors. "It always amazes me Caesar, why you continue to bring these servants with you everywhere. What nationality are you exactly? You are certainly not Roman, perhaps Egyptian might be the closest, and the accents are so unfamiliar I at times find it hard to understand you."

"We have travelled far and wide, my lord," Uriel replied. "And have gathered extensive experience and knowledge of many cultures and nations, so we can bring the most accurate possible information to the ears of the Roman Empire, and so secure the greatest victories."

"So you say," Mark Anthony said. "However, be assured you who are so 'loyal' to Rome, that such knowledge and its total accuracy is vital to your continued service, and indeed your lives. Send for that Jewish girl to fetch wine and bread, I am starving."

Adina arrived moments later and set refreshments including four silver goblets and a large jug of red wine on the table. Michael smiled at her briefly lest the officers see his clear affection. The twenty-three year old native of Jerusalem had been born on a farmland just outside of the great Jewish city, and while travelling to the coastline with her parents to seek trade and supplies, had been captured by slavers looking to expand their repertoire of 'exotic goods' for the Empire. She was separated from them as they were placed in domestic homes in Rome, and Adina sold as personal maid to Caesar. Michael believed she had been unfortunate in this circumstance as Jerusalem and greater Judah had only recently been conquered, and the Roman Senate had moved their expansionist ambitions towards Gaul instead where much greater plunder was available. She was reasonably pretty with short dark hair and a slender frame, having small breasts and being about five foot two inches. Adina was totally besotted with Michael, and he was clearly equally devoted to her as the latest reincarnation of the woman he first saw back in the lake, much to Uriel's disapproval, believing this made Michael weak and distracted him from what should be his true purpose; guiding mankind to a better destiny than the one they had set out for themselves, scrounging for scraps left over from Rome raping their resources throughout the known world.

Julius Caesar unfurled a map of Gaul and its surroundings and began pointing at various points on the diagram. "The Nervii have an impressive force of some fifty thousand men, but lack the direct influence of Vercingetorix whose interests are elsewhere in the overall campaign against us. However, one should not be complacent believing this will give us superior advantage on the battlefield as their ferocity and cunning is well known; handpicking strong children from villages and towns and training them over their lifetimes."

"Perhaps, great Caesar," Uriel said. "It might make sense to divide our forces; sending the cavalry to their rear and drive them into our phalanxes. The barbarians are not well versed in constrictive combat and prefer open field conflict instead, allowing them as much room as possible to manoeuvre."

"Maybe," Mark Anthony added. "But I believe a full frontal assault would be more prudent and use all our men all at once and finish them quickly."

"Would that be more fitting to your glory?" Julius smirked. "Leading the army to victory with you at its head?"

"I serve Caesar," Mark replied, noticing the slight smile on Uriel's face as the general was firmly put in his place. "What is it you suggest?"

"As you know I have secured the alliance of some smaller tribes including the Remi; it is they that can offer some insight into the inner mechanics of the Belgae," the Roman leader said. "We will make camp at the river Sambre until we establish those plans."

"I thought it was the job of your 'all-seeing' advisers to learn of such schemes and relate them to you?" Mark sneered.

Caesar turned to Uriel. "What can you see as to their military motives? What are the true strategies of the Belgae, and especially the Nervii?"

"Their minds are currently closed to me, my Lord," Uriel replied. "If they have ulterior plans other than amassing at Northern Celtae and awaiting your arrival, it is unknown to me."

"I hope you are correct in your assumptions, scribe," Julius said sharply. "I know you have provided accurate scrying for previous Roman leaders and the Senate for many years, but a single great failure may damn the fates of both you and your brother."

Following that threat, the Decurios, Julius Caesar and Mark Anthony promptly vacated the tent, leaving only the angels and the slave girl Adina alone in the pavilion.

Michael turned to his younger sibling. "I know what you said is not true, the Nervii plan a secret massive attack on the Roman camp at the river Sambre and catch Caesar by surprise. It is a dangerous game you play."

Uriel gave a sly smile. "You know me only too well, brother. Yes, that is the ulterior strategy of the Belgae, and so perhaps this endeavour of theirs will finally put this war to an end. A significant defeat for Rome here might affect Julius Caesar's ambitions, and perhaps in time hasten the extinction of the Empire itself."

"And what of your lives?" Adina asked. "Do they not matter if the Romans learn of your deception? Your ancient heritage and immortality cast aside?"

"Please tell your lover to be quiet," Uriel snapped. "This does not concern her."

"By your lies you also put her in danger," Michael said. "She has every right to question your motives."

His younger brother burst into laughter. "Her lifespan is so short and inconsequential compared to ours. When she dies, you can simply use the book to find her next incarnation, and this slave girl will be a distant memory when you have your arms wrapped around her spiritual successor."

Michael stared at him in rage before grabbing hold of Adina's hand and led her out of the tent.

Uriel watched them leave before he too departed and sought out the barbarian boy to pass information onto the Nervii.

Michael escorted the young slave girl into the nearby woodlands and they embraced and kissed passionately. "I am sorry for what Uriel said, he can be a bit harsh and heartless."

"And yet he spoke truth in cruelty. Your lives are so much more important than mine; that ancient knowledge you possess can be passed onto the world and bring people together."

"Your life is absolutely no less meaningful to me, and every time I have to witness your death a part of me dies with you," Michael sighed. "As regards your second point, do you really think such a concept is possible? The only thing the humans know is how to butcher each other."

"Then you need to show them a better way. Not all of them are wicked, perhaps you can devise a way to separate the evil from the good."

Michael smiled. "My love, you always know what to say. I would sometimes be mistaken in believing you are one of us; having the knowledge of the Universe."

They kissed again, harder this time and Michael lifted up her long dress and placed his hand between her legs. Adina moaned briefly, holding her hand over her mouth lest any Roman soldiers nearby might hear. He hoisted her legs up and she wrapped herself around him, her ankles crisscrossed at his bottom, as Adina slipped onto his giant penis and he entered her fully to the hilt. Her moaning became more pronounced and loud now as he thrust himself into her, pinning her against a tree. Adina grabbed onto a branch above her head and held on tight, as Michael increased his furious actions and came, with a muffled shout.

Michael relaxed as Adina sorted out her dress and kissed him tenderly on the lips, before they returned as the army prepared to move and make camp at the river Sambre. The whole operation took several hours, before the X Legion and its horses and war machinery which included light ballista made camp at the shores of the large waterway. Uriel watched the army go to sleep with the exception of a dozen sentries, before lighting a torch and waved it briefly, before outing the beacon into a bucket of water.

Michael and Adina drew alongside him as they observed with trepidation, as thousands of Nerviian barbarians descended down a hill and swept into the Roman camp, knocking down tents and swiftly killing the sentries, cutting them down with their large swords. However, several guards managed to raise the alarm, ringing bells hanging from poles before being struck down.

The Roman army was quick to respond and wake from their slumber. The angels and Adina watched with great interest, as Julius Caesar and

Mark Anthony personally had to take up arms and Uriel clenched his fists in hopeful anticipation as the Roman Commander fought off two Nerviian barbarians, knocking one to the ground with a shield, before stabbing the fallen warrior with a spear. Uriel groaned in frustration as Caesar dispatched another assailant by running him through with his sword, as Mark Anthony now defended his back.

The Roman army had now completely assembled and pushed the Nerviians back up the hill. The barbarians began to come under fire from a barrage of slings, arrows, light ballista and lances; some of the spears they managed to catch in mid-flight and hurl back at the Romans. The Nerviians attempted their traditional shield-wall tactics to prevent the assault of varied objects being flung at them, but as the hours progressed it was obvious they were fighting a losing battle. The Nerviians retreated and fled in multiple directions as the Roman army pressed on, destroying the entire Belgaen forces, and they surrendered on the threat of the total obliteration of their towns and villages.

Uriel watched the Romans begin to relax and return to their camp, and glanced at his elder brother in nervousness, as they entered the Commander's tent and awaited the certain arrival of the Roman high command including Caesar.

"It would appear your plan has failed," Michael declared in anger. "And now we will learn the consequences of your devious schemes."

Julius Caesar, Mark Anthony and two dozen armed guards entered the tent minutes later, their uniforms and bodies covered in the blood of their enemies.

"We have won a glorious victory," Mark Anthony grinned. "Forever will this be known as the Battle of the Sabis where the Belgaen army was annihilated, thanks to the bravery of the X Legion."

The guards shouted in response, cheering their general's declaration as Caesar motioned for their silence. "Indeed," Julius echoed. "But at the expense of the loss of all my standards, the majority of my Centurions dead, not to mention that I myself had to take up arms to defend my own life; one might consider such a surprise attack was well planned … from the inside."

"Perhaps you are correct," Mark Anthony added. "But certainly the 'all-seeing' accuracy of your advisors' scrying is in serious doubt."

"Have their belongings brought to me." Julius ordered to one of the soldiers.

"We have no secrets to hide," Uriel said as his elder brother glanced at him in seething anger. "Neither did we have anything to with the Nerviian attack."

"We will see." Anthony sneered as the soldier returned with a sack and emptied the contents on the ground. The general sifted through the small amount of clothes, expecting to find some notes indicating the advisors' guilt, but found nothing except a strange square book. He gazed at the peculiar cover which seemed to give off shining colours of orange, red and blue whichever way he looked at it, but upon opening found only blank pages throughout. He gave the book to Caesar who also flicked through the pages with passing interest.

"Place this in my personal tent," he ordered an adjacent guard. "I will have the scholars and mystics of the temple back in Rome examine it, and devise a way to tear it asunder and discover its potential mysteries."

The angels watched intently as the soldier left with the Book of Life, their apprehension greatly increasing as a Centurion abruptly entered the tent, escorting a small barbarian child.

"I found this Nerviian wandering around the outskirts of the camp," the Roman officer said. "He had a peculiar purpose about him that led me to believe he knew exactly how to avoid our sentries and hide in the shadows."

"Have my personal surgeon interrogate him," Caesar ordered. "Start removing fingernails followed by toes, and we will soon establish his identity and motives."

Adina suddenly grabbed a knife from the belt of a nearby guard and before the soldiers could intervene, stabbed the boy through the chest, killing him instantly. The Romans responded and seized the slave girl, forcing Adina to her knees.

"It was me," she said to Caesar. "I am responsible for the surprise attack on the camp."

"Adina, what are you doing?" Michael asked, speaking in Hebrew so the assembled Romans could not understand.

"It is as Uriel said," she replied in her native tongue. "Your lives are so much more important than mine."

"But I love you, more than anything." Michael said and began to cry, the tears streaming down his face.

"As do I," she sobbed. "We will meet again, my love. Do not grieve, for a greater destiny awaits me. Wait for me; whatever eyes I possess in my next life, I will know you immediately, and know you are mine … always and forever."

Michael pushed off the two Romans holding him and a further five soldiers moved and restrained the angel as Caesar motioned, and a guard drew his short-sword and ran Adina through the heart, killing her instantly. As she fell lifeless to the ground, Michael stared at the assembled Romans in silent rage and grief.

"Escort them to cages," Caesar said. "We will learn more of their deception in the morning, and the true origin of their scrying, if indeed it was more dishonesty than actual contact with the gods."

The soldiers brought the angels to small iron bar cages and placed them inside, only a few feet from each other and stood guard a short distance away.

"I am sorry about Adina," Uriel said. "She gave her life to save ours … at least for a while."

"That is all she meant to you. This is all your fault; she is dead because of you."

"We now have bigger problems, like escaping for one. Not to mention Caesar has the book."

"Is that the only thing which matters to you? Because of your arrogance my true love is dead. Besides, they can't even read the book."

"All the same it lies in the hands of the enemy," his younger brother replied. "And you need the book to find the birth and location of your next *true love*."

Michael was about to angrily respond when they noticed several Nerviian barbarians crawling through the high grass, and creeping up behind the sentries, quickly and silently despatched them by slitting their throats.

One of them approached the prisoners and opened the cages. "Vercingetorix has plans for you," the barbarian said, painted all in black from head to toe. "This battle may be lost, but the war with the Roman invaders continues."

"These same slavers have something precious belonging to me," Uriel said. "And which is vital to future victories for your Chief." Uriel pointed to Julius Caesar's personal tent as the angel described the appearance of the supernatural manuscript to the Nerviians.

"What you ask is difficult," one of them said. "And places not only us in danger, but risks your lives also."

"The Romans are overly confident your forces have been completely annihilated, and no longer pose a threat," Uriel replied. "They are too busy drinking and raping your captured women."

The comment drew surprise from Michael and the Nerviians stared momentarily at Uriel in rage, before six of their number left in the direction he mentioned, as the sole remaining man in black escorted the angels under cover of darkness on their knees through the grass and into the neighbouring woods. Many minutes later only one barbarian returned after killing several sentries outside Caesar's tent; the others killed, and Uriel sighed in relief when he revealed the book. Michael quickly snatched the item out of his younger brother's hands.

"What are you doing, Michael? That belongs to me; I am its appointed guardian."

"You are no longer worthy of it, from now on I will be its custodian. As you so eloquently said, you let the Book of Life fall into the hands of the enemy, all because of your arrogance and still believe you are faithfully executing the orders of The Source by interfering in the affairs of humans."

"If I give the order, these Nerviians will kill you."

"They can certainly try, whether they would succeed is another matter. And would you really murder your own brother? Perhaps you are really not that removed from Gabriel's twisted ideology after all."

"I was only trying to stop the senseless butchery of innocents."

"I will use the book and find another way," Michael said. "Even if it takes thousands of years, I will finally once and for all put an end to wickedness on this planet."

Uriel sighed and said nothing more, but watched his brother leave with the Book of Life; not knowing when, or if he would ever see Michael again.

# CHAPTER ELEVEN

"Now I understand the circumstances of how you and Uriel parted and how you came into possession of the book," Grace said, taking hold of his hand. "It must have been difficult for you nevertheless, considering you were together most of the time for millennia."

"What was more painful was watching 'you' die every time," Thomas sobbed. "Each occasion whether you passed traumatically or peacefully in your sleep tore my heart apart. It took a long time for me to get over the death of Adina … and perhaps I never have; I promised her I would find a way to rid the world of wickedness, so her sacrifice would not be in vain. This is why I do it; this is why the app must succeed."

Grace squeezed his hand in sympathy. "I still can't believe you knew legendary historical figures like Julius Caesar."

"The Roman ruler was charismatic, brilliant, but ultimately possessed a flawed character who was obsessed with his own ambition, determined to become Emperor on the backs of slaves and the murdering of innocents. It was fitting karma that lesser men who wanted the same thing killed him, and then fought amongst themselves."

"And were the Romans as evil as Uriel believed?"

Thomas paused for a moment. "Throughout history there have been many empires I have witnessed rise and fall, but the Romans learned from their defeat at the hands of the Celts, to overhaul their weapon technology and forge an iron discipline that allowed them to conquer half the world. I don't believe they were intrinsically wicked despite the awful acts they committed in territories they ruled over, not to mention the butchery of the Coliseum with bloody executions and torture of Christians, gladiators and convicts. You have to remember that nearly all Roman citizens were not free and lived under the tyranny of a line of successive dictators and a few rich men; they were as much slaves as the unfortunate countries they conquered. Any dissent or sedition was crushed instantly and violently. A soldier had to serve twenty-five years in the army to secure citizenship and own property. Most were aghast at how their politicians behaved, but had no power to change the status quo. Of all the empires I have personally seen, I believe the Nazis were the most brutal in their efficiency in terms of extermination of the Jews, gypsies and homosexuals and truly had only contempt for everyone not fitting their narrow definition of breeding. If any nation or race has displayed true evilness, then the Nazis would certainly fit that bill and I knew they had to be exterminated, for if their fabled thousand year Reich did come to pass, then an eternity of darkness would swallow humanity."

"Yes, you mentioned before your hatred for the Nazis. What was Adina like?" Grace asked, changing the subject. "Was she anything similar to me?"

"She was smart, funny and full of life," he smiled. "In many ways so much like you; all the incarnations of you were strikingly similar, it was as if the soul retained some elements of memories and personality, despite the differences such as race, nationality and personal circumstances like being born rich or poor, black or white, etc."

"Was I ever someone famous?" Grace laughed.

"If you mean were you ever Cleopatra or Helen of Troy … then the answer is no. But that is just as well, as my existence might be noted in history books."

"How many incarnations of 'me' were there?"

Thomas paused for a moment. "Twenty-six. Sometimes the gap between each life was short; your last death occurred only a year before you were born. But other times it could be quite lengthy. I had to wait nearly four centuries between Adina and the next reincarnation. Your soul in between lives floated in the aether, existing as cosmic energy without consciousness, until at random it was transferred at conception to another human, waiting to be born."

"And what of your soul and potential reincarnations?"

"I and my siblings were never born as you understand it, and indeed were never truly human, for us death is final and absolute; there is no possibility of rebirth. There is only oblivion waiting for us, it is the price we pay as angels."

Grace said nothing for a moment. "And you were never tempted to find some comfort in the arms of another?"

Thomas burst into laughter. "No, I told you before, there was only you and no other, no matter how lonely … or horny I was."

Grace smirked, but then her face became serious. "Before we return to the house, I need to ask one more thing."

"Like I assured you before, you can always ask me anything."

"Out of all my many lives, was there any of them you loved the most?"

"If by that do you mean was there competition with yourself? The answer is no. I never viewed one incarnation of you over another; I loved you all equally and without compare, for in essence it was always you; the body and face were different, but the soul was the same."

"I guess that is certainly a good response." She smiled as they began their journey through the woodland back towards the house, where Andrea was seated on the steps by the backdoor, dressed in her pyjamas and smoking a cigarette. Grace called out to her and her friend rose to her feet, and beckoned them towards the wooden table and adjoining benches. "I thought you had given up smoking?" Grace laughed as all three sat down as Andrea continued puffing, blowing a smoke circle into the air.

"Yes, I think the events of the last few days have stressed me out. I still am finding it difficult to get my head around all this ..." She said and turned to her employer. "I feel I owe you an apology for the way I spoke to you."

"That is not necessary," he replied. "You were simply protecting your best friend."

"Nevertheless, I was out of order. I know you love Grace. I was just so overwhelmed by the actions of the last few days and the fantastic story she told me about you, and I am only too aware of Grace's 'difficult' upbringing meaning she can be quite vulnerable and naïve. Can I ask you a few things?" She asked and he nodded. "Who exactly were those men that attacked us back in the apartment?"

"I am in constant contact with the federal and state authorities; not to mention Homeland Security, given your assailants seemed to be of Russian mafia origin, from the little information I gathered from my discussions with them."

"They were not interested in me or Lisa, they wanted to kidnap Grace, and they appeared to have a key to gain quick and silent entry."

"Gaining entrance would be easy for professionals, they would have appropriated a key from the doorman who they also attacked," Thomas said. "I believe they wanted Grace as leverage to use against me to stop or alter the programming of the computer application."

"Your sister Gabriel?"

"Yes, I believe so. But those lines of communication have been severed, Uriel wants nothing more to with the endeavour or the war between me and our angelic siblings. But rest assured, my family will pay for this treachery. Gabriel believes overpopulation will bring about the humans' destruction, given Earth's limited resources and living space. I actually agree with her views, but not her methods. Exterminating half of the planet's population is not the answer, rather we should use our unique knowledge and help mankind achieve a better future; perhaps building underwater accommodation in the oceans or even terraforming Mars and Saturn's largest moon Titan, because of the effects of climate change and the rising of sea waters over the next century."

"So by threatening you through Grace and perhaps even torturing her to force your hand … Gabriel believed you would then commit half genocide of the world?"

"Like I said, steps will be undertaken to punish my siblings for their crimes; this will not go unanswered. I also like her, have contacts in the criminal underground."

Grace and Andrea stared at him, afraid to ask what he meant but considered it better they not know, for in this instance ignorance was bliss and would only place their lives in potential greater danger.

"Andrea," Thomas said, breaking the uncomfortable silence. "I must say you speak very well for an eighteen-year-old; far better than your similarly educated comrades, and indeed have a grasp of modern politics, religion and history I find fascinating."

"I would normally have the same immature insight on world events as my school friends, only for my millionaire stepfather to insist on us reading encyclopaedias instead of trashy magazines every night, and all summers spent with a home tutor instructing me on subjects ranging from the Egyptian Empire to hidden secrets of the illuminati. I could speak easily and in-depth of the victories of Alexander the Great, but fail to converse on the banal lifestyles of the Kardashians." She smiled. "Likewise, I think it is simply extraordinary I am talking to someone who frequently and personally communicated with God."

"It was not a two-way conversation like a telephone. Rather it was more The Source gave instructions and you obeyed, never questioning or debating the righteousness or logic of such divine decisions."

Andrea started laughing. "So, it was like being in school. What did it sound like?"

"If you are expecting for me to say it sounded human, then the answer would be no. It is like the noise the wind makes through the trees; a deep kind of 'musical' whisper that vibrates throughout your entire being, there is no mistaking it … or denying it."

"Do you miss it? The lake that is."

Thomas said nothing for a moment. "Every day. Having that incredible purpose and responsibility; being the guardian over humanity all at once and everywhere … and then suddenly it was gone. But being amongst humans is without compare, not to mention the lives of Grace I have shared throughout time."

"Still, it must have been lonely during those periods when you were without her."

Thomas glanced at Grace and smiled. "Yes, those were the hardest and seemingly longest times, but I occupied myself with learning and exploration of the planet and helping mankind whenever and wherever I could. I found employment in as many professions as possible, from such low positions as lavatory cleaner to the personal scribe of kings. I even once tried my hand at being a literary agent, but found their obsession with Twitter perplexing, and mystified how they managed to function at work while consuming daily two bottles of white wine from bucket-sized glasses."

"I understand," Andrea smiled. "I imagine the Catholic Church would have loved to get their hands on you or your family, and use an angel as proof of the divine and to further their twisted ideology across the world."

"Indeed," Thomas replied. "Keeping ourselves hidden from the Church and other historical scribes was not easy, religious fanatics were everywhere and eager to provide justification for their worst murderous intentions like the Spanish Inquisition, and the Protestant nobility who treated Catholics with such contempt in medieval England and even throughout Ireland's tragic history. I was not going to allow myself to be coerced into being a pawn for such an insidious organisation that values money, male power and sexual child violence in such high regard and secrecy while dominating the poor and vulnerable, and sucking up to the rich and elite in society who believed they could pay their way into Heaven and absolve themselves of their awful sins."

"Speaking of the supernatural, I find the concept of reincarnation fascinating. Is this my first life or was I born before, and is there an infinite amount of souls and lives?"

"No, there is not an endless supply of souls; like humanity itself there is a finality to all Creation. When the Chamber of Guf produces the last soul, then mankind will cease to exist, for no child can be born without a spiritual life-source. That is why throughout Earth's long history, there have been far more people born and dead than are currently alive today, despite the planet's seven billion plus population. When the figure alive levels with what has gone before into the grave, then reincarnation will cease to occur, and the end of all human life will be sudden and swift; not unlike something resembling the Rapture."

"The Rapture?" Grace asked. "I thought that was a myth to frighten people into Church?"

"An exaggerated biblical metaphor like so many other parables and stories in the Bible," he said. "Nevertheless, its arrival will be no less traumatic and final, destroying the planet in a mixture of global earthquakes, volcanoes and tsunamis. This will occur when the first baby born without a soul will die instantly; in effect a stillborn and nothing and nobody can prevent it, for this was decided at the beginning of human creation. Even those humans who reside on other worlds and in space will not escape; their lives forfeit as if they too were on Earth as it was destroyed."

"Then exactly what is the point of it all?" Andrea frowned. "Why create such wonders on this planet like life in all its splendour and variance, only to extinguish it all in an instant without a care, and with a simple wave of the Almighty's cosmic hand?"

"I have wrestled with the insane logic of it myself, and debated with Gabriel and my brothers for long periods. However, they believe it is not our place to question The Source's decisions, but to simply obey. Samael said to me once that it was a great empyreal joke that this 'God' the humans so adore and worship, ultimately has nothing but contempt for them all, and pokes and prods at humans, bestowing upon them incurable diseases and natural disasters outside of their control for Its own amusement. I believe this theory was not lost on many ecclesiastical scholars and the biblical tale of Job represented this viewpoint; his life beset by tragedy and hardship that no normal human would endure, but did so without complaint for a God who denied Job of his daughters and sons, his livestock of sheep and cattle, and was shunned by society. In reality this poor unfortunate bastard's only crime was to worship without question a cruel bored deity."

"Interesting perspective," Andrea said. "And what of your own origins? How long exactly is your lifespan and that of the other archangels?"

"So far two hundred thousand years, give or take a millennia."

"And you did not exist before that?"

"The dinosaurs and insects did not require guardian angels. We were created to oversee mankind, nothing more and nothing less. We watched the destruction of your two previous great civilisations; that of the ancient Atlanteans who fled to Antarctica and Tibet after their home was flooded, and the race of giants who built the pyramids in Egypt and South America before their extinction."

"Two hundred thousand years spent gazing into a lake, that must have been boring. One thing though; historians told us modern humanity only really existed for fifty thousand years or so."

"Many archaeologists now realise advanced races existed for much longer than that, the Egyptians did not build the great Sphinx which originally was created as a lion to represent an animal hunted in a region more similar to rich marshland than the lifeless desert it is today. Bones of giants measuring at least seven metres have been found throughout the world, for it was them that moved the heavy blocks of Stonehenge and other structures as no human today could move such objects without an arsenal of large machinery and logistics. But to answer your other question, I was never bored in the lake. It was my appointed sacred duty for all eternity, or at least for the length of time mankind existed, and I had my siblings for company. Indeed I would still be there performing those same tasks but for Samael destroying the realm and forcing us to leave. I sometimes had wishes to explore the Earth and its many wonders first-hand, but I was bound to this 'Heaven' and would never have done so."

"I can only imagine the extraordinary events you must have witnessed over the course of human history."

"Yes, I have seen the creation and fall of magnificent empires such as Egypt, Rome, Troy, etc., and personally walked the gardens of Babylon; one of the lost seven wonders of ancient civilisation. I have had conversations with great minds such as Socrates, Copernicus and Einstein, and attended concerts of Beethoven, Bach and Mozart … and the

Beatles. To bear witness to such splendour like Greece and Rome at its peak which are now mere ruins fills me with melancholy. But it is a tragic reminder that everything has its time and nothing lasts forever."

"Speaking of which … what if this computer program does not work? What happens to all those 'evil' souls if they are not extinguished? And indeed, what are the true consequences if the application performs to your specifications; will all wickedness be forever removed from this planet? Won't new deviant souls be created to replace those ones and the cycle go on for all time, not to mention what about those souls stuck in this aether as you call it, waiting for their turn to be reborn?"

"No, your spiritual essence along with theirs was forged at the moment of 'The Big Bang' at the initial creation of the Universe; it cannot be duplicated or replicated later, it was a one off moment in time and space. Their lifeforce and souls will be eliminated simultaneously and forever. I am simply performing now what would inevitably be done later when they died, when their malevolent deeds would decide their eternal fate, and also those people who had not committed sinister acts who would have gone on to be reincarnated and given another opportunity in their next life to carry out that wickedness, they too will likewise be damned as if they had indeed acted upon those evil deeds. As regards the actual computer program itself, I have gone to extraordinary lengths and coding testing to make certain it does as required in all forms of technology, even satellites to reach everyone on the planet. And as regards future incarnations; the software is so sophisticated, it will be forever integrated into computer mainframes, and duplicate itself into technology not yet developed, as users will be using existing software and hardware to invent next generation computers."

"I understand, and are you not doing this because you despise God?"

Thomas started laughing, taking the two women by surprise. "I don't have any real feelings towards that religious deity to which you refer, and certainly not hatred. It is mankind throughout the millennia that has twisted the notion of God as an excuse or provocation for their greed, lust and violence against minorities, the poor, homosexuals and especially women; the deliberate subjugation of women I find somewhat amusing, as it is men's inherent insecurity and fear that drives this obsession as they know deep down that women are the stronger sex, and live in constant terror that women will rise up and take over."

"I think you will find that is commonly referred to as Small Dick Syndrome." Grace said and they all smiled in reply.

"Speaking of women," Andrea said. "I was always taught Gabriel the Archangel was a man, at least that is how it is portrayed in the sermons told by the priests."

"Of course they would teach an anti-women viewpoint," Thomas replied. "The same false ideology behind portraying Mary Magdalene as a prostitute. However, many secrets lie within the Vatican archives that show something else entirely; it just does not fit their twisted agenda, so it remains hidden."

"On a more personal note, why did you not simply activate the computer program first, and then make contact with Grace at the school? Why place her in danger, not to mention she could be used as leverage against you … was it so she could join in your victory parade?"

Thomas gave her a stern glance. "I know you are best friends, and her safety is important to you, as indeed it is to me, so I will overlook that comment. The Book of Life suggested her identity was compromised and Gabriel was coming for her soon. It was never my intention to place her in harm's way; it was simply the lesser of two evils to locate her earlier than planned, and by keeping her close to my side, best maintain her safety."

"I understand, I apologise. So, getting back to our original discussion, where does Jesus fit into all this?"

"He doesn't. While the Roman Empire kept meticulous records including the executions of such 'prophets;' thus his existence is not in dispute, the very concept that a supreme being such as The Source with its infinite lifespan would interfere on such a minor scale and have a human child is absurd, especially considering the entire history of mankind is barely a blink in Its cosmic eye in comparison to Its own eternal existence. Besides, in my own personal experience of God, It never required a 'messenger boy' or 'semi-divine' postman delivering what was in effect *junk mail*."

"So, all those people who gave their lives for their faith were fools?"

"They arrogantly believed they knew the inner mind and reasoning of a deity who would look kindly upon their self-sacrifice. Martyrs who died blissfully; fixated on the ridiculous idea they would see God's face in reward, but in reality it was the worms and maggots eating out their eyes would be the only response for their naïve ideology. The simple truth, which has been the same for Christians who willingly threw themselves and their families to the lions, and likewise especially in modern times violent cults like Islamic State, who believed blowing yourself to pieces would guarantee a hundred virgins in the afterlife, as long as you took a thousand innocent victims with you; is more to do with their own narcissistic personalities than actual genuine devotion to their twisted version of their chosen religion. As if a supreme being who created something as magnificent as the Universe would care for such false and petty expressions of piety, not to mention chanting 'God is Great' as you merrily carve off someone's head would make the deed any less heinous or more religiously significant."

"And those people who claim they are Jesus Christ reincarnated?"

"Clever charismatic conmen. Recent history has especially seen a rise in these 'false prophets' with the advent of mass media and the Internet, giving a perfect platform for their shallow sermons, and coercing weak-minded followers. It is amusing at this very moment there are several so called Christ incarnates; from the former policeman in Russia, to the Australian who conveniently labels every new girlfriend the reincarnation of Mary Magdalene. Like David Koresh, they start preaching peace but ultimately it always comes down to money and sex, particularly a paedophile obsession for the youngest and most vulnerable members of their followership, often with the blind allegiance of their parents."

"And the ones who witnessed visions of Jesus such as Madeleine Aumont in Dozulé in the nineteen seventies?"

"I always found it a remarkable 'coincidence' that all these so called visionaries were fanatically devout poorly educated simpletons who after staring too long at the sun suddenly saw angels, and immediately ran to the parish priest who was only too eager to manipulate such delusions for his own aims. The 'Jesus' in question in Dozulé conveniently spoke of land ownership arguments between the local padre and his parishioners and how to resolve same, and even arranged further visions for very specific times, as if catering for the priest's duties and his mealtimes."

"How many people have you killed personally?"

"There were moments when my life was in genuine danger and I was forced to act; and other times when a truly wicked individual deserved death, but I never enjoyed it; taking a person's life is a monumental thing and should not be considered lightly."

"And yet you plan to murder millions …"

"It is not murder, but preventive justice on those that are unworthy of the gift of life, and I take no pleasure in their destruction."

"Speaking of which, if you have such incredible power at your disposal in the form of that all-knowing book, then why did you not eliminate the terrorists before they crashed the airplanes into the New York twin towers?"

"The Book of Life is not prophetic and cannot see into the future, and scrying the minds simultaneously of everyone on the planet is impossible."

"That's very convenient and absolves you of any potential guilt," Andrea said. "Getting back to my original question, you were going to mention my own previous incarnations …"

"I examined the book only briefly when it came to your origins because of your close friendship to Grace; you were a seamstress in your previous life, had four children and were relatively content."

"Was he rich; my husband?" Andrea smirked.

"He was a carpenter, worked on several famous buildings including the British Museum in London. You were not wealthy by any means, but comfortable and enjoyed a happy marriage until he died quite young of meningitis at age fifty four. You lived until you were nearly seventy. That would have been the year nineteen sixty eight."

"Speaking of getting old, I imagine not all of Grace's incarnations died young, you must at times have been shagging a granny … and then some."

Thomas glanced at Grace who turned red with embarrassment. "Our relationship throughout the ages was based on more than just the physical. I tried my best to keep Grace's previous incarnations alive as long as possible and protect them, however that was not always possible as circumstances like what happened to Adina were outside of my control. But as you so 'eloquently' mentioned a few did live to be quite elderly, especially Elizabeth, who was Grace's former life whom departed just a few months before your best friend was conceived. Elizabeth lived to be eighty four years old."

"And did you always wait for those girls to become of age, by that I mean were they eighteen years old like Grace is now?"

"I don't think I like what you are inferring," he glared at her. "I am not a paedophile and seducing children. Those women were always of a mature age, at least seventeen years old. Nobles like 13th Century King John of England might have been raping twelve year olds like his second wife Isabella of Angoulême, but I was not. Such an idea is abhorrent to me. It is worth mentioning we were punishing such deviants back in the lake, and in quite a severe manner."

"I meant no offence," Andrea said, placing her hand on his arm. "Let's talk about something else. You are essentially human, am I correct in saying? By that I mean you bleed and can be killed like any man; except you do not age, cannot have children and are sterile, and are much stronger than a normal person. And also you are incapable of getting sick or ill, from the common cold to more serious diseases like cancer, etc."

"Yes, our angelic DNA is the original evolutionary starting point or 'missing link' which scientists keep referring to from which mankind was devised. That divine genetic structure was integrated into apes, forcing their evolution into humans. However, over many millennia that superior heritage was lost, causing humans to become weaker and more susceptible to illness; their original long lifespan was henceforth significantly reduced. What is it you exactly want to know?"

"I understand all that. But one thing I find perplexing is if you and your siblings are as fragile as us mere normal humans, how is it you or your family were never killed or even seriously hurt or maimed, given the amount of wars and senseless violence perpetrated throughout the ages? I am aware you have advanced intellect and strength compared to ordinary people, but I find it inconceivable that none of you died through deliberate fights with soldiers, or some accident not of your own design; falling from a huge height, being hit by a horse and cart, or vehicle; etc."

Thomas laughed. "Do you mean did us guardian angels have guardian angels?"

"Is that so impossible to consider? Yesterday I was an atheist, certain in my opinions that no God existed … and here I am conversing with a real-life archangel; the very physical proof of the divine. It is as if my entire core belief structure has been torn apart. Of course, I myself have yet to see you in action; I have only Grace's word on it, but I have never doubted her or known her to be delusional."

"I see what you mean, but trust me when I say my family of angels are unique in the entire Universe. The Source clearly viewed humans as special and required protection, otherwise events such as natural disasters like asteroids, super volcanoes, etc., would have wiped out your species long ago, not to mention the necessary extinctions of the dinosaurs and other creatures whose world domination would have prevented human evolution, and also the existence of the Moon which regulates your tides, and the axis of the Earth creating your seasons in conjunction with the 'Goldilocks' zone of your planet from the sun. All these have encouraged the growth and safety of humans; it is not blind luck these exist."

"Interesting," Grace said. "Does that mean the Bible is real?"

"All stories steeped in legend and myth have some basis in fact, whether that be vampires and werewolves; or tales of gods and demons, but even I know Earth was not created in six days, and I never saw anyone rise from the dead. The Bible and religion have been twisted and used as provocation for man's greed and ambition like the Crusades, and the persecution of the Jews and homosexuals. One intriguing event happened however some years ago, when I encountered someone who claimed to be the actual biblical character Cain who killed his brother Abel, he was on the run from the illuminati and their leader Samuel Carson."

"That's certainly a fascinating tale, but I won't be rushing off to church and praying like an altar boy just yet," Andrea smirked. "How is it after so many previous incarnations, I have no memories of my husbands or my children?"

"All humans enter a new life with a 'blank slate' as it were, having no recollection of events experienced by their former selves. It is better that way; imagine grieving over dead spouses and kids you knew before this current incarnation, and that would greatly affect your attachments to future husbands not yet met or children unborn. Besides, mistakes can be forgotten and new skills can be learnt whether that be art, music, literature, etc. The future becomes an unwritten page and full of wonder; experiencing things again for the first time."

"So, there is no choice involved in where I end up? Rich or poor, black or white and my nationality or time period?"

"Yes. It is completely random, everyone ... even Grace."

"So, this Book of Life is how you knew where and when she would be born again. Can I see it?"

"I'm afraid not. It is locked securely in a vault in Marsh Tower."

"And yet you showed it to Grace. I am only kidding, I am not jealous," Andrea grinned. "Something I have always been curious about; if everyone is reincarnated, besides the evil souls who are destroyed ... then how do you explain ghosts if they do indeed exist?"

"The 'Spirits of the Dead' do exist, but do not have a consciousness; the tremendous force released at their traumatic death is caught in a perpetual loop or spiritual echo, meaning the 'ghosts' are endlessly revisiting the same event and place because of a violent act that brought about their death. The energy expended at the point of their awful demise has caused a tear in the space time continuum which can never be repaired."

"So, us humans and even animals all have a soul and will be reincarnated forever until the end of time, but you angels do not … what does that mean when one of your family dies?"

Thomas paused for a moment and glanced at Grace. "We disappear completely."

Andrea frowned. "Well, that kind of sucks. So, that means The Devil is also gone forever."

"I did not know him as that; he was not only my brother, he was my friend and I grieve for him every day. I had no choice in my actions, he was a tremendous danger to us and humanity."

"Don't blame Grace for telling me the story, I can be a persistent bitch and have a knack of dragging secrets from her," Andrea smirked. "So, I guess that means former President Donald Trump is not the Antichrist after all."

Thomas started laughing and the two young women quickly joined him. "Considering the legendary son of The Devil is supposed to be a genius at politics and possess supernatural charisma, then you guess correctly about Trump. Besides, that odious swamp creature may be sinister and utterly corrupt like the fabled Antichrist … but is simply too fucking stupid to fit the title. Donald Trump however bears one trait with the Antichrist in that he is the ultimate narcissist, and has such an unwavering admiration in his persona he probably finds his own reflection sexually attractive and masturbates to himself in the mirror."

They were still giggling when Lisa appeared, carrying several shopping bags, the logos on the packaging instantly recognisable with high street clothes companies.

"Don't stop at my account, continue the joke about me." Lisa said sharply.

"Girl, you are really not that important that every conversation is about you," Andrea sneered. "I would rather discuss the ecological benefits of used toilet paper than fill my time talking about you."

Lisa threw one of the shopping bags onto the wooden table in front of them. "Care to borrow some proper fashion, considering you always wear clothes you stole from your grandmother."

Andrea glanced at the contents of the bag as one extravagant blouse was evident, before looking up at Lisa. "I always say you can smudge the most expensive makeup and put on the priciest dress on a pig … but at the end of the day it will always be a fucking pig."

Lisa glared at her, before picking up the bag and walked away, returning to the house.

"One final thing I must ask before we go back inside," Andrea said, turning towards her employer. "Are you certain that computer program is the only way to stop the evils of the world? I know we discussed it already, but perhaps humanity should discover their own path and bring these criminals to justice?"

"Justice?" Thomas echoed. "Those are laws that were conceived by idealistic naïve men who believed fair play would always be adhered to; the guilty would be punished and the innocent protected. But the truth is mankind is divided clearly by those who have and those who have not; the poor and minorities will always will be downtrodden and treated unfairly, and the rich and the nobility will escape proper castigation. Tyrants like Syrian President Bastard al-Assad and North Korean Supreme Lardass Kim Jong-un will continue unhindered in their butchery because of weak corrupt men, but my program will give their people the true justice that has always been denied them. Humanity as a whole believes if a common global threat like alien invasion were to occur, they likewise as late President Ronald Reagan once declared before the United Nations, would rise up as one species; united under a single war banner and combat this extra-terrestrial menace. But the truth is in a very short space of time they would turn against each other, as total panic and chaos reigned upon losing forever all Wi-Fi signals on their smartphones."

"And now you will use that very same technology against them; corrupting those same signals through your computer program and filtering into every television, radio, mobile phone and all types of computers," she sighed. "You have a very cynical view of mankind."

"I have watched humans tear each other apart since their creation. This is truly the only way," he said sternly. "Enjoy the brief pause in the solitude and beauty of this forest before we must return to Marsh Tower, you are safe here and no harm will come to you. No one knows about this place."

Andrea went back into the house, leaving Grace and Thomas alone on the bench.

"Thomas, why does your family hate us so much? What did we ever do to them?"

"It is not you, my love," he sighed. "Gabriel believes I turned away from the true path."

"For not killing Samael when she demanded?"

"That ... and for others. I showed mercy when perhaps it was not deserved. I chose not to kill people in Malaga in the middle ages."

"The Spanish Inquisition? When you saved Ramiel from certain death?"

Thomas nodded. "And yet it was not enough to satisfy her bloodlust ... it was never enough."

## CHAPTER TWELVE

"In all the godforsaken places we had to end up; it had to be Spain at the height of the Spanish Inquisition under the infamous Tomas de Torquemada, the Grand Inquisitor himself." Raguel said.

"Well, our time in England had come to an end," Gabriel replied. "Anyway, cease your fretting; anyone here who might have been told of our angelic existence is dead."

"We hope," Sariel added, as they walked through the brown cobbled streets of Malaga, and entered an alleyway. "For if not they are telling all secrets on the rack."

"Those 'unfortunate' nobles who despised the Inquisition required proof we were angels to risk their lives and give us safe haven," Gabriel said. "Those bloodthirsty religious hypocrites only persecute rich people to confiscate their property, and line their own pockets to fund mistresses and their own lavish lifestyle."

"You certainly gave that proof to those nobles," Raguel said and they all laughed. "Pulling the arms and legs off that inquisitor we kidnapped with your bare hands ... and the fucking mess afterwards, not to mention the screaming; my ears are still ringing."

"He deserved nothing less," Gabriel smiled. "These sons of bitches think they know God and are acting on Its behalf, but rather they are fuelling their own dark desires."

"They're scared, like all humans." Michael said as he suddenly appeared in the alleyway.

"Well, look what crawled out from a fucking rock," Gabriel sneered. "I hoped to never set eyes on you and Uriel again, thousands of years has not been enough."

"It's good to see you too, sister," Uriel said, also appearing out of the shadows alongside his brother. "Long have I dreamt of this moment since ancient Egypt."

"So, the family reunited once more," Ramiel said. "And not 'all together' since the last time we met we buried Samael in an unmarked grave in the desert."

"And was that slave girl in Babylon all you hoped for?" Gabriel asked. "Was her pussy so sweet that you would leave us?"

"You as the almighty leader exiled us," Uriel said. "You made it very clear we were not welcome."

"And the Book of Life?" Raguel asked. "Do you still have it after all this time?"

Uriel sighed. "I gave it to Michael for safekeeping."

Raguel and the others stared at him in shock and disbelief. "You were its appointed guardian; it was your sacred duty to own for all of humanity's existence, not a simple possession like a chair or table to give away."

"I abused its trust," Uriel said. "I was using it to further my own personal crusade and change the course of mankind through violence."

Gabriel started laughing. "And what did you think we were doing all the time in the lake, if not altering the destiny of humans by whatever means necessary?"

"I am not that man anymore," Uriel replied flatly. "I intend to learn from mankind and let them find their own path without interference."

"You are a fucking archangel," Gabriel snarled. "Christ, what a disgrace and weak bastard you have become. I was right to exile you, the very sight of you now turns my stomach."

"That's enough." Michael said.

"And you dare speak to me as a leader?" She sneered. "You lost that potential title a long time ago. At least Uriel has some principles, even if they are wrong and twisted. But you brother, look at yourself. The humans believe the Bible; a ridiculous work of fiction and lies portray you as the one who defeated Lucifer and saved Heaven. If only they knew the truth of what you are; a pale imitation of that fantasy, spiritually weak and following a human woman's incarnations through history like a lost puppy. I should cut your fucking head off too and leave it for the desert rodents to feast on like Samael."

Michael smiled in response. "I am confused as to why you have not set the record straight with the Holy Inquisition as to the true facts, instead of cowering like scared cowards in this alley?"

Gabriel struck him square in the chest, sending Michael flying across the wall and onto the ground. He swiftly rose to his feet and prepared to attack when Uriel interceded.

"Save it for the priests of the Inquisition."

She glared at the two brothers in temper. "We will continue this discussion later. Tell me what you are doing here, it was no accident you discovered us."

Michael dusted himself down and turned towards them. "I found Uriel in northern Granada, and learnt of rumours of the Spanish Inquisition investigating witchcraft and heresy in Malaga including stories of angels. Believe it or not, I was worried about you."

Raguel laughed. "That's very sweet. I presume you have a house nearby."

Michael nodded and led them through the streets and red bricked houses to a dwelling overlooking the Mediterranean Sea, and up the mountain in a remote location a short distance from the town. Before them was a three-storey building, surrounded by a two-foot wall and a garden to the right of the entrance filled with small trees and flowers suited to the warm temperatures of the region.

"Selling antiques seems to be lucrative," Sariel said. "I am curious that Torquemada has not made up excuses to seize your estate."

"Finding witnesses that know me to organise false crimes has proven difficult," Michael replied. "And I have made it my business to make court informants are too frightened to sniff around."

"I thought you did not advocate violence." Gabriel said.

"Making implied threats is often enough, it is not necessary to rip limbs off to make your point."

An attractive woman aged in her mid-thirties appeared at the top of the stairs and watched the visitors enter. The angels with the exception of Michael and Uriel, looked on in bemusement as the woman descended the wooden steps. Gabriel could see the woman had long curly dark hair tied to a single ponytail, which was hanging over the right shoulder of a slender frame with pear shaped breasts and hazel eyes. She smiled at her guests revealing near perfect teeth, clearly paid for by the best dentist Michael could easily afford; quite different to her Spanish contemporaries, as dental work was both too expensive for the majority of the populace, and only foreign teeth doctors such as from England would have sufficient expertise for the middle ages.

"I welcome my family to our humble home," she said, her elocution again evident of a good education. "Please come to the kitchen where I have bread and wine refreshments."

"My family?" Gabriel frowned and caught hold of the human's hand, noticing a gold band.

"My name is Marianna," the woman said. "And yes … Michael your brother is my husband."

Gabriel sneered. "Is it not enough you lower yourself to fornicate with these creatures, that you must marry them as well?"

"I love her, as I have done with all her former incarnations," Michael replied. "Perhaps finding such emotions with a human would not be so remote for you also?"

"I would lay with the swine in the mud first than love a human," his sister growled. "At least the pig's motives are obvious and not deceitful."

"You have desires the same as I. That leaves only the option of sleeping with one of your own kind."

"Incest is strictly forbidden, to do so would be the moral equivalent of the sodomites Torquemada has rightfully burnt at the stake. I would in all conscience have to join him in the Inquisition, or perhaps even hand myself in for heresy."

"Do you ever tire of hearing yourself?" Uriel asked.

She glared at him as Marianna handed them each a goblet of wine. They sat in silence at the table; eating bread and drinking, Gabriel glancing at Michael and Uriel every few moments as if in disapproval. They had just finished when loud knocking could be heard from the front door. Michael stared at them all in surprise and fearful curiosity as he expected no other guests.

"Open up in the name of the Holy Office of the Inquisition," shouted a man from beyond the door. "By order of the Grand Inquisitor Tomas de Torquemada."

Gabriel and the others rose from their chairs. "We cannot allow ourselves to be captured," she said as they all revealed swords, drawing them from the scabbards. "Prepare for combat."

Michael put his hands up to motion for calm. "Let me speak to them, it is clear we were followed and they know of your presence in Malaga." He led Marianna to a hidden compartment under the stairs before opening the front door.

Forty armed soldiers entered the building one after another until they were all assembled in the main foyer area of the house. They were dressed in white tunics bearing the circular crest of the Spanish Inquisition; a rough appearing wooden cross flanked by an olive tree and a sword surrounded by a Latin inscription. All were armed with swords and were clearly professional soldiers.

The captain spotted the guests in the kitchen and called them out. "Drop your weapons and produce identification."

"There's no need for violence," Michael said. "We are all prepared to cooperate with the Holy Inquisition."

"That is good," the captain said. "I would hate to tear this place apart to find the woman I know resides here, or if I fail in that task, burn the building to the ground with her inside."

"That is not necessary, and besides you would not then be able to confiscate the house and sell it, which is your familiar method of thievery," Michael said and turned to his family. "Go with them peacefully; I will pay for your imprisonment, that seems to usually suffice."

"We have no papers, brother." Raguel said, speaking in Enochian; the language of the angels so the soldiers could not understand.

"Speak not in the words of witches," the captain ordered. "It will only add to your guilt and sentence."

"Now I really want to kill them," Gabriel said. "And fucking slowly."

"What part of no witch speak did you fail to understand?" The chief guard roared. "Seize them."

Three soldiers moved to take Gabriel into custody, but as they did so, Ramiel hit one of the men in the back of the head, severing his spine and killing him instantly, such was the force of the blow. The action took the others momentarily by surprise, but they swiftly recovered and the angels were soon completely surrounded.

"I don't know how you managed such a feat of strength, but it is clear this previously held belief that witchcraft was purely rumour should be re-examined," the chief guard said. "Torquemada himself will be most interested in your interrogation."

The soldiers disarmed the angels and placed them all in irons, including Michael and Uriel, fastening their hands at the wrists with heavy metal handcuffs before escorting them out of the building, and marched them down the mountain.

After nearly an hour they arrived in the town square and approached a huge building situated in the very centre of Malaga; one of the coastal settlements of the Granada region of the Spanish nation. The guards and their captives were escorted inside the grandiose mansion, and Michael was stunned by the luxury and expense poured into the structure designated for the Grand Inquisitor. The house appeared to be four storeys covering a large area which must have contained at least fifty rooms. The walls before them were lined with tapestries of former popes, and in particular Queen Isabella II, the current reigning monarch of Spain and her husband King Ferdinand of Aragon. Religious icons gifted to the nation by Pope Sixtus IV, who instigated the Spanish Inquisition at the sovereigns' request could be seen, including golden crosses hanging over the windows.

The prisoners were marched into an enormous windowless room completely composed of solid oak shined to near mirror effect where against the far wall was six throne like chairs, upon were seated old men dressed in brown robes, and a large silver crucifix around their necks. The soldiers and their captives came to a stop in the centre of the chamber, and the captain approached the head of the Council of the Supreme and General Inquisition, whom the angels believed was none other than the Grand Inquisitor himself; Tomas de Torquemada.

The sixty-eight year old man before them was dressed in the familiar attire of a monk, but his brown robe was hoodless and had a white collar like that of a priest. He had however the traditional shaved bald head save for the crown of short hair over the forehead and ears and around the back of the head. The Grand Inquisitor had the fearsome stern look of a man who had sent thousands of Jews and converso-Christians to the burning stake for the petty 'crime' of being forced to change their chosen religion to Catholicism while still secretly practicing Judaism. After the captain whispered in his ear, Tomas de Torquemada turned towards the congregation of assembled soldiers and prisoners.

"This is most unusual and against established protocol," the head of the council of six members declared. "Before guilt is achieved, the accused must be first detained pending trial and witnesses will be called against them, and if they refuse to acknowledge their crime, they will be tortured in the method of the rack, cloth water drowning and tied up by the wrists until dislocating of the arms."

"Sounds like fun," Ramiel interrupted. "When can we start?"

A nearby soldier punched him in the stomach, causing the angel to fall to his knees.

"Such impertinence and disrespect of the tribunal will not be tolerated," Torquemada said.

"Any further outbursts will be dealt with severely. To continue, confession will be found at torture and sentence then carried out which may range from exile, to confiscation of all property to death for the truly wicked. However, seeing as it appears you are clearly witches I think we can proceed straight to the latter."

Michael let out a sudden cough and Torquemada turned towards him directly. "We are not witches."

"So you say, as many others have done so before you," the Grand Inquisitor chided. "But all evidence points to the contrary."

"Perhaps we are the fabled angels of which the rumour speaks," Ramiel said. "If so, as divine beings we should not be detained."

Torquemada laughed. "To mention such is the greatest of heresies, next you will say you are Christ himself. If you are an angel, then produce your wings, golden armour and flaming sword and strike us down. Rather I say you received your superhuman strength from Lucifer."

The soldiers began to move their prisoners out of the chamber for the destination of the cells and later the gallows, until Ramiel abruptly stood out and roared at the council.

"I wish to confess."

Torquemada stared at him in interest. "Speak for time is short and the stake awaits."

"My comrades are innocent, they were deceived by me," he said and the others motioned for him to be silent, but he waved them off. "Free them in the name of the risen Lord and I will tell everything of my infernal dealings with Satan."

"What are you doing?" Gabriel asked, talking in Enochian so the Spaniards would not understand.

"Saving your lives," Ramiel replied. "It serves nothing us all being condemned, and will afford you the opportunity to petition my release."

"These savages will not listen to reason," Raguel said. "Rather we seek a chance to fight our way out of here."

"Then perhaps that opportunity will present later when we are not surrounded." Ramiel said.

"Cease the witch speak and your deception if you truly wish freedom for your friends," Torquemada ordered. "Your sincerity will be put to the test. The others will be detained in cells until such time a honest confession is withdrawn from this witch, and we will ascertain if more than his life is required to stop this prevalence of sorcery."

They were escorted out of the room and Ramiel was separated from the others, being led to a cell in an adjacent wing of the prison. The guards placed Michael and his siblings in cages, two at a time together. Michael was imprisoned with Raguel in an eight-foot square cell lined with thick iron bars surrounding them. They could see Gabriel and Uriel in another cage alongside them while two soldiers stood nearby.

After the majority of the armed men had left, Raguel reached over and suddenly grabbed Michael by the throat and pinned him to the far end of the cell. The two sentries seemed to take no notice, pain and suffering was intrinsic to the Inquisition and if prisoners wanted to assault each other, then it was not their business.

"How is it we were discovered in the mountains?" Raguel growled. "Did you lead us there to trap us?"

"The town is full of spies and informants," Michael replied, pushing his sibling back. "If they do not fill a monthly quota of so called fake conversos and heretics, then they too will be arrested and detained indefinitely."

"It seems very convenient that such a large force of soldiers would descend on your house mere minutes after we arrived, as if we were watched from the moment we stepped into this godforsaken nation?"

"Everyone is under observation here," Michael replied. "All the time. You can't shit without a spy taking note."

"And how do you presume to get us out of here?" Gabriel asked in the adjacent cell. "Every minute spent puts Ramiel's life in danger."

"I promise no harm will befall him," Michael said. "Despite our differences, he is still family."

"We will see." She sneered.

"I want you and Uriel pretend to fight and he will strangle you," Michael said. "When you appear dead, the soldiers will respond and open the cell to investigate. Then you can seize your chance."

"They weren't too concerned when you two were fighting." Uriel said.

"Violence and pain is nothing new here and the prison regularly has to be cleaned of bloodstains," Michael said. "But if a prisoner should die before trial and sentence, then the guards will be severely punished."

Raguel burst into laughter. "What a charming quaint country you settled in."

"I follow wherever Marianna's reincarnations go," Michael said. "This path has led me to some of the most remote and hostile locations on Earth, from the deserts of Egypt to the jungles of Africa, to even high society in England."

"What an adventure you must have had," Gabriel frowned. "Fucking your way through the millennia while simultaneously remaining faithful to the same *woman*."

"I wouldn't expect you to understand."

"I understand only too well. You convinced this weak piece of shit next to me to give up the book, which was his sacred duty for all time to protect."

"I believe that's my introduction to get ready." Uriel said.

"Yes, I tire of speaking with you two cowards," Gabriel said. "Any more time spent in your odious company and I will need to vomit."

Seemingly encouraged by the comment, Uriel pushed his sister against the metal bars and grabbed her by the throat. The two sentries stood and watched with some amusement, perhaps with the vague hope they might witness some female nudity, even a rape. However, as Uriel attempted to choke her and she appeared to lose consciousness, the soldiers responded and opening the cell, pulled Uriel off his sibling. While one guard kept the male prisoner at bay with the point of his sword, the other sentry tried to resuscitate the woman.

There was a startled look on his face when the woman suddenly seemed to come to life and he pulled back in fright. Gabriel punched him straight in the chest with her right fist, breaking his ribcage and splitting his heart, such was the force behind the blow. The man screamed and fell back dead and the other soldier turned, taking his attention off Uriel, giving the angel an opportunity to grab the guard's arm and pushed the sword upwards and into the man's stomach, the blade coming out of his back. The Spaniard fell onto Uriel as he died and the angel heaved his corpse off and onto the ground.

Gabriel took the dead soldiers' weapons and opened the other cells, freeing her brothers. The only other remaining sealed cage contained what appeared to be an old man who had clearly starved to death awaiting trial, his skeletal cadaver covered in cobwebs and a rat running over his bony legs. It was a gruesome sight and a grim reminder that the welfare of captives of the Inquisition was dependent on relatives paying for their imprisonment; obviously the money had run out and the unfortunate individual was left to rot.

They carefully opened the metal door leading out of this wing of the prison and were momentarily startled by the intermittent screams of prisoners being tortured throughout the structure. The building was huge and sprawled over a large area meaning searching for Ramiel would take time. Gabriel motioned for them to split up to increase the chances of finding their sibling and leave before their absence was noted.

Considering the mutual animosity amongst the company of angels, Michael decided to go with Uriel. Some doors were locked and required force to enter, their superhuman strength proving useful gaining entry. Some cells revealed a miserable sight: captives of both sexes and differing ages hanging from the ceiling bound at the wrists behind the backs to increase discomfort and encourage dislocation of the arms at the shoulders. Uriel pointed out it was not their business to interfere and to do so would waste precious time which they could not afford. Other rooms had the torturers themselves still inside committing various acts of brutality, such as pouring water over bound prisoners on their backs on a wooden table, a cloth covering mouths which provoked a form of simulated drowning; a medieval type of waterboarding. Gabriel spent a few seconds disposing of the inquisitors, the screams of the prisoners hiding her entrance. Michael did not frown on such activity, knowing the torturers deserved their fate and acknowledging his sister's hatred for them. Of course, it was also an outlet for her aggression and he considered at least it was directed at them, and not him and Uriel ... for the moment.

Gabriel returned about twenty minutes later and to Michael's relief had Ramiel with her. She passed the injured angel to him for safekeeping, evidence that he had been placed on the rack and stretched could be seen, including dark bruising around the upper and lower joints and rope burns at the wrists and ankles. Ramiel mentioned it took more than three men on each side at the wheels to pull him on the rack given his strength and resilience to torture. However, he was clearly in a lot of pain and could not stand unassisted.

"We will secure the path ahead." Gabriel said.

Michael nodded as the rest of them including Uriel went on in front. Finally they could see the main exit and sighed with relief. However, a nearby door abruptly opened and one of the council of six ruling members that judged them back in the mansion appeared. The inquisitor revealed a short dagger from beneath his monk like outfit and moved to stab Ramiel in the chest. Because Michael was half-carrying his brother, he was unable to block the blow or drop his sibling in time and kill the inquisitor. He had a mere second to decide and by instinct turned himself, and the knife entered his right side a few inches below the ribs. Michael let out a cry of pain as blood flowed down onto the floor. The action however allowed Ramiel to reach out and hit the monk square in the face, breaking his jaw and knocking him out. Michael fell to the ground as Raguel came to his aid.

"You saved my life." Ramiel said, grimacing in agony as striking the monk with a limb that had only an hour ago been dislocated was extremely painful to accomplish.

"You would have done nothing less." Michael smiled.

"I hope that is true," Ramiel replied. "Nevertheless, I won't ever forget it."

Raguel tore a piece of his tunic and wrapped it around the wound, stopping the flow of blood. Michael gritted his teeth in pain as he was helped to his feet and Sariel who arrived, picked up Ramiel. Gabriel and the others were waiting at the exit of the prison building. A brief glimpse outside onto the street showed no soldiers in sight and they all quickly moved into the adjacent alleyway.

"This looks exactly like the place where we first met earlier before the arrest." Ramiel said and they all laughed, including Michael, despite the injury.

"We should have stayed here." Sariel added.

"Yes, very amusing," Gabriel said. "But we are far from safe, and this town is crawling with soldiers and spies of the Inquisition."

"Thanks for stating the obvious," Michael said. "We are going to return to my house and then find a boat out of Spain. It is time for new scenery."

"The guards could be waiting for us back at your residence," Gabriel growled. "It is foolish to go there."

"I am not leaving Marianna to die there alone," Michael said. "Or to be tortured by the Inquisition."

"Can't you just get another version of her later?"

"Fuck you, Gabriel. Besides, for your information, the Book of Life is in the basement and I am certain you don't want that falling into the wrong hands."

His sister sighed. "This just goes to prove that the book should never have been in your keeping. I will take ownership of the book. That is the deal for my help, take it or leave it."

Michael nodded in agreement and they began the journey up the mountain towards his home, hiding in back gardens and alleys until they finally sighted the building. Michael groaned upon seeing several armed soldiers patrolling around the house and outer grounds.

"Christ, are you sure this girl is worth it?" Gabriel asked. "It is appropriate we are sterile and can't have children, for if you were to actually have offspring with these women, fuck knows what they would be like; as a prophet once said to me: if you breed with a dog ... then it is a dog you will have."

Michael glared at her. "Once again you remind me why I did not join your merry group of fanatics."

"What does that mean?" Sariel asked.

"You so blindly follow our sister, you cannot see the true face of hysteria?" Michael asked.

Gabriel laughed. "Are you seeking converts for your own cause?"

"I just want them to examine their path and know there is always another choice," Michael replied. "Things have changed since the lake, we cannot alter humanity to our liking anymore; that divine vocation is gone forever."

"You are a hypocrite, brother," Raguel said. "You seek a similar destiny for mankind with your obsession with the nature of evil, travelling the globe attempting to right the wrongs of the world; dispensing 'justice' on murderers and rapists ... all you lack is the means to kill them all at once."

"Don't you realise there is both good and bad in every man and woman; one cannot exist without the other," Gabriel added. "It makes more sense to kill the rich and so called nobility; the true evil of the world. If the 'Holy' Inquisition has demonstrated anything, it has proved ambitious men will manipulate greedy royalty to influence politics and the destiny of nations for their own nefarious means. With the wealthy removed from society, then the downtrodden can reclaim their stolen birthright and live free."

Michael was about to respond when they saw two soldiers remove Marianna from the house, her hands bound at the front. He moved out of the bushes from where they were hidden and advanced on the men. Gabriel motioned for Raguel and Sariel to help him, while she and Raphael would confront the four guards at the side of the building. They left Ramiel behind as his injuries prevented him from being of any use to the attack.

The two soldiers saw Michael and his brothers and drew their swords. The first guard swung at Sariel's stomach, but the angel jumped back and Raguel punched him in the back. The man let out a scream as he was sent flying across the ground and the other soldiers inside the building came running. The second guard held his sword to Marianna's neck and began to back away, the three angels facing him.

"Let her go if you want to live." Raguel ordered, but the man shook his head in fear.

"I give you my word you can leave safely if you release her," Michael said. "Otherwise I will castrate you with your own blade."

The soldier hesitated for a moment before dropping his weapon and ran off. Michael severed the rope binding her hands and they embraced. Three more guards appeared at the entrance to the house, but were cut down from behind by Gabriel and Raphael, the angels driving swords through the surprised men's backs.

Michael sighed in relief. "That was close. You disposed of those other soldiers at the side of the house already?"

Gabriel sneered. "While you were letting one of them go free and making sweet talk, we were busy killing. Now, remember your promise ... give me the book."

Marianna glanced at her lover in confusion as Michael entered the building and returned a few minutes later.

"Here is my book," he said, handing his sister a folded over leather bag. "Enjoy the read."

They made their way down to the harbour and paid a ferryman for passage out of Spanish territory, Gabriel and the others boarding a small fishing vessel.

"Where next for you?" Michael asked, as he watched the craft begin to leave the pier.

"Somewhere quiet," Gabriel said. "Perhaps Africa or even Russia, a big country to get lost in and avoid the Inquisition."

"Queen Isabella is terrified of England," Michael shouted back as they were now some distance from the stone wall. "So maybe there for Marianna and I ... or even Ireland."

"Just stay out of history's way and my path, and you will be fine," she said and opened the bag, revealing not the Book of Life, but a small leather bound manuscript. "What is this?"

"My diary," he shouted. "Like I mentioned … enjoy the read."

Gabriel motioned for the ferryman to return to the pier. "This is not what we agreed. I should have checked the bag; I should have known you could not be trusted."

"I promised you my book, and that is what you got. The Book of Life is hidden up in the mountains where no one will find it. Read my diary, perhaps it will offer you a different perspective on humanity."

They began to approach the stone wall, but then spotted a large detachment of soldiers at least fifty strong marching nearby, and Raguel instructed the ferryman not to land, but continue out to sea.

Gabriel glared briefly at Raguel, but realised to return would be suicide. "Don't interfere with my plans, Michael, and you will be safe to love your women in peace."

Michael just waved in response, before he and Marianna left the harbour in the direction of the mountain to retrieve the book … and then leave Spain forever.

## CHAPTER THIRTEEN

Gabriel gazed across the metal table at her assembled siblings, eating the contents of a Chinese takeaway, some of them struggling with chopsticks to pick up noodles and pieces of chicken.

"I can never understand the logic of these flimsy wooden instruments," Raphael said, much to his brothers' laughter. "Why make such interesting and delicious food and then hamper the experience with torturous devices."

"All the time you spent in Asia, and you never learnt how to use them," Raguel laughed. "Just use a fucking fork."

"But that would 'take away' from the experience." Raphael smirked.

"Will you shut the fuck up," Gabriel said, scattering the collection of tinfoil containers and Styrofoam cups onto the floor, much to her brothers' dismay. "I am waiting for a phone call from Sariel."

"Two years have passed since we set eyes on our wayward brother," Ramiel said, staring in annoyance at his dinner strewn on the dirty stones. "And now we wait upon his communication like a hungry dog begging for scraps; eager for news of the outside world."

"Not to mention cowering like scared rabbits in this abandoned church," Raphael added. "Frightened of Michael's rage … and his revenge."

"I for one fear not our sibling's retribution," Gabriel replied. "And Sariel is acting under my orders."

Raguel sneered. "Are you really that naïve, sister, to believe he stills follows your commands? He has his own agenda now; not to mention his hired army of mercenaries, it is only vague loyalty that he does not send those men to kill us also."

"This is why I am the leader, and not you." Gabriel replied with a stern glance, before standing and moving away from the rest of them. She stared out at the overgrown grass that covered the forgotten tombstones of long dead residents from New York, from the broken tinted windowpane and let out a deep sigh of frustration.

Raguel stood alongside her. "I apologise for being impertinent, I was out of line. I know the pressures you are under as we get closer to that computer program becoming operational; I am aware that time is short."

"Look at those abandoned graves out there," she said and he gazed out at the eroded stones, their names stripped away from the wind and rain. "No one visits or cares for those dead people who once breathed air and had beating hearts like them; the humans are too busy, thinking their lives are so hectic and full they will never die, and it is more similar to an indignation for them that nature or a deity would deny them of that ebullient life often without warning or meaning of a higher purpose," Gabriel said and clasped the edge of the broken glass fiercely, causing a thin stream of blood to flow down her wrist and onto the grey cobblestones of the ancient church, as Raguel could only watch in troubled fascination. "And yet as certain as this blood leaves my body, then it will surely leave theirs on the final day of their lives, and like them one day we too will be forgotten and discarded like those corpses in the graveyard; our divine knowledge, personalities and experiences turned to dust."

"However, they at least have the salvation of reincarnation, and an opportunity to live again, though without that previous wisdom that must die also with their former bodies."

"Again something denied to our kind," she echoed. "Which is why our angelic lives are so much more important than theirs, and we have therefore only one opportunity to make our lives count and have meaning … and change the world for the better."

"And Michael knows nothing about Sariel?"

"He only has vague suspicions about our plans, and believes Sariel has left our group and vanished, at least that is what his spies have told him. That is why Sariel had to go into deep hiding and remain apart from us to bring these schemes to fruition without Michael's interference."

"And now our very lives depend on his discretion." Raguel said, reaching out and rubbing her right cheek with the back of his hand.

Gabriel flinched at the sudden touch. "Don't do that, please."

"Don't deny what I feel for you … and I know what you feel for me."

She stared at him sternly. "It is forbidden."

"And so you say every time after we are together, even when we made fierce passionate love in that hotel room when we left the others here. Remember how they feared something had happened to us, we were gone so long."

Gabriel laughed. "I was faking all that time through."

"Sure you were," he grinned. "Especially those moans when I gave you oral sex."

She grabbed hold of his hand, pulling it away from her. "It was still wrong and we cannot do it again. We are archangels sworn to a higher purpose; common lust belongs to the humans, we are greater than that. It is not our way."

"Gabriel, I know more than anyone how alone you have been all these many millennia and how you long for the same companionship that humans take for granted, indulging in casual sex without meaning or thought for consequence."

She stared at him in reply. "We are brother and sister, it is incest."

"Mankind's laws built on hypocrisy," Raguel responded. "Every day the humans with their 'civilised' notions of fairness and equality dance around these rules, and deceive each other for money and sex."

"That may certainly be the case for mankind, but we should not use their failures of character as an excuse for our own actions; we alone are responsible for our desires and must bear the consequences for same."

Their conversation was broken as Ramiel stood alongside them. "I am wondering … what of the degenerates in society like rapists, murderers, etc., should we not include them also like Michael plans to eliminate, in our own version of the computer program?"

"The 'evil' humans that our wayward brother so obsesses over is his remit alone." Gabriel said.

"I don't understand, why not let his plan come to fruition and exterminate these deviants, for surely that will significantly decrease the world population, and in essence kill both birds with one stone; solving our dilemma as well."

"It won't be enough," Gabriel replied. "Our brother's computer program might account for millions, but in order to save this planet we need the population decrease to be in the billions. Besides, the real hidden problem that has always been at the core of humanity won't be resolved, that being the super-rich; whether it is the Illuminati or the Bilderberg Group, or whatever fancy name these elitist fucks call themselves that truly hold mankind in low-wage bondage, and being the backroom kingmakers of presidents and prime ministers, while orchestrating wars and fake pandemics to keep the populace asleep to their true enemy. It is this vermin that needs to be extinguished for humanity to be finally free."

"And what of the living space expansionism schemes Michael mentioned in his diary he gave you in Spain?" Ramiel asked. "Building underwater cities and terraforming the Moon and Mars? They might solve Earth's population problems."

"Yes, they would work … to a degree," Gabriel replied. "But this planet simply does not have sufficient time for governments to put such grand plans into fruition; such proposals would take centuries. The humans have mere decades left because of pollution, overpopulation, damage to the environment and global climate warming. This is the only way. I have made my decision and it is final." At that moment her mobile phone rang and she glanced at the device noticing it was their absent brother. Gabriel let out an audible sigh before swiping the screen and answering. "Sariel, at long last. Let me put you on speaker," she said and returned to the table as her three siblings took their seats. "What news have you?"

There was a brief pause and everyone glanced at each other, believing their brother was not going to answer, before finally a rough voice boomed from the mobile phone, startling all, even Gabriel.

"How fare you in that ruined church?" Sariel shouted. "Comfy and cosy in your forced isolation?"

"We are eager for information." Ramiel said, breaking the uncomfortable silence that followed such a strange question.

"Things are proceeding to plan," Sariel said. "Despite the 'unfortunate' failure of my men to secure the girl."

"Unfortunate?" Raguel snarled, much to his sister's surprise. "Your soldiers could not even capture a schoolgirl, and worse still were killed and their bodies left behind for convenient identification by the authorities; a spotlight our kind could do without, especially at this most important and critical time."

"Don't let it upset you, brother," Sariel said sarcastically. "Homeland Security and the Federal Bureau of Investigation will spend enormous time chasing their tails in that direction. My men were of Russian origin, and it is in that pathway the American police will be focussing their attention, believing they are either some rogue mafia or foreign agents seeking industrial espionage into Marsh Tower, my involvement in this matter is without trace."

"So you say," Ramiel said. "And what of the attention you have provoked against us by way of this schoolgirl's boyfriend? We never authorised you to kidnap the girl; you are acting on your own, and now you have placed us all in jeopardy."

"None of you ever considered that when we put this plan of genocide into formation, so consumed were you with your grand schemes to change the world." Sariel laughed.

Raguel leaned across the table, placing himself directly above the mobile phone. "It would be stupidity to disregard Michael's rage in this matter; we are all too aware of his feelings for this young woman and will do everything in his power to keep her safe, even if that means punishing ... or perhaps killing us."

"Relax, brother, don't fret," Sariel said. "I have taken great steps to maintain your safety and your location is secret. Neither Michael's spies nor the police know where you are. Just because I have been away from you all these past years does not mean I have forgotten that you are family."

"Speaking of which ..." Gabriel said. "Have you encountered Uriel in your travels, is there any possibility he might be persuaded to join our crusade?"

"That is a lost cause not worth pursuing, sister," Sariel replied. "He has made his intentions and non-participation quite clear, both with us and Michael. Uriel prefers to stand idly by and watch from the side-lines; for our brother was always the aloof observer."

"We need to talk about Michael," Gabriel said and they all stared at her in interest. "By that I mean what exactly are we going to do with him when we capture Marsh Tower? Our sibling is simply not going to step aside and let us take possession of the Book of Life and use his computer program to wipe out half of mankind. I am uncomfortable with the thought of killing him."

Sariel laughed. "You had no such qualms murdering family members before."

"That was different," Gabriel snarled. "Samael was a psychopath and could not be reasoned with, he would have killed us all given half the chance."

"Very well," Sariel replied. "We will instead hold Michael in bondage."

"And the soldiers guarding the vault?" Raguel asked. "They are highly trained and armed mercenaries, they will not be easily subdued."

"They are expendable," Gabriel said. "As are the three young women."

"Yes," Sariel echoed. "But it makes more sense to use the women as leverage in case things don't go to plan."

"And do you expect our schemes to go awry?" Ramiel asked.

"This is in essence a military operation, and as such one should expect things to fuck up," Sariel said. "Especially as we need our brother's hand signature to access the vault and his private authorisation at the computer directly connected to the book for the application to work and be altered."

"Has anyone ever considered simply severing his hand?" Raphael asked. "If we are too squeamish for the task, then Sariel's men could do it."

"He is still our brother and no harm must come to him," Gabriel said. "He may be deluded, but he is an archangel and divine like the rest of us."

"And what if Michael does not return to Marsh Tower in time, or if ever?" Gabriel asked. "Then we too are fucked."

"Leave that worry to me, sister," Sariel laughed. "I will give our arrogant sibling a push in the right direction. I will be in touch."

They were about to enquire further what Sariel meant when he abruptly hung up, leaving the angels to stare at each other in confusion.

"I don't like this, Gabriel," Ramiel said. "Sariel has become too unstable and can't be trusted."

"What choice do we have?" She replied. "Besides, I am the leader and he will follow my commands."

Raguel turned to her. "It sounds like he is following his own orders."

Gabriel put her hand up, motioning for their silence. "Enough debate. Go to the basement, and take some time for yourselves; make your peace as it were, for in a few days we will change the world, and every one of us needs to be prepared."

They all left and went to the basement of the church, the most secure part of the dilapidated building where separate areas had been organised to give some privacy, especially for their sister. Gabriel had just sat down against the concrete wall when Raguel appeared, also sitting down next to her.

"I apologise if it seemed I contradicted you earlier," he said. "That was not my intention, I was simply expressing my concern. In hindsight, we should not have put Sariel in this position; I fear he has been compelled to make difficult decisions on our behalf, much to his own disadvantage."

"You should put more faith in Sariel. He is no longer the foolish comedian we knew back in the lake, our brother is cunning and devious and has the ruthlessness to do what needs to be done. That is why I chose him and set him apart from the rest of us, so Michael's spies would believe he was either dead or no longer interested in our mutual scheme. We have all changed over the millennia, forced to commit terrible acts to survive against our many enemies and done things we are not proud of."

"I understand," Raguel said, as he ran his right hand through her hair and touched her cheek. "But my feelings for you have not altered despite these many centuries. It may be hard for you to admit, but we gave up being archangels after the lake was destroyed and became essentially mortals when we fell to Earth. Apart from our enhanced strength, inability to age and conceive children, we are now the same as everyone else with similar desires and physical needs."

"But we are not the *same* as the humans," she said sharply and gently knocked his hand away.

"The feeding of carnal impulses is the obsession of the animals of this planet."

"So you say." He smiled, as he suddenly kissed her.

Gabriel tried to push him away, but realised he was too strong and relaxed as he slipped his hand beneath her panties and grabbed her bottom. Raguel shifted himself and slid down beside her as she pulled off her underwear, roughly shoving her tongue into his mouth. He responded by grabbing the back of her hair and shoving her head back, before licking the front of her neck and running his tongue up and sucked on her earlobe. Raguel quickly removed his clothing and cuddled up alongside her, and they kissed hard as she wrapped her legs around him and he entered her to the hilt, both of them giving out a simultaneous groan of pleasure. Raguel pressed himself up onto the palms of his hands above her and began to thrust hard into her, almost removing his penis entirely from her with each movement, before penetrating her deep. Gabriel was moaning loudly now and kissed him fiercely as he suddenly exploded inside her and let out a sharp cry, such was the strength of his orgasm.

"Sorry about that," he whispered and kissed her gently on the lips. "I guess I got carried away."

"I'll bet you are truly apologetic," she laughed. "Oh Raguel, what have we become? We have developed into the humans now ... complete and absolute."

"We have fallen in love, my sister. We were thrown into the darkness after our home in the heavens was destroyed; forced to survive in an alien world that fears and despises us, and we have only each other to depend upon. This love became natural due to unnatural circumstances beyond our control, for you and I could never have found each other otherwise."

"It is I who should say sorry, I was very harsh with you. I am a hypocrite; spouting grand gestures and higher principles of truth and loyalty to which as archangels we should aspire, but then not following them myself. I am a liar and a fraud."

"You are too hard on yourself. We have all become lost in this wilderness; this world belongs to the humans, we were always meant to oversee and guide it from afar, never thread it in the flesh amongst them." He said and ran the fingers of his right hand through her blonde hair. "I know you are conflicted and afraid; we all have been since our arrival on this planet, but the others are not so different from you and I. Ramiel and Raphael have both had girlfriends over the millennia, and even Sariel has frequented brothels on many occasions; much to your distaste, so be more forgiving of yourself."

Gabriel was about to reply when they abruptly heard loud footsteps on the floorboards above them, knowing all the angels were downstairs in the crypt. She and Raguel swiftly dressed themselves as their brothers within moments appeared, their faces full of concern.

"It appears we have unwelcome visitors." Raphael said.

"Nosy kids?" Raguel asked.

"Not unless they are dressed in full body armour carrying automatic machineguns," Ramiel said. "I could see them from the bottom of the stairs."

"Cops?" Gabriel asked. "Or Federal agents?"

"My guess is neither," Ramiel replied. "They have no identifiable lettering on their jackets. I think they are mercenaries, American by the accent. I heard the leader giving orders."

"Michael." Raguel said and they all stared at him in apprehension.

"And you were so dead-set against harming him," Raphael sneered. "And now he plans to kill us."

"We don't know that for certain," Gabriel said. "But neither can we allow ourselves to be captured. Almost all our guns are with Sariel, as he is arranging purchase and going to distribute them amongst us just before we enter Marsh Tower. What weapons do we have?"

"The 9mm Glock handgun with a full magazine of seventeen rounds," Ramiel replied. "And the ten inch army knife."

"Not much against machineguns," Raguel said. "Give me the gun. How many did you see?"

"At least eight soldiers," Ramiel said as he passed over the weapon. "But there could be more outside."

"There is only one entrance and exit from the crypt," Raguel said. "They will have to come down the stairs to search the basement of the church. If we can get at least one of them as he descends and confiscate his firearm, we might stand a fighting chance. The jeep is out in the woods, they may not know of its existence. We are fortunate the church is so open with no roof and windows, otherwise they would likely use tear gas to force us out."

"If they found the jeep, they will surely have sabotaged it." Raphael said.

"Well, it's the only working plan we have at the moment," Gabriel said. "Move to the underside of the wooden stairs and get ready."

"I can't believe Michael would want us dead," Ramiel said as they prepared themselves for combat. "Especially as he once saved my life."

"That was a long time ago," Raguel said. "And considering we through Sariel placed his 'soul twin' in danger, he probably feels justified."

Gabriel motioned for their silence as the noise upstairs increased and heavy footsteps could be heard approaching the crypt entrance. They watched with trepidation as two soldiers began descending the open steps, in close formation. Raguel watched them reach halfway and reaching through, sliced the right leg at the thigh of the second guard. The man let out a scream and fell into his colleague, causing both of them to fall the short distance to the floor. The second soldier collapsed onto his friend, and before they could rise and react to the assault, Gabriel grabbed one intruder by placing her hands at either side of his head, and twisted it, snapping his neck. Raguel drove the ten inch blade through the back of the neck of the mercenary he already injured, killing him instantly. Although their attack was swift and relatively silent, the angels waited with nervousness for the other guards to respond, but they did not.

"What now?" Ramiel asked. "Do we wait for the other soldiers and ambush them too?"

"I would not press our luck," Gabriel whispered. "We are essentially trapped here with no windows and exit doors. It is only a matter of time before the mercenaries above realise something is wrong and respond with all guns blazing, or even send tear gas down here. Ramiel and Raphael, get their machineguns and let's see what awaits us in the main church."

The two brothers armed themselves with the automatic weapons and all slowly crept up the stairs. Gabriel peered around the corner, but could see nothing but darkness. They ascended the steps completely and stood in the hallway, gazing at the closed door ahead which gave access to the altar and what remained of the ruined church. Carefully opening the old door, she glanced into the main area and could see two guards at the far end with no obvious sign of any other soldiers. She motioned for her brothers to get on their knees, and crawling along the left side of the church in the darkness, made their way to the exit at the opposite end.

When they nearly reached their destination, she beckoned for them to stop and remain silent, as the two mercenaries resumed their patrol and made their way towards the crypt, presumably to check on their friends and their long absence. The angels waited for a few minutes and crawled towards the main doors. Raguel slowly opened one of the double doors and glanced into the night, before ushering his siblings into the nearby grass and out of sight of the church. Again there seemed to be no sign of any other guards, much to their puzzlement and relief. They crawled for a short distance before rising to their feet and fleeing for the woods and the jeep parked in the trees.

Gabriel smiled as she sighted the vehicle and all began to enter, eager to leave the church behind and any danger within. However, just as Raphael was about to open the front passenger door, he noticed a soldier run towards him, his weapon raised. The angel realised he had no choice and bringing the machinegun up, fired in the direction of the mercenary. Gabriel and her brothers were startled by the sudden loud noise as Raphael proceeded to fire several rounds at the guard. Much to his shock and disbelief, instead of falling to the ground, the soldier simply came to a halt and lowered his own weapon, and did not respond by firing back. The angels all entered the vehicle and Gabriel quickly started the ignition. They sped off as her brothers watched in astonished fascination as the mercenary stood motionless only a few feet away, making no sign of attack and no indication of injury from Raphael firing on him. Gabriel drove for about five miles at high speed through the winding dark country roads before finally coming to a halt, certain they had escaped their assailants.

She switched off the engine and turned towards Raphael. "How did you miss? He was only a few feet from you."

"I didn't," he replied. "Maybe he was wearing a bulletproof vest."

"That doesn't explain why he did not fire back, he had you right in his sights," Raguel said. "Give me the machinegun, I want to look at that magazine."

Raphael passed back the weapon as Raguel removed the clip and started emptying the rounds into his left hand. He stared at them in confusion as the tip of the bullet was missing from each one, revealing only the vacant shell.

"These are all blanks," Raguel frowned. "You did not kill him because you were firing empty rounds."

"That's not possible," Raphael said in dismay. "It makes no sense. Why attack and not mean to harm us?"

"We killed two of them back there," Raguel said. "For nothing."

"They were only humans," Gabriel said sharply. "And clearly dispensable. It would appear Michael was sending a message."

"Well, we can't return to the church," Ramiel said. "Our brother seems to know our every move."

"Then let's do something he does not expect," Gabriel said. "We won't wait a few more days for Michael to return to New York. We go now to Marsh Tower and prepare our assault. I will contact Sariel when we get to the city and tell him to get his Russian mercenaries ready. It is time to finally put an end to all this."

# CHAPTER FOURTEEN

"So, the Spanish Inquisition was as terrible as was described in books and movies?" Grace asked.

"Even those media could not adequately describe the barbarity," Thomas replied. "Torquemada would be proud if he knew future historians would regard the Spanish Inquisition, and him in particular as the epitome of religious intolerance, exploiting a bigoted young princess for his own diabolical ambitions, and the intense fear of a nation against a potential Ottoman invasion. During his reign up to four thousand innocent people were tortured and burned at the stake. Later other inquisitors like Diego Rodriguez Lucero in 1506 in Cordoba rose to power, and even had two men put to death simply because their wives became Lucero's mistresses and after one of them became pregnant by the inquisitor, their existence became an embarrassment."

"Speaking of Gabriel and your brothers; you essentially saved their lives?" Grace asked, changing the subject. "And now they repay your generosity by trying to take ours?"

Thomas sighed. "So it would seem. I warned my brothers about this path they had chosen and now they will pay the price. There will be no second chances this time."

"I can see Andrea from the kitchen window," Grace said. "I think she wants to have a chat. We will talk more about this later. I want to be fully part of this endeavour, Thomas. I want you to know, and be fully aware that I am your partner, not your sidekick; I am not your naïve subordinate, I and no one else will define my life for me, guardian angel or not."

Thomas nodded in reply as Grace left and entered the house. Andrea took her hand and brought her upstairs to the bedroom, so to ensure some privacy.

"That was some story," Andrea said. "The incredible events and people he must have witnessed and conversed with, if indeed I am to take him at his word, or perhaps he is simply nuts and dragging me along for the crazy ride."

"I understand you need proof," Grace said. "It seemed all so fantastic to me at first until Thomas showed me the Book of Life in the basement of Marsh Tower."

"Yes, about that … our employer has made some powerful enemies in the criminal underworld and that sister of his; what was her name?"

"Gabriel."

"Yes, that's the name of that bitch. We were always taught Gabriel was a man, I guess that was a lie like so many other falsehoods the Catholic Church shoved down our gullible throats. However, I'll bet Fr O'Mahony would love a theological chat with our archangel boss."

"He's too busy chasing sexually frustrated housewives to think about God." Grace laughed.

"Speaking of which, have you spoken with your parents? How has your mother been, now alone to defend herself against that monster of a husband?"

"We have not spoken since I left home. I thought it was better that way, and I have not returned their calls."

"Well, I think it may be time to reach out," Andrea said as she sat on the edge of her bed and beckoned her school comrade to sit alongside her. "At times like these a person should have the ear of a loved one, if only to know they care."

"And what of your parents? I know you are close to your young brother."

"Yes, Paul is just about to turn seven years old, I was going to ring him on his birthday. It's hard being away from family, I even miss my stepfather moaning about money all the time, and my mother's incessant nagging of my clothes and makeup seems a pleasant memory. So, despite your parents' apparent hatred for each other, deep down they still see you as the centre of their world."

"I seriously doubt they do," Grace said as she sat next to her friend. "At least I know Thomas loves me, and that is enough."

"Yes, he seems to adore you. It seems like some extraordinary love story greater than Romeo and Juliet; he has protected and worshipped your lives throughout history and never even remotely considered the touch of another woman, no matter the gap in decades and centuries between your former incarnations."

"It is hard to comprehend at times; how one person could love another so absolutely that they would follow that 'soulmate' throughout the ages and love that woman no matter the different face and personality, simply because they represented in spirit their chosen one."

"Yes, it is a bit crazy," Andrea said and they both laughed. "Though when you consider men in general, any man will tell a woman they adore them at the point of ejaculation."

Grace smiled. "I'm really glad you are with me on this journey, I could never have imagined taking this grand adventure without you, and that sarcastic humour I would miss."

"Jokes aside, that boyfriend of yours no matter how gorgeous or rich he may be has placed all of us in real danger because of his obsession with evil and changing the world, even the safety of that bitch Lisa Swanson."

"Thomas knows what he is doing, he will keep us safe."

Andrea watched her companion get up from the bed and leave the room and sighed. "I hope you are right."

Grace did not hear but made for the bedroom she shared with Thomas. He was not there and she assumed he was busy making lunch before their planned walk in the forest. She reached for her mobile phone and hesitated for several moments before finally ringing home, breathing heavily in apprehension. The call was answered after about a minute and her mother called out, her voice full of excitement.

"Honey, I am so glad you called," Christine Anderson said. "We have missed you."

"Me too, Mam. I am sorry for not answering your calls. Things have been somewhat crazy here."

Her mother paused for a moment. "Your father has changed since your absence, he has become like himself before, you know ... the accident."

"And the drinking?"

"Gave it up the day after you left."

"I'd like to believe that," Grace sighed. "And also accept the memory of the bruises on your body would fade so readily too."

"You would understand if you were married. Sometimes a wife has to tolerate the badness in her spouse for the greater good; to hope one day the husband will change and love her the way he used to."

"Thomas would never treat me like that, and neither would I ever tolerate it."

"So you are together then?" Christine asked. "Believe it or not, I am glad."

Grace was surprised by the comment and did not speak for a moment. "I did not think you would approve, especially of an older man; not to mention my employer."

"I just want you to be happy … you deserve at least that."

Christine passed the phone to her husband. "Grace, it's me," Charles said. "I am desperately sorry for the way things ended between us when you left. I have been a bad father, I feel terrible guilt and am worthy of your hatred."

Grace sighed. "Perhaps I have also not been the best daughter in the world, and I should apologise for that. I was always too eager to leave the town and my life behind."

"I thank you for that; it is more than I deserve, I have not been the parent you loved as a young child and it is that bittersweet memory I should aspire to," Charles said softly. "How have you been? I am a little surprised you called, delighted you did of course so I could say these things to you and beg for your forgiveness."

"We can talk more about our past and moving forward as regards even mutual counselling when I get home. I rang because I may be in trouble."

"Do you need money?"

Grace laughed. "Dad, I am dating a billionaire."

"Is it legal difficulties? Do we need to hire an attorney?"

Grace paused for a few moments. "It's nothing, honestly. I should not have said anything. I will work it out, please don't worry about me."

"Okay, honey. I know you have a good head, you will figure it out. And please, be safe and call us again soon ... for any reason."

"I will. Perhaps I will come home for a while when this blows over."

"We would very much like that, we can talk," Charles said. "I love you."

Grace did not answer back and pressed call ended on her phone. She left her bedroom and suddenly bumped into Lisa who responded with a glance of discomfort at the encounter.

"Excuse me." Grace said and moved past her towards the kitchen.

Lisa Swanson stopped in the hallway and called out. "Wait, please wait."

Grace threw her eyes up to the ceiling in frustration, expecting another argument.

"Just because Andrea and I are enemies, does not mean we have to be," Lisa said, standing in the corridor in her striped pyjamas. "I never had any issue with you directly, simply you being friends with that sarcastic bitch meant you sometimes got caught in the crossfire."

"Andrea is my best friend," Grace replied. "I know she can be hard work to get along with at first, but it is worth the effort."

"Why exactly are you so close to that spiteful cow? You have nothing in common with her; you are from the poor working class part of town and she is upper class with a big house and millionaire stepfather. Word is he is ripping off his clients to fund that expensive lifestyle and huge mortgage."

Grace sighed in frustration. "I thought you actually were being conciliatory and wanted to make amends."

"You really don't know anything about what is really going on, and are way in over your head, you stupid little girl," Lisa said sharply. "Walking around with blinkers and so love in with our boss. You and that evil friend are due for a big fall."

Grace was about to respond, but Lisa went back into her bedroom, closing the door loudly behind her. Grace shook her head and returned her path towards the kitchen area of the house. Thomas was busy making a collection of cereal, French toast and sausages.

He smiled at her arrival as she sat on a high stool, and continued to place cutlery and glasses of water on the table in front of her.

"I spoke to my parents." She said and he glanced at her in surprise.

"I am pleased to hear that, sincerely. It is important both for you and them to mend those fences. Speaking from someone who never had a real mother and father, I am only too aware how vital that connection is and should not be dismissed so readily."

"Apparently my own father has stopped drinking if you can believe that, and even learned to control his temper, which is even more extraordinary."

"That is good, if it is indeed true. Time will be the truth of it however."

"Thomas," she said and he stared at her. "Do you believe people can change, or are we forever slaves to our desires and failures of character?"

He paused for a few moments. "I believe a person must be genuinely willing to alter their behaviour and attitude, but most adults are too set in their ways and habits; they may know these patterns are morally wrong, but are generally incapable of giving them up. Only a very young child can be taught to alter their conduct as their personality is still at an infant stage of development, but once they reach puberty, it is almost impossible to change their nature and they will stubbornly fight to the death to preserve their obsessions. The Chinese have a proverb that the last thing a man will give up is his suffering; but that also applies as much to any other strong emotion, especially anger and hate which blinds them to any other path of decision making."

"I understand, so we are doomed to perpetually repeat the same mistakes?"

"Usually. However, your father's alcoholism is a learned adult behaviour, and as such can be unlearned as other men and women have similarly put aside that addiction with proper support and guidance. Then perhaps he can atone for those sins of violence against your mother and find redemption in her potential forgiveness ... if indeed she finds it in her heart to do so."

"So, do you think I should forgive him?"

Thomas sighed and reached over, grabbing hold of her hand. "Only you can decide that for yourself, my love. That decision is yours alone."

"Do you believe your sister Gabriel is capable of change?"

He stood back against the kitchen sink and glanced at her before turning and staring out at the red-leafed trees which filled his vision from the single large window. "Gabriel and my brothers, and indeed I as well are unique. We were created for a sole purpose: to monitor and alter humans through direct intervention in their daily routines on the specific orders of The Source; from when they rose in the morning and tended to their families and animals until they slept at night. Even their dreams were not an escape from us as we interceded, creating imaginary worlds and scenarios that might affect their waking lives. It is for those reasons my siblings have been spiritually conditioned for a certain way of thinking, and it is that steadfast twisted rationale that guides them without contradiction on that prescribed destiny; leaving the lake for them in essence changed nothing, the planet and its lifeforms are their playground, always now and forever … coming to Earth only altered the landscape, not their perverted viewpoint."

"And does that apply to you also?"

"What do you mean?"

"You also have an obsession of your own," she said. "You wish to modify humans also in your own way."

Thomas sighed. "You think I am a hypocrite."

"No, that's not what I meant; I am not placing you and Gabriel in the same category, I know how you feel about their opinions and motives. I am just concerned that this fascination with evil will ultimately destroy you."

"I understand. It was wrong of me to involve you in all of this, not to mention Andrea and Lisa."

"We can take care of ourselves."

"I don't mean to be patronising, my love, but these are dangerous people and I have placed you all in great jeopardy."

"I thought you were planning to scare Gabriel and the others, at least enough to buy us time to finish the computer program."

"It is in process, but I fear nothing will deter my siblings from their determined path."

"I love you, Michael," Grace declared, catching him by surprise as she called him by his true name. "When I signed up to all this and accepted both the good and the bad together, I knew in my heart I was in it until the end."

Thomas smiled. "I love you too, Grace Anderson. You mean everything to me, you cannot imagine the pain every time I had to watch you die; a piece of me went with you on every occasion. Sometimes I had you with me for decades, other times only for mere months and had to wait perhaps centuries to see you again with a new face, that is why I want you and your friends to stay here safe and hidden in New Haven where no one knows us."

"No. We will meet this together, whatever the outcome." She took his hand and led him to their bedroom.

"The food will get cold." Thomas said.

"Breakfast can wait." Grace smiled as she opened the door and pushed him onto the bed.

Thomas grinned at this dominant position which he had never seen before in her and was a pleasant surprise. Grace removed her pyjamas and threw them on the floor before climbing naked on top of him, his top half lying flat while his legs dangled over the end of the bed. She lent down and kissed him passionately and he responded, their tongues intertwining as he pulled off his own pyjama top. She ran her hands over his chest and kissed him gently on the nipples and he laughed as it tickled him.

Thomas caught her and rolled Grace over onto the covers and kissed her first on the lips and then the side of the neck before moving further down on her body, kissing her breasts and holding onto her nipples with his mouth and pulling on them softly with his teeth, causing her to moan. She giggled as he moved and nuzzled at her stomach, before gently parting her legs and kissed the inside of her thighs before licking ever so slightly at her outer vaginal lips, teasing her.

Grace grabbed the back of his hair and forced his head down further and he responded, snatching hold of her lips first with his mouth before moving onto her clitoris, causing her lower back to rise off the bed in ecstasy. She started shuddering, grabbing onto the blanket fiercely as an intense orgasm ripped through her entire body. Before the enormous feeling could subside, he came up and abruptly entered her to the hilt. She tapped his shoulders as if to say it was too much for her, but he ignored and started to thrust deep into her.

Again he rolled over, placing her on top position. Grace wrapped her feet and lower legs under his bottom and began to ride him strongly and he reached up, holding onto her breasts and pulling on the nipples. She continued to rock back and forth, and had another orgasm, catching even Grace by surprise and he momentarily laughed at her reaction. Grace grabbed onto the bed covers and was moaning loudly as Thomas let out a sudden shout as he came hard inside her, his teeth clenching such was the strength of the orgasm, almost on the point of extreme pain.

They laid like that for at least twenty minutes, just enjoying the intimacy when they abruptly heard a loud noise coming from downstairs. Thomas thought Andrea or Lisa had dropped something, causing a breakage and decided to investigate. He swiftly dressed in pants and a jumper and his shoes, and instructed Grace to do the same as she put on jeans and a navy blouse and her own shoes. He encountered the two other women just outside the bedroom and they too were startled by the now increasing sounds coming from downstairs.

"What is going on?" Andrea asked.

"It would seem we are not alone," Thomas said. "Get dressed and stay here with Grace upstairs. It would appear my security system has been disabled."

He began to descend the steps, but stopped upon seeing several men in black combat attire and carrying machineguns. Thomas could hear them talking and realised they were Russian. He softly went back upstairs and met the three women, now fully dressed and very frightened.

"We can't stay here," Thomas whispered. "The easiest exit from upstairs is through my bedroom. The largest window looks out onto a short tiled roof where I will jump down and catch you one by one."

"That's insane," Lisa said. "You intend to catch us as we leap?"

"Trust me," Thomas replied. "I am much stronger than the average person."

"How is that possible?" Lisa asked.

"I don't have time to explain," he said. "We have to go now."

Thomas led them quietly into the bedroom he shared with Grace, and opened the main window, swinging it wide. They could see brown tiles sloping down leading to the grass and a short distance away the forest; the red leaves beckoning to them a potential escape from their assailants.

Thomas went out first, climbing onto the tiles and slid down to the edge before jumping to the short grass. He briefly peered around for a glimpse of their attackers, but they seemed to be exclusively in the downstairs section of the house and at the front entrance of the building. He waved to Grace to follow and she slowly crept onto the short roof before turning and placed her legs and waist over the edge, as Thomas reached out and caught her as she pushed herself off. Andrea quickly followed and she too landed safely. Lisa began to climb through the window as the noise inside the house intensified, but hesitated in fright.

"Lisa, come on," Grace said. "We don't have time, let's go."

"I can't." She replied and disappeared from view back into the bedroom.

Andrea and Grace continued to call out until a sudden burst of gunfire rang out and a shrill scream startled them. They glanced at Thomas in terror, fearing the worst.

"We have to help her." Grace stuttered.

"She's dead," he said, much to their shock. "And if not, we can't help her, not against several armed men."

They ran for the woods, Thomas holding onto Grace's arm and she in turn snatching onto Andrea's hand fiercely. He could hear their attackers following through the undergrowth as they fled through the red trees. Grace glanced around her. In another time, this forest would be peaceful and beautiful, and a leisurely walk talking and laughing would have been lovely in such a magnificent setting. But now instead they were running for their lives; once again in great danger, and Grace began to wonder when it would ever end.

They ducked down beside a fallen tree as a soldier came nearby and Thomas crept out behind him. He grabbed the guard around the throat and with his other hand snapped the mercenary's neck in one swift motion. Thomas took the man's handgun and checked the clip, identifying fifteen live rounds inside and one in the barrel. He made sure the safety was off and beckoned the two women to come out of hiding. They started to run further into the forest until another soldier suddenly appeared from behind a tree.

The guard pointed his handgun straight at Grace. Thomas raised his own weapon and shouted at her to get out of the way, but Grace was petrified to the spot and could not move in fright. However, just as the mercenary shot off a round, Andrea jumped in front of Grace and took the bullet in the middle of her chest. Grace screamed as Thomas shot the soldier in the face, the round exiting out the back of his head as he fell down dead.

Thomas picked up Andrea and carried her to a nearby tree before gently placing her against the wood. She was coughing blood as Thomas examined her injury. He groaned in frustration and anger, realising it was fatal and close to her heart and the blood loss was too great, the red liquid pouring furiously out of the wound and down onto her waist and legs. Andrea clasped onto Grace's hand and smiled through the agony at her best friend as Grace was crying, the tears streaming down her face. They watched the young woman's life ebb away before Thomas rose to his feet.

"We have to go, Grace," he said. "There's nothing more we can do."

"We can't just leave her here." She sobbed.

"I'll make sure she's taken care of. But for now we must save our own lives."

They continued through the forest until they came across a carpark. Thomas spotted a shop and found a phone inside. He returned to Grace as she stared on; her gaze vacant, speechless and in shock.

"I've rang for a car, and we will return to New York."

Grace looked at him, her face streaked with a mixture of dried blood from her friend, dirt and red leaves. "I want you to promise me, Thomas, after the computer application has been switched on … I want your sister dead."

He sighed heavily. "What you ask is difficult."

"If you want a future with me, Michael," she said flatly. "You will promise me."

He paused for a moment. "I vow whoever is responsible for this will pay with their life … whoever it is."

She nodded, apparently satisfied with his answer. They sat on the ground in silence until the car arrived about twenty minutes later and they began the long journey back to New York. She vaguely listened as Thomas made phone calls from the limousine, making arrangements for her dead friend, and to let the family know in a few days once the computer program had been activated and things had calmed. There would be time then to reflect and mourn over Andrea.

The chauffer dropped them off at Thomas's penthouse apartment where they showered and got clean clothes.

"We can't stay here," Thomas said. "If Gabriel found out about the house in New Haven, then it is certain she will attack here next."

"What do you suggest?"

"I have booked a hotel room which overlooks the entrance to Marsh Tower under false names. We will enter the basement at dawn and activate the program. I have received notification from the technical staff responsible that the program is nearly ready for deployment; the virus will infect simultaneously all satellites in space, mobile phones, and all computers and televisions; ensuring it reaches everyone in the world."

"Then let's finish this," Grace said softly. "Let's not wait, we should go right now."

"The program is not completed yet, it will be ready by early morning," Thomas replied. "And it is too dangerous to go at night, my siblings are sure to be watching us enter. At least in the morning, there will be people around. Gabriel won't appreciate the intrusion of public and police."

They left the apartment and got a taxi to the hotel. Once they entered Grace opened the blinds and could see her former workplace Marsh Tower just across from them, the huge structure filling her vision as if blocking everything else from sight. She sat in a chair facing the window and said not a word for the entire night. Thomas occasionally glanced at her, but dared not break her silence and obvious grief, but stared himself at the tower he had created, and knowing in a matter of hours, he would have to destroy it, and face his angelic brethren who wanted him dead.

## CHAPTER FIFTEEN

"Remember your promise," Grace said as she stared at Marsh Tower in the near distance. "You vowed there would be no second chances for your family, they must pay for Andrea."

"I have not forgotten," he replied and kissed her forehead. "And I am sorry about your best friend."

Grace turned and sat on the edge of the bed, which was still perfect as she had not slept a wink. "We had known each other since we were small children in playschool and never once had a fight or falling out. That bitch Lisa Swanson told me just before the attack and her own death that Andrea had nothing in common with me, that Andrea was a spoilt brat from the wealthy part of town. But Lisa did not know the inner deep loneliness beneath the facade of sarcasm; it was a mask to hide Andrea's true feelings. Her stepfather may be rich, but he is a cold heartless bastard. Andrea doted on her little brother, how am I going to tell him his big sister he idolised is dead?"

Thomas sat next to Grace and put his arm around her. "She must have truly loved you, that is what you must always remember … not her final moments."

"It's my fault, if she had not followed me to New York, she would still be alive."

"No, you should blame me," Thomas said. "It was I that offered her the job, knowing from the book that you two were inseparable. It is entirely my fault, and I am truly sorry."

"It was Gabriel and your brothers that killed her," Grace replied. "You were only doing what you thought was right. Besides, job or not, Andrea would still have followed me to New York and everywhere."

Grace stood up and wiped away the tears. "That diary you gave Gabriel in medieval Spain, do you think she ever read it?"

"Honestly I have no idea, I had hoped she might as it contained my own opinions and views on humanity that differed from hers and might give a new perspective on her crusade."

"Well, clearly it did not work."

Thomas nodded. "Do you want breakfast before we go?"

"I can't eat anything. Let's just get this over with."

"Are you certain you won't stay here in the safety of the hotel? They might be waiting for us."

"I am beyond caring about that. But I am still going to give Gabriel the fight of my life."

Thomas smiled at her comment as they left the hotel and walked the short distance across the street to Marsh Tower. There was no sign of the other angels anywhere, and Michael hoped the dawn entry to the office block would therefore go unnoticed. He opened the main entrance glass doors with his key and they entered the main lobby. Grace noticed it was eerily quiet, not a single soul being present.

"None of the employees and staff will be here until at least two hours," Thomas said. "And I have instructed the normal office security to not come in until later as well. They are not equipped or trained to deal with professional soldiers armed with machineguns. I will not have their deaths on my conscience. The combat guards below at the vault will be enough to deal with any scenario."

"And the computer application, is it ready?"

"I have been informed it is fully operational and ready for deployment; satellites are aligned and eighty percent of the world's population already have the dormant software unknowingly installed on their mobile phones, tablets, televisions, vehicles and computers. It is secretly placed on their systems through aggressive malware viruses to ensure one hundred percent saturation. The application through the Book of Life will even filter into radio waves so no one on the planet will escape its attack. I expect ninety-five percent capability immediately upon activation, and even those living in remote areas whether it be Australia, Africa, isolated small islands, etc., should feel the effect of the program within hours or days at the most," he said as they approached the elevator leading to the basement and the vault. "It is only required to press right Ctrl key followed by enter to activate. The computer's motherboard and hard drive will incinerate directly afterwards, ensuring no one can stop or alter the software."

"And you have ensured their souls will not simply be reincarnated and in their next life they can continue their wicked ways?"

"Of course, for if not it would defeat the entire purpose of the computer application if their future incarnations carried out terrible deeds. The Book of Life will extinguish both their lives and souls upon activation, there will be no rebirth for these monsters; the cycle of reincarnation will be severed for these people."

They ventured into the lift and began their descent, the elevator slowly making its way to the basement.

"Scared?" He asked, taking hold of her hand.

"More nervous than anything," she replied. "It is hard to imagine in mere minutes from now, we are about to change the world and kill millions."

"Nobody innocent … and instantly painless, which is more than most of them deserve; something they did not afford their victims."

"Governments and national security agencies won't see it that way, we will be the planet's most wanted people if they discover it was not some sort of global accident or epidemic."

The elevator reached the basement and they entered the short corridor leading to the vault and the Book of Life. Thomas keyed in the numbers into the console and the door opened. However, what greeted them was not armed soldiers standing guard, but an empty chamber devoid of life. Both of them glanced around in surprise and puzzlement.

"I don't understand," Thomas uttered. "There should be several men here."

Grace opened the door marked canteen and let out a sudden scream, and he came running. On the floor just inside the tiny room were two soldiers, both clearly dead. Broken cups and milk were also strewn on the ground. Thomas knelt down and examined them and groaned in anxiety.

"They've both been shot in the head at close range," he said. "Obviously the work of professionals. But that does not explain the absence of their colleagues. They also don't seem to have had the chance to fire their weapons as they are still holstered, which suggests they were taken by surprise."

Thomas went to the enormous safe and opened the colossal metal round door by keying in at the console and placing his palm on the fingerprint recognition screen, causing the vault to automatically swing wide open. Everything appeared normal inside, the antiques and other priceless objects he had collected over the aeons still in the same place and unmoved. The single metal reinforced door leading to the book and computer equipment for the activation of the program also seemed undamaged, as he briefly peered through the square bulletproof window built into the door at head height.

"Thomas," Grace whispered in fright. "What the fuck is going on?"

"We're getting out of here," he replied. "I will make a phone call from my office upstairs and send for reinforcements."

However, as they approached the door leading out of the chamber and access for the elevator to return to the lobby, it suddenly swung open and in walked his sister Gabriel and brothers Raguel, Raphael and Ramiel.

"How nice it is to see you again, Michael," Raguel said. "Since our last encounter at the Cathedral Church of St. John the Divine in New York City in which we parted in such 'unpleasant' circumstances."

"But at least you were generous enough to open the vault for us." Gabriel laughed. "I thought we would have to wait for your eventual arrival, and bring you down here unconsciousness and place your hand on that console."

"You bitch," Grace roared and ran to hit Gabriel, however Michael swiftly grabbed the young woman and held her back. "You killed my best friend."

Gabriel stared at her, perplexed at the outburst. "Michael, please restrain your human girlfriend," she said and the others grinned. "My dear, I can assure you I have no idea what the hell you are talking about."

"You attacked us at the house in New Haven," Michael said. "And killed Lisa and Andrea."

"That wasn't us," Ramiel said. "You should really keep an eye on all these enemies of yours. Though it might have been justified on our part after you sending those American mercenaries to assault us at the ruined church just outside New York."

Michael glanced at him in anger. "I didn't send any men there, I didn't even know your location. I was in the process of arranging a scare to frighten you off, but did not get the opportunity to organise such an operation."

"Interesting," Gabriel said. "Though if you had arranged same, it would explain why the men were carrying blanks in their weapons as if they only meant to drive us out of hiding, and not mean any genuine harm."

"American mercenaries?" Michael asked. "The soldiers that attacked us in New Haven and the women in their apartment in New York City were Russian, or Ukrainian mafia."

"The men at the apartment you mentioned were exactly that, perhaps even Crimean hired goons," Gabriel said in a nonchalant manner. "And likewise were to frighten you in the hope you might advance the program, and even come here to Marsh Tower and open the vault … which you have kindly done for us."

"It would appear Sariel was a bit heavy-handed in that matter," Raphael said. "Speaking of which, where is Sariel? I thought he was going to meet us upstairs and give us weapons."

"It does not matter now, he has served his purpose. Not to mention I never instructed him to launch an attack at New Haven," Gabriel smiled in amusement.

"I don't see how you can be so flippant," Michael said. "You led me to believe Sariel has been missing for years, and now I discover he is out of control and killed Grace's friends."

"Calm yourself, brother," Gabriel said. "They were only human and therefore not important. Speaking of which, I think it is now time you opened that door and allow me access to the program."

"So you can wipe out half of humanity?" Grace asked.

"So I can finally shape mankind into what it should have always been; a fair and equal society without the confines of the rich and elite," Gabriel replied. "Surely you must realise the world is rotten to the core … simply killing 'evil' people is not enough."

"I won't do it, I refuse to give you the code for the door," Michael said. "You will have to murder me first."

"You are divine like us," Gabriel replied. "No harm will come to you. Rather if you don't open the door, I will kill that precious human playmate of yours; Grace Anderson."

Michael moved to attack his sister, but Raguel interceded and punched him in the stomach, followed by a left hook to the jaw, sending him back against the wall. Gabriel grabbed Grace and placed her right hand at the young woman's throat while Raguel held Michael down onto his knees, as Ramiel and Raphael held his arms behind his back. However, at that moment twenty men dressed in full body armour carrying machineguns and wearing all black, complete with what appeared to be motorbike helmets covering their heads and faces abruptly filled the chamber. They raised their weapons and pointed the guns at all present, including Michael and Grace.

"What … who the fuck are these guys?" Ramiel roared and moved to assault the nearest soldier and seize his machinegun.

Another guard struck Ramiel with the butt of his weapon across the side of the angel's head, knocking him to the ground. Gabriel released Grace as all were placed against the wall and forced to their knees. The soldiers instructed everyone to put their hands behind their heads and interlock the fingers. Every person had two guards at either side of them and had a machinegun barrel put to their temples. The remaining guards stood nearby, watching their prisoners' every movement.

Just then a single individual entered the room. The person was tall and hooded, wearing what seemed like a stage magician's cloak, all black and open at the front and draped to the floor, revealing a dark jumper and jeans underneath with brown shoes. The features were obscured and he carried a small zipped canvas bag which he then placed on the ground at his feet. It was all clearly done to promote a dramatic entrance like a famous celebrity appearing on a music or acting platform to the cheers of the crowd.

"I can't leave you alone for a moment before someone gets excited and threatens everyone, spoiling the party." The hooded figure laughed, appearing to speak directly to Gabriel.

"Sariel?" Gabriel asked. "Release us, that is an order."

"Your time of giving commands is over, sister." The man said sharply.

"I told you he was unstable and could not be trusted." Raguel said.

"You didn't have a lot of faith in Sariel, did you?" The black cloaked individual laughed.

"Sariel?" Michael asked.

"Guess again, brother." The man said and pulled back his hood to reveal himself.

Everyone gasped in shock. The figure had shaved black hair almost to the point of being bald, but there was no mistaking the piercing blue eyes and the handsome strong features. It was Samael.

"No; no, it's not possible." Michael said, his voice quivering in disbelief.

"I told you back in the lake, brother …" Samael said. "I am unique, even among all the archangels."

"You had me believe all these millennia you were dead and I killed you," Michael said. "You lying bastard."

"Actually that was our sister who killed me," Samael growled. "Cutting off my head and burying me in the desert in an unmarked grave like I was a piece of trash."

"How is this possible?" Gabriel uttered in amazement. "Where is Sariel, for it seems I have been conversing with 'you' these past years instead?"

"Oh, I am afraid decapitation was a bit more *permanent* for him." Samael laughed and opened the canvas bag to reveal the severed head of their brother Sariel, his flesh quite decomposed, but still somewhat recognisable as he held it high like a trophy.

"You murdering bastard." Michael said, staring at the gruesome sight; Sariel's eyes gone, revealing vacant sockets.

"You can talk after what you all did to me. Imagine your own brother you loved and trusted running you through with a sword, and then your sister removing your skull from your shoulders," Samael said, pacing around the chamber in front of his kneeling prisoners; in essence having a captive audience for his rant. "The last sight I had was the desert as my head rolled across the sand and then everything went dark. Time had no meaning; I don't know how long I was in that hole, it may have been days, months, years or even centuries before I suddenly woke up and took a mouthful of dirt. For hours I spent all my energies establishing a physical connection with my headless body, having my fingers dig blindly through the sand until I reached the surface, and then claw again to locate my severed skull. I stumbled for days through the desert heat, carrying my head like a football under my arm until I came across a family of nomads, all the time in excruciating agony. They almost ran off in terror only for the fact I managed to grab the youngest, a five year old boy and held him hostage and forced the father to sow my skull to my neck," Samael said, pulling down the turtleneck black jumper to reveal a horrible sewn neck not unlike the twisted knots of skin a post-mortem coroner would leave on a cadaver after an autopsy. "Yes, I know it is not pretty, he was no cosmetic surgeon. The nomad had to wash the wounds to remove the sand and insects before reattaching, though still I feel a terrible itch at times, as if dirt and bugs still reside there deep inside. For years I spent in that tent in torment as my nerves and spine became whole again, and even another millennia before I was at full strength, forcing successive generations of desert nomads to feed me, wash me and even wipe my arse. But during all that time, the one thing that kept me going was revenge; vengeance against you all for what you did."

"So it was you that sent those American mercenaries to the church?" Gabriel asked. "We killed two of them even though they had only blanks in their weapons."

"They were expendable and served a purpose," Samael said. "Not that you would cry over dead humans. It was necessary to frighten you to come here immediately."

"If you despised us that much, why not simply have had us killed there and then?" Ramiel asked. "Why the elaborate charade?"

"That would have been too easy, I wanted you all to suffer; like you made me suffer. Thousands of years went into the planning for this precise moment. It was I who subtly and discreetly orchestrated your every movement and pushed you into a specific direction, like how the Spanish Inquisition knew of your existence and arrested you, and how you were left alone with only two guards, making sure of your escape. It has all been an intelligent game of cat and mouse; you believed you had 'free will' like the naïve humans, but in reality your every action was my doing."

"I don't understand," Michael said and Samael stared at him. "In all this time not once did your presence come to light in the Book of Life, I should have known or at least suspected at some stage an indication that you were alive."

Samael burst into laughter and they all glanced at him in puzzlement. "You stupid fuckers, don't you get it … you were in the lake, every day altering humanity at the direction of The Source and it never occurred to you that all this; the history of mankind, the intricate details of this planet that made intelligent life possible; that perhaps it was all orchestrated. My resurrection also so this exact moment could occur … The Source planned all this, down to the minute detail. This 'God' you worship told me how to destroy the lake, and even how to write an incantation into the inside sleeve of the Book of Life when I had possession of it in Egypt, so my presence and intentions would be hidden."

"I don't believe you." Gabriel choked in shock.

"There's more," Samael grinned. "I spoke back to The Source, we had many conversations. For the rest of you it was one way instructions like a radio, but for me it was like a telephone and we chatted often."

"Now I know you are lying," his sister replied. "That's not possible."

"I told you, I am unique. We had hundreds of conversations, and debates about the nature of the Universe, and It even once divulged a secret, as if by genuine accident; an extraordinary slip of the tongue not unlike a human might do."

"What do you mean, what secret?" Michael asked.

But Samael put a finger to his lips. "That tale for another time … perhaps."

"What else have you been doing all this time, besides planning our downfall?" Raguel asked.

"Oh, I have been busy," Samael replied. "Playing with mankind has been fun … they are such easy chattering monkeys to manipulate; a slave to their desires: greed, lust, anger and especially hatred. By fuck do they despise one another, crawling over each other for position and power like fucking ants. It was remarkably easy to create religious wars and persecutions like the Crusades and the Spanish Inquisition, playing to their prejudices and fears. But my near greatest achievement was the Nazis, under my direction they came close to conquering the globe; a simple push to 'conveniently' blame all their problems on the gypsies, homosexuals and other deviants, and of course the wealthy Jews. However, that stupid bastard Hitler, he stubbornly refused my advice not to invade Russia. I told him to bide his time and isolate Stalin and starve them out, but he just would not listen. So, I left the Nazis to their fate. But modern American politics is much easier, those corrupt Republicans would sell their own mother for government status and big business donations; if Donald Trump is a swamp alligator, then they are the putrid lichen stuck to his back. Of course the self-righteous Democrats are not much better; obsessed with wokeness and promoting fake news, all to further their own twisted agenda." He sneered. "On a personal note, I did my very best to experience every dark desire mankind could offer. I raped men, women and even children, sometimes all at once; entire families restrained together … you can't imagine their faces helplessly watching what was happening to their loved ones and knowing they were next," he laughed and they shook their heads in disgust. "But *killing* … that was by far the most pleasurable experience; extinguishing a person's life and robbing them of their hopes and dreams was truly a beautiful thing. I tried shooting humans with every manner of firearm, stabbing and dismembering with knives, swords, axes, etc., even using explosives and every known type of torture including burning and drowning alive in acid. However, I always found manual strangulation using my own hands rather than rope or wire my clear favourite; watching a person's life slowly ebb away, the look of sheer terror and disbelief on their face when they realise they were about to die, as I push my thumbs ever further into their throat. Sometimes I would stop so they would return to consciousness and start all over again. It is amazing how people on reflection think they will react in such circumstances; that they will be brave and not weep, but in the end they all beg and cry like a baby."

"You're a monster." Gabriel said.

"Says the person willing to wipe out half of humanity," Samael replied. "But now enough of this dithering, it is time for business."

They all watched as another individual entered the room and Grace gasped in surprise.

"Lisa, you're alive." Michael declared.

"And kicking, boss," the young woman smiled, and to everyone's amazement turned and kissed Samael on the lips. "Surely you must have realised an insider was needed to get admittance into Marsh Tower for my lover."

"You don't have any security access," Thomas said. "And certainly not for entry into this room."

"It wasn't necessary to have permission for prohibited areas in Marsh Tower like the basement," Lisa grinned. "I only had to get official headed paper and make a few phone calls for a 'cleaning crew' to get validation into the building, and gain entry to the computer mainframe. Nobody pays any attention to people mopping floors and scrubbing toilets, making hacking into forbidden rooms go unnoticed. Such hubris on your part; you went into such extreme measures for security for the basement, but forgot to place additional guards on the mainframe. Hackers may not be able to get to that computer directly connected to the book, but they were able to download software to it from the mainframe; now all is required is to activate a new program. For someone so intelligent, it was rather stupid."

"And you did it so brilliantly," Samael said and patted her on the bottom. "Sneaking into your office and using your personal phone and email account to set it up, while you were so busy screwing your chattering monkey."

"Don't tell me you actually love this psycho?" Grace sneered.

"Nothing so romantic," Lisa said. "But like marriage, promises were made and mutual interests exchanged. I got my angel and his army in, and he eliminated Andrea for me. Christ, did I hate that spiteful cow, I wish I could have seen her die. But I had to pretend I was killed back in the house. However, that stupid soldier nearly shot you instead; not that I would have cried over you dying, Grace Anderson ... but you were not the true target."

"You fucking bitch." Grace growled.

"Answer me this, brother," Michael asked. "How is it the Book of Life suggested the three women were friends, for if I suspected they were not, I would never have even interviewed Lisa back in New England?"

Samael laughed. "For someone who had the book in their keeping for so long, you really know so little about its nature. The writings and foresight of the book are easy to manipulate from afar, if you are clever enough; a subtle breadcrumb here and there to confuse its scrying. In the weeks leading up to your arrival at the school, I had Lisa make extra efforts to befriend Grace, enough to confuse the readings of the book and make you believe they were true companions in spirit."

"I should have been awarded an Oscar for my acting performance," Lisa smirked. "And now for your other promise ... I can't wait for my present."

Samael frowned. "I think you misinterpreted me, I don't make promises to humans."

"But the sweet things you said when we made love," Lisa pouted. "You said you would make me the queen of the world."

Samael laughed. "That was just pillow talk ... a woman will believe anything when they are in the act of being fucked by a man they naïvely think could actually adore and be attracted to them."

"You said I would be the last human on Earth after you kill everyone else and I could live in Buckingham Palace like a princess." Lisa sobbed.

"What?" Michael asked and the other angels stared on in speechless shock. "You are going to use the program to wipe out *all* of mankind?"

Samael sighed. "This is what you get when you entrust information to a chattering monkey. I was actually going to let you live; Lisa Swanson, for all the deeds you dutifully carried out ... but now you are a liability."

A look of pure terror came on the young woman's face. "Please don't kill me, honey," Lisa said, crying. "I promise I will do as I am told. You can do whatever you want, I won't even scream anymore when you beat with me with the barbed-wire whips."

"I'm afraid that won't be enough anymore, especially having to endure your endless fucking whining." Samael said flatly, and punched her in the middle of her chest with his right fist.

Lisa dropped to her knees in the centre of the chamber, clutching at herself and gasping for breath, several of her ribs fractured. She glanced at her former classmate as if for assistance.

"Goodbye, bitch." Grace said, her expression devoid of emotion.

Samael struck Lisa in the face, breaking her jaw and snapping her neck, sending her head so far back it nearly rested between her shoulders. She collapsed on the floor in a heap.

"Remove that mess." The archangel ordered one of the soldiers, and the mercenary picked up the lifeless young woman and carried her out of the room.

"And now the truth is revealed," Gabriel said. "You are still the megalomaniac we stopped in Egypt, always trying to rule the world or destroy it."

"I was hoping Michael would open the door to the book before that little secret came out," Samael said. "I had been practising this speech for years; what I would say and observe your face, sister, when you realised I was going to eradicate your humans and therefore your true reason for existence; so obsessed with altering mankind and trying to make society a 'better' place. This was to be my revenge … and now that stupid chattering monkey has spoilt it."

"For God's sake, why?" Michael asked.

"For God's sake is exactly why," Samael said, his face to their surprise becoming quite sorrowful and full of emotion. "None of you can imagine what it was like; two hundred thousand years The Source screaming in my head; ordering me as the Angel of Death to kill this man … or this woman … or this child; all for some unknown greater scheme that I was not privy to. It was no wonder I went insane."

"So, the conversations with The Source," Gabriel asked. "Did they really happen, or were they a figment of your demented imagination?"

"Oh, that part was true, again for some higher purpose that I was clearly unworthy to know. But now I will have my vengeance upon God as well, and destroy Its greatest creation that It took so much time and effort to nurture."

"You don't have to do that," Michael said. "Mankind as a whole is worth saving, despite what was done to you."

"You always had such a good heart, brother," Samael said. "But you have a loftier view of humanity than they deserve. They are not the noble creatures of justice and honesty they profess themselves to be … the things I have seen them do to each other for petty reasons."

"But they have created incredible artistry too," Michael replied. "Wonderous crafted items of art and literature, and technology to bring people together like the Internet."

Samael laughed. "Most inventions were inspired to enable them to destroy one another; gunpowder, explosives, the atom bomb, more advanced guns and planes, etc. And as regards pictures and literary works; books featuring a creepy rich handsome boss spanking his shy secretary sell in the millions above more worthy novels, and some of the things they call art; if I fed a dog a bottle of whiskey and tied a wet red paintbrush to its tail, and let the animal loose in a white room it would create something far better than what most humans produce. The Internet is purely a tool for governments to spy on their citizens; for big companies to sell shit people do not need, and for perverts to masturbate over the darkest of depravities."

"They are all not guilty," Michael replied. "Some are innocent and good natured."

"Only babies are truly innocent," their captor said. "For they have not yet been hypnotised by shiny objects of materialism they are deceived into believing will make them content; force fed a strict diet of daytime television and social media that teaches them to obsess over their looks and mobile phones and view themselves as gods, and the only way to rise in society is to treat the poor like dirt, especially if they are not white. Prejudice and greed is indoctrinated into them from birth and they would no sooner let it go than chop off their own head."

"That's truly inspiring," Michael said sarcastically. "But it doesn't explain your desire to commit genocide of the entire human race."

"Maybe I am fulfilling their view of me as The Devil," Samael laughed. "To quote the French philosopher Jean Rostand; kill one person and you are a murderer, murder millions and you are a conqueror, and kill everyone you become a god. But the simple truth is I want to rest, for I am so fucking tired, my head still aches from my time in the lake and every part of my body still hurts from my death and resurrection."

"If you want to die," Gabriel said. "Then I can certainly do that for you."

Samael poked the kneeling Gabriel on the forehead several times with the index finger of his right hand, causing her to glare up at him in rage. "Yes, I imagine you would love another attempt at that," he smirked. "But I have other plans for you."

"Leave her alone," Raguel shouted. "Unless you want that physical pain you felt in Egypt to be a pleasant memory compared to the agony I could inflict."

Samael glanced at him in curiosity. "How interesting; your statement suggests more than sibling loyalty … are you shagging her?"

"That's none of your business." Raguel replied.

Gabriel turned to her captive sibling. "I can fight my own corner, brother. I don't require any protection, especially from the likes of him."

"How delightful, brother and sister in a 'happy' union; though you must have been pretty desperate to hop into bed with this hypocrite and tyrant," he smirked, pointing at Gabriel. "And I'll wager you kept this incestuous relationship secret from your brothers while at the same time dictating they abstain from any sex with the humans … not to mention frowning on Michael for daring to love the 'same' woman."

"Tell me the real reason why you want the whole world dead." Michael said.

"Because The Source wants all humans gone," Samael said. "Start the planet afresh without the influence of mankind and the catastrophic effect they have had on the environment; they have abused their gift and it is now time to put things right."

"You are so full of shit," Ramiel said. "The Source would never want that."

"How would you know? Perhaps it told me so," their captor said and burst into laughter. "Okay, the truth is I want them dead. I want to punish The Source for Its screaming in my head for countless millennia, and for revenge against you all for the betrayal."

"You're clearly insane, brother," Michael said. "Give up this craziness, let us all go and we will help you find the peace of mind you so desperately need. You don't have to become the monster and mythical Devil mankind has labelled you."

Samael smiled down at him. "That's very kind of you, Michael. You were always my favourite and I could always confide in you, but the brutal truth is there is no hope for me; there never was and there never will be. Now please open the door. I promise to bring Grace in with me and if she lays her hand on the Book of Life as I activate my version of the program, then she will be protected and you two can leave, and go on with your lives. Reincarnation will end for her as everyone on Earth will be dead, but at least you will still have her for this life … for however long that lasts."

"And what about our siblings?" Michael asked.

"They can leave safe and sound also," Samael said. "Except for Gabriel, she has to die for what she did to me."

"Then there is no deal," Michael replied. "Get your hacker friends in here and open the door for you."

"Now you are pissing me off and treating me like an idiot," Samael snarled. "I know that console is boobytrapped, a wrong number entered and the computer system inside the room is wired to explode. My hacker friends as you describe them may have entered the mainframe above in Marsh Tower and planted alternate software, but it still requires user control at that isolated machine inside the chamber to launch the new program. You think you have been so fucking smart and thought of everything, but you never planned for this moment."

"And what about your soldiers?" Michael asked. "They too will die along with everyone else. Perhaps they should be told of their own impending doom."

"If you believe you can converse with them, good luck with that," his captor replied, pointing to the single earpiece mobile Bluetooth over his right ear. "They can only hear my orders through those muffled motorbike helmets, and if you think you can persuade them to change their allegiance and attack me, you are mistaken. Which is what happened to your guards, their loyalty was bought for far less. We watched them leave Marsh Tower and made them an offer they could not refuse. They were only too willing to kill their two comrades that could not be bribed and executed them in the canteen adjacent this chamber. They then returned home; convinced of a big payday, but received a bullet instead in the head for their treachery … for such men cannot be trusted."

"You have thought of everything," Michael sighed. "Except my resolve. I won't open the door."

"It is my unbreakable determination you are trying to put to the test," Samael said sharply. "You will watch helpless as I rip Grace's arms and legs off like a house fly, and we will see the true measure of your resolve."

Michael struggled against the soldiers pinning him down, as his brother tapped on the Bluetooth and ordered the guards to raise Grace to her feet and move her towards their cloaked leader.

Out of the corner of his eye, Michael could see Gabriel smile and wondered for a moment if she was enjoying the show, but it was the sudden appearance of a lone figure at the exit to the chamber which caught her attention. Michael watched as their brother Uriel lent just inside and threw several smoke canisters across the floor, a thick grey cloud beginning to fill the room.

The mercenaries responded, and despite the smoke managed to fire off several rounds, successfully hitting Uriel in the chest as he fully entered the chamber in an attempt to assist his captive siblings. The angel slumped to the ground as Ramiel went to help him. Gabriel, Raguel and Raphael attacked their own captors who were startled by the sudden assault, and moved their weapons from the heads of the kneeling prisoners, giving the archangels the opportunity to snatch the machineguns from their hands. They shot the soldiers in the neck which seemed to be the only unprotected area of their bodies, blood spraying across the walls. Gabriel saw Samael through the cloud and attempted to shoot her brother, but three guards interceded between them and Gabriel was forced to turn the weapon on them instead, giving her sibling a chance to escape the line of fire.

"Grace, come with me." Michael said and caught hold of her hand, their own captors also leaving their position to face the oncoming threat.

He approached the computer room and quickly keying in the code at the console, ushered her inside and shut the door behind her. Grace stared through the foot square window at her lover as he keyed in another set of numbers to deactivate the boobytrap, and then drove his fist into the numerical panel, smashing it beyond use.

"Thomas, what are you doing?" Grace asked. "Come inside with me."

"It's too late for that," he replied. "Activate the program using the command keys I told you; simply press Ctrl key and Enter. I will try and hold them off and give you time. I have to help my family and not just let them die. Be strong, my love … you can do this. I believe in you."

She cried out after him as he disappeared into the grey smoke. Grace could only watch on helpless and yet protected inside the impenetrable small chamber as the angels attempted to fend off their assailants, but they were hopelessly outnumbered and within a few minutes were subdued, and were knocked to the ground. When the cloud had dissipated, Grace could see the soldiers dragging the lifeless bodies of Uriel and Raphael into the centre of the room in front of their leader. The remaining guards raised the other prisoners back up onto their knees and placed heavy metal handcuffs around their wrists, too thick even for their incredible strength to break. Eight mercenaries also lay dead, strewn in various positions throughout the basement.

Samael caught Gabriel by the throat with his right hand, and raised the angel several inches above the floor and slammed the woman against the wall, causing her to cry out in pain. "That was foolish," he growled. "And utterly pointless. You scarified the lives of two of our brothers for nothing, and delayed your own death only for a while. Now witness the end of your life's mission as I completely eradicate the human stain from existence on this planet."

She responded by spitting in his face and he moved to strike her, but was interrupted by a nearby mercenary who pointed towards the computer room. Grace gasped in fear as Samael released his sister, allowing her to slump to the floor and instead approached the young woman trapped inside the tiny chamber.

"Well, this is quite the conundrum," Samael said as he stared directly at Grace, only two feet from her face through the small window. "Open the door, this is not the business for humans. The console may be smashed, but I know you can unlock this chamber from the inside."

Grace had never been this frightened in all her life, but nevertheless shook her head in refusal. "I can't do that, you want to murder everyone."

Samael's face turned bright red with rage and the young woman was shocked and startled by the intensity of the hatred shining out of his eyes. "I'll wager Michael told you to activate his version of the program, the fucking coward that he is. You're not capable of killing one person, never mind millions."

Grace was quivering in fear, but continued to shake her head, denying the angel access. She could only watch on helpless as Samael approached Ramiel and removing a handgun from a nearby soldier, placed the barrel of the weapon to the kneeling angel's head. The captive sneered in response before his brother pulled the trigger and a bullet entered Ramiel's forehead before exiting through the back of his head, sending a spray of blood, bone and brain matter across the wall. The archangel slumped dead to the floor as the remaining three prisoners screamed in rage and anguish.

"Now you understand the nature of my resolve, after what I just did to one of my own family," Samael said. "Imagine what I will do to you when I finally gain entry to that room."

"Am I supposed to be impressed, as if you need to clarify how much of a psycho you truly are?" Grace roared. "I know you can't force your way into this chamber without the computer self-destructing and ruining your crusade to eradicate all mankind, so why don't you crawl back into that desert hole you came from?"

"I am going to flay you alive and rub your skinless body in salt for what you have done," Raguel said. "You will know agony like no human has ever experienced, though something tells me you would probably enjoy that."

Samael smiled. "You don't have the stomach for torture, for I could certainly teach you the ways of true pain which I have discovered are more exquisite when inflicted on loved ones, and making the victim watch on helpless to their screams."

"There is really no redemption for you," Gabriel said. "You have become so removed from the divine concept of an archangel that the only remedy is to put you down like a rabid dog or lame horse; you truly deserve no other fate."

"My dear sanctimonious sister," Samael replied. "You should be more concerned with your own precarious destiny at this moment, as I now kill your boyfriend and eradicate all of mankind; your life's purpose completely destroyed, and finish you last so you can bear witness to oblivion."

Gabriel observed in dismay as her errant sibling pointed the gun at Raguel's forehead and prepared to fire the weapon and kill yet another member of their angelic family.

"What is your answer, girl?" Samael growled towards the sealed room. "Will you have another death on your conscience? These matters do not concern you, open the door and go on with your life with your lover."

"I told you, I can't," Grace said. "Executing him will make no difference. Besides, I care nothing for Raguel and his sister."

"What an interesting choice of words." He smiled and picking up Michael, marched him towards the sealed chamber and slammed his face into the small window, the impact on his nose creating a smudge of blood onto the pane.

The sudden action took Grace by surprise and she jumped back, nearly knocking the box containing the Book of Life off its table in the centre of the tiny room. She could only watch on in heartache as Samael forced his brother to gaze at his soul twin through the glass, helpless to save her from observing his anguish at what was transpiring. Grace placed her hand on the pane as if to touch Thomas as it was the closest she could get to him, and he smiled in reply briefly, before his captor revealed a ten inch bowie knife and put the blade to his prisoner's throat.

"Now for the last time," Samael shouted. "Open it ... open the fucking door!"

Grace shook her head again in refusal despite her absolute terror as Thomas smiled at her.

"It's alright my love," Thomas said softly. "Don't be afraid. Remember what I told you. Activate the program and you will be safe from harm. My brother will not be able to use the machinery as it will be destroyed directly afterwards."

"But he will kill you." Grace sobbed.

"But you will go on," Thomas said, a tear running down his left cheek. "You will find a husband and have children which I could never give you and be happy."

"I don't want that. I just want you; you are my soul twin for all eternity, we are meant to be together."

"This is all very sweet and utterly pointless," Samael said. "You are very naïve if you believe this man truly loves you. He was desperate to leave the lake, you were simply his excuse that he gave himself to absolve him of the guilt he felt at that desire. He was too much of a coward to destroy Heaven, you cannot imagine his secret joy and relief when I forced our exile to the planet. Finally he was free of the sacred duty he hated and could experience all the Earthly wonders denied to him. It was never about 'good and evil;' saving humanity from themselves and easing suffering. Ultimately it was always about himself. The untimely death of Adina was a stark reminder that a path of loneliness awaited him after her demise until the reincarnation of another you, and it was that dilemma he was trying to avoid or prolong, not for any other altruistic reason. Michael like mankind is selfish to the core. At least I am honest in myself and in my actions. In essence he stole from your incarnations the choice of another life with a human husband and the potential of children, removing your former lives from a destiny where they might have been happier. But after these stupid girls met my brother, who could have competed with the love of an archangel? In truth, he fancied many others that co-existed with the timeline of your first incarnation who he sought out after leaving the lake; you stood out from the rest because he could act the hero and save you from perceived hardship and persecution, or at least that is what he told your former lives to get inside their knickers. You were never anything special or unique, even now I still laugh at his cunning; Michael is more alike me than he would admit."

"That's not true," Thomas said. "There was never anyone else for me."

"Grace, you have a choice," Samael said. "My version of the program or your lover's life, for believe me I have no qualms about killing another sibling. Go to the computer and press Ctrl and Backspace; the other software my hackers installed in the mainframe will override my brother's program, and you can leave and Michael will be alive. But no more delays or denials."

Grace approached the keyboard and could see personal profiles of various people being flashed on the computer screen, their pictures as if just taken from their social media accounts; their entire history detailed including wives, husbands, past loves, children and deeds committed both good and bad, and in some cases truly horrendous acts of violence and depravity carried out on their fellow beings. These were the genuine wicked individuals designated for death by the application in conjunction with the Book of Life sitting on the narrow pedestal behind her. With two simple keystrokes their very existence would be exterminated, even their souls obliterated and their path to reincarnation ceased.

"I am sorry, Grace," Thomas said through the grille in the door and she turned to face him. "This was never your burden to bear; this was to be my task alone. It was selfish of me to even ask you to be witness to such a tremendous and terrible venture, and now you have to carry out the deed yourself in my absence."

"I told you before, my love," she replied. "We are in this together."

"Yes, Michael always wanted to be the hero; foolishly trying to save his siblings' lives, instead of casting them aside like I would have done and gone in there with you. Now the dirty work is left up to you. Make the right choice, girl," Samael ordered as he began to cut slightly into the neck of his captive, causing a small trickle of blood to flow. "Let me see you enter the correct keystrokes or watch your 'eternal twin' die for all time. There will be no afterlife for my brother; his existence along with his soulless body will rot and be lost forever. Neither you or your future incarnations will ever see him again."

As commanded, Grace sidestepped so their captor could see everything to avoid any potential deception.

"I know you are hesitant; the sheer enormity of the decision before you," Samael said. "Do not think about it, just press the buttons and in a moment it will be all over, and you and Michael can be together again. Your future incarnations may not come to pass with the death of all mankind, but at least you will have the precious years of this life to spend in peace and harmony. Besides, in your heart you know it is the right choice, humanity was never a positive effect on this planet; they are parasites that care nothing for animal life or the environment, they have neglected this almighty gift they were given and did not deserve. The Earth will go on and be a better place for their absence."

"It's alright, Grace," Thomas said. "Be strong, I know you can do this."

Grace pressed the Ctrl key and held her finger over the Backspace key to eradicate all mankind, and Samael smiled in delight as he turned back to laugh at Gabriel, much to the woman's dismay, realising what was happening as she and Raguel struggled at their bonds.

Grace stopped pressing the button and their captor glared at her in confusion. "I never really paid any attention to what the nun told me back at the convent school," Grace said, as she faced the door. "Sister Greta was after all an evil bitch who probably hated God even above us girls for the life she believed had been forced upon her ..."

"What the fuck are you talking about?" Samael roared, shoving the blade deeper into his prisoner's throat. "Enough of the nonsense, finish the program or your lover dies!"

Grace smiled in response, despite his threats and her own fear. "But if there was one thing the nun said that stuck with me ... it was never do deals with the Devil."

Samael and his captive could only watch as Grace ignored the Backspace button and pressed the Enter key instead, activating the original designated application which Thomas had created. The Book of Life inside its box let out a fantastic burst of white light that seeped through any cracks and its lid, showering the small room and they had to shield their eyes, such was the intensity. The computer screen went blank as the motherboard and hard drives within the machine burned out, destroying essential hardware and any possibility of halting the program and altering its outcome. Any chance of making new software from this computer or the mainframe above was gone forever, as evident by the black smoke that began to rise from the back of the machine through its rear fan slots.

Gabriel and Raguel could only watch as three of the soldiers suddenly fell to the floor, their lives and souls extinguished instantly. The remaining guards fled, leaving their kneeling prisoners behind, not knowing what had transpired. The angels knew above them and all over the globe millions of people were dropping dead wherever they were; driving to work or in business meetings, lounging on the beach or watching television, in the middle of sex or playing with their children, surfing on their phones or playing computer games, and some even in the act of rape or murder; the very acts that had promised their demise and the obliteration of their souls. Their victims finally acquiring some type of justice which had been denied them because of the courts or they had escaped without any witnesses to their diabolical crimes. However, many of the fallen would be children or even babies, much to the anguish of their parents; not realising their offspring would one day commit terrible acts of violence, only knowing ultimate grief in that moment. All however knew the world and humankind had changed irrevocably, and would never be the same again.

"I am certain at least a few on your list would have perished," Raguel whispered to his sister as they both pushed themselves to their feet. "We should be thankful for that ... I suppose."

"It is small consolation," she replied. "However, their heirs will simply replace them and the endless cycle of greed and poverty will continue forever. An opportunity to finally make society an equal and fair realm has been shattered; for the poor and dispossessed nothing will change, their misery and injustice will only flourish."

"Let him go, it is over," Grace said to their captor who still held a knife to her lover's raised neck. "Your great plans of genocide have vanished, you profit nothing with further bloodshed on your siblings."

"You bitch," Samael said. "You have ruined everything. An eternity spent planning this event and all wasted because of some stupid schoolgirl crush. However, I will witness your agony as I kill

Michael, and then my last remaining brother Raguel before taking my sister's life. It will only remain then to commit suicide and let the legacy of archangels come to an end."

Grace moved to the window. "No, please don't."

Despite their bondage, Raguel and Gabriel tried to attack their brother, but too late as Samael began to cut deep into the throat of Michael and ran the blade right across his neck from ear to ear, cutting deep into the flesh. Michael gave one last smile in response at his soul twin through the glass, as Grace began screaming before Samael let his lifeless body fall to the floor, a large pool of blood beginning to form around the entrance to the vault. Grace finally opened the door and exited into the main chamber. Samael could now get access to the Book of Life and the computer, though its purpose was now beyond him. Instead he took a step back, and let the knife fall from his hands as his siblings could only stare over the corpse of yet another of their kind, his divine knowledge and experiences gone forever.

Grace knelt down and picked up her lover's head and cradled it in her lap, the tears running freely down her cheeks.

"Was it worth it?" Gabriel asked their captor. "Was the cost worth it?"

But Samael had no words. He only stared motionless at his dead brother at his feet.

Raguel pushed into Samael, knocking him against the wall. "Go on then, finish us off like you promised. You are after all a man of your word."

However, Samael only glanced at him before slumping to the floor in apparent dismay at what he had just done, much to the confusion of Raguel and Gabriel, for he had not shown any remorse for his awful actions up until this point. "For what it is worth, I am sorry. I never wanted him dead," he said as he turned towards the kneeling grief stricken young woman. "He was more than a brother, he was my friend. I should not have done that."

"I don't want your apologies, you fucking psycho," Grace shouted, not even looking at him, but continued to hold her lover's head in her lap. "Thomas was much more than that; more than an archangel, more than his divine knowledge and long memories, more than his incredible intelligence and wonderful personality; he was mine ... he was always mine."

Nobody could find speech to respond, but remained in their positions without moving, as if time itself had ceased and the Universe in a microcosm was contained complete in that very moment in that chamber with nothing else existing. They were however shaken from their 'catatonia' by a tremendous earthquake as tremors ripped through the building and plaster began to fall from the ceiling and walls around them.

Raguel watched in curiosity as cracks began to form in the basement structure and he feared the enormous tower above was about to come crashing down upon their heads.

"This is not a result of the computer program," Gabriel said, noticing her brother's apprehension. "My understanding is the software was designed to affect human life only, not the tectonic integrity of the planet. This is something else entirely."

They suddenly heard a loud groaning noise like a large animal in pain, and turned to see a pool of silvery grey liquid begin to appear out of nowhere in the centre of the chamber. It continued to form until reaching about two metres in diameter and appeared to be very thick in nature, almost like oil. Gabriel approached it and despite her arms still bound at her back, managed to kneel and peered into the puddle only a few inches from her face.

"I could be mistaken," she said. "But I think it is pure mercury."

Samael seemed to break out of his trance and stared at her, before rising to his feet and also inspected the pool. "Oh no … no, it can't be."

Raguel watched him roam the room in fear. "It's not that I don't enjoy seeing you frightened, but what exactly is going on?"

Samael stopped his nervous pacing. "Mercury is a conduit, it provides a portal for magickal creatures to pass from one plane of existence to another."

"So?" Gabriel asked.

"Something ..." Samael replied. "Or *someone* is coming ..."

Grace was not even aware of what was transpiring between the angels and their preoccupation with the miniature lake of mercury, such was her grief as she continued to cradle her lover's head and rocking back and forth with the sobbing. It was only when a bright white light similar to when the computer application went online filled the entire chamber did she raise her head in half-interest. She could see the three remaining archangels standing back from the pool as it started to congeal into a solid form and continued to rise until it stood at six foot, the full content of the puddle now transformed into this bizarre humanoid-like figure.

The angels gasped in shock as the mercury almost seemed to melt away, revealing a young human woman approximately thirty years old. She was incredibly beautiful having silver hair atop a slender frame, and wore what looked like a single white dress that barely concealed her nakedness. Her entire body was glowing in a mixture of orange and white, as if her aura and the Book of Life was composed of the same supernatural material. It was however the bright red eyes that gave the indication that she was not human, but something else altogether. Gabriel immediately dropped to her knees and ordered Raguel to do the same. Samael on the other hand continued to back away in terror.

"My son," the silver-haired woman said in a voice similar to the sound the wind makes as it whispers through the trees; certainly beyond the capabilities of any human or angel could possibly mimic. "Not since your creation two hundred thousand years ago have I presented myself before you."

Samael tripped over himself and fell on his ass as he stared up at the woman peering down at him, and even began sliding backwards on his bottom as if to escape. "Please don't kill me, I could not bear to die again. I did everything you asked of me. I even killed Michael; the one person I ever loved and never wanted dead."

The silver-haired woman smiled. "You were always the dutiful servant, my son. But perhaps you enjoyed killing the humans and your brothers a little too much."

"But *you* made me this way," Samael replied. "Constantly shouting in my head like a giant bell, driving me to madness. What else was I to do, murdering these chattering monkeys was my only mental release from the memory of that agony. Their suffering was merely a faint echo of my own; they should be grateful as I did them a favour and a service in sending their souls back to you."

The other angels rose to their feet. "Was this all orchestrated, like he said? Did you plan all this from the beginning? His impossible resurrection? The destruction of the lake; our exile and forcing us to hate each other?" Gabriel asked.

"The lake had served its purpose," The Source replied. "Try as we might to alter humanity, they always reverted to their true nature of good and wicked. It was necessary to devise a way to eradicate all evil souls from the world, and start anew. Besides, did you really think a deity which had forged the Universe would not see this outcome, and even plan for it? Samael's rebirth was essential and inevitable."

"Why not just destroy those wicked individuals instantly yourself, for you certainly had the power to do so?" Raguel asked. "Why the elaborate charade?"

"You and Michael had to be set at polar opposites to guarantee he would create the program, he had to be utterly convinced of the moral importance of his scheme. Simply annihilating those evil people by divine intervention would cause a massive tear in the Space Time Continuum. It was necessary for the humans to create their own instrument of destruction, like nuclear weapons. Yes, the Book of Life was needed to reach the relevant people across the planet, but neither would it have been possible without the human invention of the Internet. Left on their current path, this planet and ultimately all life would have been obliterated through human selfishness and greed; a way had to be devised so only the evil would perish, and yet not involve my direct participation and prevent that spatial rift had I used my powers directly."

"But our brothers are dead." Gabriel said.

"What is done ... can be undone." The Goddess smiled and put out her hands.

They watched in amazement as Uriel, Ramiel and Raphael awoke from death and rose to their feet. Even Sariel's rotting skull vanished and he appeared as if out of nowhere; all angels alive and completely unharmed as if they had never been killed, with the exception of Michael who still remained a corpse in Grace's lap.

Sariel immediately ran to attack Samael. "You bastard, I am going to smash every bone in your body for what you did to me."

The Source pointed her right index finger and the angel was stopped in his tracks as if he was frozen. "No more violence. Archangels you were, and so you will become again."

The Source then reached out her hand to place it on Grace's head, but Grace turned and knocked it away with scorn.

"The angels may fall in worship at your feet," Grace said as she stared up at the Goddess through eyes bloodshot from crying. "But I do not recognise any deity that would force me to kill millions for Its own amusement, and in reward allow the death of my beloved."

The Source smiled. "I can see why Michael chose you above all others. You have a fire and spirit I admire, which is why you were the perfect choice for activating the program. You performed the act with conscience, reluctance and honour, knowing it was the right decision under difficult circumstances. Only an ethical human could kill millions of their own kind, despite knowing such souls were evil and deserving of 'permanent' death; an angel or god could not have done so, that is why you were chosen. Would you really have done it without sufficient and appropriate pressure, such as your soul twin's life held to ransom?"

"You sound more like a politician than an all-powerful deity capable of solving such dilemmas instantly. Atheists have the correct moral standing for disbelieving your existence, for the truth is worse than considering the no-god scenario. And what of those children born with deformities of no fault of their own, and cancers that mean their short lives are full of pain and misery in which their only relief is usually death … where is their justice and fairness?"

"Without adversity mankind would never have struggled to rid themselves of these illnesses as they have done so for others; it is that which means no goal is beyond them as they strive for the stars. As regards children born with deformities, they will have another chance for health when they are reborn again and again for all time. Reincarnation has to be random in order to be fair and just. Life is a great test both for the individual and for humanity in general, that is why I created them that way."

"You brought the other angels back to life. Why not Thomas? And what of the innocent humans, like my friend Andrea?"

"To return your friend would destroy the Universe as her soul has moved on into another body, born only a few hours ago. There is a supreme order to creation but it is also very fragile, and some things cannot be undone. The angels do not have souls so it is only their bodies I am bringing back to life. Michael strayed from his true course unlike his siblings, so has not proved himself worthy of redemption."

"So, you let his psycho brother live but not Thomas? And what of Gabriel and her incestuous relationship with Raguel, was that all part of the great plan?"

"Gabriel too has fallen somewhat from the divine path, but did not associate herself with mankind and its desires to the same degree, unlike Michael."

"Please give my brother another chance. Give him the opportunity to prove himself." Gabriel pleaded.

The Source paused for a few moments before reaching out her hand and placed it on top of the head of the dead man on the floor, his skull still in the lap of his grieving lover. Grace watched in amazement as his injury began to disappear, the deep wound on his neck healing itself and the colour returning to his face. Thomas suddenly opened his eyes and breathed hard, rising up in shock before seeing his girlfriend and embraced her. He turned and gasped when he saw the Goddess smiling down at him and quickly rose to his feet, continuing to stare at the deity in astonishment.

"I don't believe it," Thomas said. "You are really here! I guess I should be grateful for my life which you have returned, but I don't understand what has happened."

"Your friend can explain all," the Goddess said. "But from this moment, things are going to change. No longer will archangels interfere in mankind's affairs; humanity will discover its own path without help or hindrance. Gabriel and her brothers will become the Lords of Karma; standing in judgement over the souls of men and women when they die, and pass sentence on them based upon their actions as read from the Book of Life. The innocent will go on to be reincarnated and the new evil souls not yet born will become the property of Samael, who will see fit to perform whatever torture he likes upon their bodies in an underground realm; a place of fire and darkness deep in the bowels of the Earth where they will never escape."

"So Samael is effectively to be rewarded for his own diabolical deeds?" Raguel asked. "And why even create new evil souls? The Book of Life and the computer program Michael instigated would have stopped their reincarnations as well."

"Samael was only obeying me after all," The Source replied. "Even if he was a little too eager in the pain he inflicted upon humans, but now only the truly guilty will feel his wrath. As regards the new souls forged from the Chamber of Guf; humanity has been given a fresh start as it were, and they must be allowed to learn from their mistakes, otherwise they will never progress as a civilisation."

"And what of me?" Thomas asked. "Am I to re-join my brethren in this new career move?"

"I have stripped you of your divine heritage; you are no longer an angel. You are now a human with a soul, you have lost your great strength and immortality. You will age and get sick like any normal man, but you will still retain your memories and experiences along with your knowledge of all languages to guarantee your success on this planet. In addition, you can now have children and even die like an ordinary human and one day be judged by your siblings and even reincarnated. You are no longer the Archangel Michael, but now simply and forever Thomas Marsh. Go now, and be with Grace Anderson and forge a new life for yourself."

Thomas stared at her, speechless, but embraced his former siblings one after another, even Gabriel and Samael, though Gabriel did it reluctantly. Grace caught hold of his hand and they left Marsh Tower and returned to the busy street. They could hear sirens all over the city as emergency services responded to people spontaneously dying in their offices, homes and cars. Frightened citizens of New York ran past them, rushing to get home to see if their loved ones met a similar mysterious fate.

"I don't understand," Samael frowned, back in the basement. "Bringing him back to life; making him human … that was never part of the original plan."

"My son," the Goddess smirked. "Sometimes; just sometimes, I like to do the … unexpected."

Back on the street, Grace turned to her soul twin. "What are we going to do now?"

"Whatever we want, we are finally free." Thomas smiled as they went into New York City, away from the angels and their former lives … and never looked back.

Lightning Source UK Ltd.
Milton Keynes UK
UKHW022210180722
406045UK00011B/223

9 780993 424748